Readers love the
Fabric Hearts series by KC BURN

Tartan Candy

"…a captivating read with characters I really enjoyed, steamy sex, interesting secondary characters and a sweet love story."
—Open Skye Book Reviews

"The ending was perfect—pretty much like the entire story!"
—Prism Book Alliance

"Sweet, romantic love story you will enjoy very much if you like hot men, kilts, and true emotions."
—Three Books Over the Rainbow

Plaid versus Paisley

"*Plaid versus Paisley* proved to be a satisfying, worthwhile read…"
—Just Love: Queer Book Reviews

"I was quickly immersed in their story and kept turning the pages to see just what would happen between the two men."
—Long and Short Reviews

"KC Burns gave us two lovable characters with flaws and struggles that not only endeared me to them but I cheered for on the sidelines."
—Diverse Reader

By KC Burn

Grand Adventures (Dreamspinner Anthology)
One Pulse (Dreamspinner Anthology)
Pen Name – Doctor Chicken
Rainbow Blues

FABRIC HEARTS
Tartan Candy
Plaid Versus Paisley
Just Add Argyle

TORONTO TALES
Cop Out
Cover Up
Cast Off

Published by DREAMSPINNER PRESS
www.dreamspinnerpress.com

JUST ADD ARGYLE

KC BURN

Published by

DREAMSPINNER PRESS

5032 Capital Circle SW, Suite 2, PMB# 279, Tallahassee, FL 32305-7886 USA
www.dreamspinnerpress.com

This is a work of fiction. Names, characters, places, and incidents either are the product of author imagination or are used fictitiously, and any resemblance to actual persons, living or dead, business establishments, events, or locales is entirely coincidental.

Just Add Argyle

Cover Art
http://www.lcchase.com
Cover content is for illustrative purposes only and any person depicted on the cover is a model.

ISBN: 978-1-63533-567-5
Digital ISBN: 978-1-63533-568-2
Library of Congress Control Number: 2017901629
Published April 2017
v. 1.0

Printed in the United States of America
(∞)
This paper meets the requirements of
ANSI/NISO Z39.48-1992 (Permanence of Paper).

For those who've ever felt they didn't belong.

ACKNOWLEDGMENTS

So many people to thank, but I have to start with Alex and Dottie, whose rock-solid support I couldn't do without. Also my book club and my breakfast bunch—I love you all. I also have so much gratitude to Dreamspinner, for getting my stories out there, and to the wonderful editors who help make them stronger.

CHAPTER ONE

"HEY, GINGER-BABY, I'll give you twenty bucks to suck my dick."

With a disdainful sneer, Tate Buchanan flipped his middle finger at the asshole in the car that had slowed down beside him.

"Going rate's fifty." Tate's sneer turned into a grimace. That was the sort of thoughtless reply that was going to get him in trouble—again.

But seriously, twenty was just insulting. At least he thought it was. Money—or anything with numbers, really—confused the fuck out of him more often than not.

Still, he wasn't a damned crack whore, and if he wanted to have sex with some perverted old goat, there were a number of his mother's "boyfriends" who wouldn't have objected to taking him for a spin. A shudder shook him. When he was younger, before he figured out how to use his fists, he'd had a few narrow escapes. But now that he was no longer a teenager, those dickless wonders his mother dated were a little more circumspect when they eyed him up. No one had tried to cop a feel since Tate had broken a few of the last guy's fingers for his trouble.

"C'mon. You're real pretty and I've only got a twenty."

"Fuck off." Tate kept walking, somehow managing to hold on to his temper and not lob a chunk of broken asphalt at the car. Did he fucking look like a charitable priest from the Church of Needs a Skanky Whore?

"Bitch." The car squealed away.

Tate clenched his fists before continuing on, scuffing his shoes along the sidewalk. Even though it was well after sunset, humidity had thickened the air and katydids sang, audible even over the rush of traffic on the nearby highway. The night was aglow with neon signs and streetlights.

He didn't know where to go. He'd gotten fired—again. Going home this early on a Friday night was a bad idea on so many levels, not the least of which was having to deal with his mom and her latest flavor of the month and their intoxicant of choice. In a few hours they'd have passed out and he could find his way to his room. Pathetic to still be living at home, but right now his options were his mom's place or the street. Even if he was as stupid as everyone seemed to think, he was smart enough to know that even in Orlando, living homeless was no picnic.

He fingered the small amount of money in his pocket. He didn't think he had enough to go to a bar, and there weren't too many places around here to hang out cheaply. Not outside of library hours, at any rate. The whole area was designed to suck money out of unwary tourists. On the other hand, living so close to the tourist schlock meant a number of places he could try to get hired on, although at the rate he was going, the options were getting slimmer.

As he walked past the decaying, boarded-up motel that had found less success than other nearby motels, he realized there were two nearby options. This strip of motels and collection of stores offering tacky shell souvenirs fronted a small residential area and, more specifically, a playground. A little farther up, on the other side of Irlo Bronson Highway, was a classic sci-fi-styled minigolf course called Area 52, yet another touristy venue he'd been fired from. He hadn't understood the meaning of the name before he started working there, but the manager, Mr. Singh, had explained it without acting like Tate was an idiot. He didn't think it was nearly as clever as Mr. Singh did, but he would never tell him that.

More importantly, though, was the patch of dirt with some battered picnic tables the staff used for breaks during the day. Located behind the operations area and below the level of the greens, it wasn't well lit enough for anyone to bother with at night, and he could easily get there without being seen.

He didn't think any of the local dealers used either of those spots, at least not regularly, although he really only paid attention to the seedy underbelly of the tourist trade to make sure he avoided them. His life might be sort of shit, but following in his mother's footsteps wouldn't make anything easier. Getting hassled by them was no treat either, and he was already in a shitty mood. No telling what his temper would goad him into if he didn't get some peace and quiet to wait out until well after midnight, when it would be safe to go home.

Spending a few hours in the dark didn't sound like a whole lot of fun, but it was better than the alternative. At least he was wearing a long-sleeved shirt and his increasingly shabby work pants. Mosquitos loved him, and having his skin covered would help.

The last thing he wanted to do tomorrow was pound the pavement and look for yet another job. Most of the places he was qualified for didn't bother putting ads online, so he didn't even have the excuse of spending the day in the library, away from his mother's recriminations.

Spring could be tricky. On one hand, there were a lot of tourists around for spring break, making all the fast-food joints and gift shops busy. On the other hand, most places had already hired on their extra staff. But if he could hang on to the next job for a couple of months, he'd be almost guaranteed a position throughout the summer. Maybe.

Tate sighed. Wishful thinking. The more time people spent with him, the less patience they had for him. No matter what job he got now, he'd likely be looking again in a couple of months, if not sooner.

Deep in thought, Tate rounded the wooden fence surrounding the outdoor trash bins and rocked to a stop. A flare of anger bloomed in his chest as he realized his anticipated haven was already occupied. Then his brain began to take in details. Three guys, two of whom were a little older than him, and a much younger third, who was bent face-first over one of the picnic tables, mostly naked. He had a spiky thatch of blond hair and blue eyes, wide and tear-filled, and more shockingly, a lurid "alien" green Area 52 tank top stuffed in his mouth, gagging him.

Fucking hell. Tate's anger morphed and flared bright and hot. Even if he hadn't recognized Kris from his short stint as a cashier at Area 52, it was obvious he wasn't there by choice, and he didn't have a chance of escaping his attackers. Tate didn't have a phone, and even if Tate took off at a dead run, this kid would be violated and/or dead before he could get any help.

At that moment Kris's gaze landed on Tate. On the off chance Tate was the sort to leave him to his fate, that pleading, terrified gaze would have changed his mind. A quick glance found him a broken piece of wood that would help, and he snatched it up and hurled himself into the clearing, yelling wildly.

He slammed the wood against the shoulder of the guy holding Kris down, knocking him off-balance. It was enough for Kris to wriggle away as Tate spun to face the other guy, who had already recovered from his surprise.

"Jealous? Don't worry, we could have fun with both of you."

Tate curled his lip, making sure he kept the two of them in his sight line. "Like I want any piece of your diseased worm."

If there was anything Tate was good at, it was making people mad, and the burly one was no exception. He snarled and swiped but moved too slow, and Tate batted away the meaty paw with his board, causing a howl.

"Tate?" Kris asked behind him, voice shaky.

"For fuck's sake, Kris, get out of here." Tate didn't have time to help Kris any more than he was, or he was going to get the beatdown of his life.

The scuff of dirt and gravel told him Kris had hightailed it away, and Tate grinned at the two men. "Think all us twinks are interchangeable?"

He hated guys who assumed one twink was the same as any other almost as much as he hated the guys who thought their cocks were made out of gold and therefore deserved to dip in whatever hole they fancied.

"Since you chased away our first choice, you'll have to take his place."

Like fucking hell. These assholes would soon learn the difference between an innocent kid earning money for college and a rat who'd been fighting for his virtue since puberty.

They flanked him but obviously hadn't done this often, or they'd have moved simultaneously. Tate lashed out a foot, landing a vicious kick at the side of the taller one's knee before swinging his makeshift bat at the burly one.

The taller one went down with a yelp, but the bigger guy kept coming, face red and scowling. Tate danced back, swinging again, hoping to catch him in the ribs. At this rate he was going to have to go for head shots, but he didn't want to risk accidentally killing one of them. Jail wouldn't work for him.

Suddenly someone grabbed his arms from behind. The burly one smiled, making fear bloom big enough to swamp Tate's anger. He writhed and screamed obscenities at the top of his lungs, trying desperately to raise the board, but the taller guy was stronger than he looked. Instead, Tate kicked, but even the burly guy was bigger than he was and was able to avoid his legs.

"Let's see how pretty you are with a fat lip. Or missing a few teeth."

The burly one swung and landed a fist in his face. For a moment everything in Tate's face went numb, but Tate knew better than to relax. The pain exploded, and Tate couldn't hold back a shout.

"Fuck you! Motherfucking piece of shit!"

Each obscenity goaded the big guy into hitting him again, in the face and stomach, but Tate only stopped when one good blow knocked the breath out of him. He hung limply in the taller man's grasp and desperately tried to suck air into his lungs.

The burly guy hooked his fingers in the neck of Tate's shirt and pulled, ripping it into rags. Would have been a more impressive feat if the shirt wasn't already threadbare and on the edge of disintegrating, but the loss of one of his few pieces of clothing—with no means to replace it— brought his anger roaring back. Instead of trying to kick the guy in front of him, he jammed his foot on the instep of the taller guy who'd imprisoned his arms, taking care to scrape along his shin on the way down.

The move was painful enough—the guy was wearing shorts—to free Tate's arms, and he swung again, this time slamming the board against the side of the taller one's face. He was too short to get a lot of leverage, but it still knocked the guy out, and Tate spun to face his remaining foe. His own vision swam and the sight in one eye wasn't clear, but the scowl on the burly guy's face was easy to distinguish.

"Goddamn tourists," Tate snarled. These guys were maybe college guys, but they might be even older than that.

A familiar snick made sweat pop out all over Tate's body, slicking his grip. He'd brought a piece of wood to a knife fight, and he was having difficulty seeing out of his left eye. If he lost his grip on the board now, he was a dead man.

He crouched, hoping he'd be able to block this guy long enough to get away while his companion was down for the count. He wasn't stupid enough to stick around if running would save his life. Unfortunately, they'd turned, and the only easy way out—the way Tate had come in— was past the burly guy.

Then circles of light illuminated the area.

"Police! Drop your weapons!"

FUCKING HELL. So fucking close to getting out of here with his skin intact and without yet another run-in with the cops. Opening his fingers, he let his makeshift weapon slowly slip from his hand, gaze never leaving his opponent. If the dude opposite him was going to ignore the law's directives, Tate wanted to be ready to drop to the ground when they opened fire.

Big and Burly wasn't stupid, though, and he let his little switchblade fall, hands raised.

With some effort, Tate resisted the urge to turn tail and run. The last thing he needed was yet another arrest. He'd been lucky so far in that nothing had ever stuck, but he couldn't rely on luck forever, and sooner or later his temper was going to land him in jail.

Yet another thing he was too stupid to do—control his temper like a sensible person.

He didn't know if Kris had exaggerated the threat when he called in the cavalry or if the Kissimmee police were having a slow night, but there were way too many cops for him to risk doing a runner.

Leaning back against one of the picnic tables, he waited while officers dealt with the two other guys. A couple of EMTs hovered around the edges, moving closer as the two other men were zip-tied. If Tate had accidentally hit one of them too hard, he could be in real trouble. Funny how he'd wanted someplace to hang out until it was safe to go home. Jail was pretty much last on that list, well after just going home and dealing with his mom.

Despite the warm, humid evening, his fingers were freezing and wouldn't stop shaking, so he folded his arms across his chest, tucking his fingers into his armpits.

One of the cops he'd run into a few times before, Officer Hernandez, glanced over as he finished with the big guy's zip ties, and shook his head. Tate shrugged.

When he spoke, though, he directed his comments to Tate's opponents. "Pretty stupid, guys, bringing a knife with you on vacation. Gonna make these charges a whole lot worse."

The big guy gestured at Tate using his shoulder. "What about that guy? He had a weapon. He attacked us. We were just defending ourselves."

Officer Hernandez glanced down at the ragged piece of wood lying at Tate's feet. "The guy you tried to rape called 911. And I don't see any other weapons besides the knife of yours we just confiscated."

Tate relaxed just a bit. Over the years, he'd picked up all too much information about how the law worked, and weapons were a big no-no, especially one that actually made contact with someone. Tate never started the fights… well, he never started the physical fights, at least, but even still, he'd expected to get arrested just the same. Hernandez's words gave him hope that if he stayed quiet and out of the way, this would all be over soon.

The big guy sputtered as Hernandez handed him off and waved in the EMTs.

"All clear." Hernandez pointed at the skinnier guy. "That one's still out cold, so take your pick."

"Thanks, Diego," the male EMT said. *Diego.* Interesting. Tate had never heard Hernandez's first name before.

The EMTs, a man and a woman, conferred briefly, the man glancing quickly at Tate before saying something else to his partner. She nodded and unexpectedly crouched down beside the unconscious man, leaving the other guy to approach Tate.

Tate backed up as far as he could—which wasn't very far. This wasn't supposed to happen. Everyone was supposed to ignore him, although if it had been anyone other than Diego Hernandez, he stood a good chance of getting hauled in anyway. He tensed up, poised to run if it became necessary.

"Hey there. My name is Jaime. I'm just going to set my kit down here on the bench."

Tate blinked, not entirely sure what to do with Jaime. Although his voice was soothing, he also approached like Tate was rabid or something.

Jaime set the large plastic case down, snapped on a pair of gloves, and pulled a few instruments out before slowly entering Tate's personal space. "What's your name?"

"Why do you need to know?" Tate couldn't stop himself from sounding belligerent, but people knowing things about him never went well. They either thought they could get something from him or thought they could interfere in his life.

"Okay, okay, we can start with something else. I want to check your vitals, and then I want to take a look at that eye."

Tate swung his head around—too fast—and winced. Between the shadows and his rapidly swelling eye, he couldn't see clearly what Jaime looked like, and for some stupid reason, he wanted to.

"Are you dizzy? Feeling sick?" Jaime asked slowly while shining a light in his eyes, then doing various other medical-type things. Jaime was a good bit larger, both in height and bulk, than Tate, and Tate had learned all too well that the bigger his opponents were, the harder Tate fell. Yet Jaime's simple clinical touches calmed him in a way he'd never experienced, although he could hardly call it soothing, because it wasn't.

Tate contemplated not answering, but something told him it would take a lot more to keep Jaime from pressing. "No. I'm fine."

Jaime snorted, the unexpected sound almost coaxing a laugh out of Tate. "Okay, well, I can see you're not exactly fine, but probably not concussed."

After a few more minutes of Jaime's quizzing, poking, and prodding, Officer Hernandez walked over. "What's the verdict, Jaime? Is Troublemaker Tate heading to the hospital? Angelica's going to need some help getting that other guy on the stretcher."

Tate grimaced. So much for not telling Jaime his name. *Thanks ever so much, Diego.*

A moment hung between them, a sense that Jaime had questions he wasn't willing to voice, but Tate wasn't interested in offering up any more answers, and he hoped Jaime would go where he was needed.

"Thanks, Diego." Jaime's attention prickled at his skin, but Tate refused to look at him again. Fucker probably thought he'd won. "So, Tate, most of your injuries appear superficial, but I'd like to take you to the hospital, get a doctor to take a closer look at that eye."

Hell no. He wrapped his arms around his body again. The couple of times he'd ended up in the hospital were times he'd been too out of it to refuse, and even the good drugs they gave for the pain didn't make the cost—a cost he could ill afford—worth it. If the pain became unbearable, he could swipe some of his mom's weed. She rarely used it, as alcohol was usually her favored method of oblivion.

"No."

"Tate." The way Jaime said his name, without any smugness but with a trace of pleading, made him shiver. Then he curled his lip in irritation. Jaime was the last in a long line of officious uniformed jackasses who just wanted to tell him what to do.

Mutinously, he stared over Jaime's ear while also avoiding Officer Hernandez's gaze.

Jaime sighed and handed him an instant cold pack before he efficiently packed up his medical case. "Keep that over your eye for about twenty minutes. If you have problems with your vision once the swelling goes down, if the swelling doesn't go down, or if you start getting dizzy, please promise me you'll go to Emergency or Urgent Care."

"Fine."

That prompted another sigh from Jaime. "A man of few words, you are, Tate."

Hernandez laughed. "You're just lucky all the ones you're hearing are clean."

Which made Tate want to scream a few obscenities, but he bit his lip to keep them contained. He was already squeaking by without an insufferable ride in a squad car, and he didn't want to mess that up.

"Can I go?"

Jaime grabbed his case and stood up straight just as Tate swung his gaze to Hernandez. The portable lights the police had set up to illuminate Area 52's almost-sort-of outdoor break room hit Jaime full-on, and Tate sucked in a breath. Jaime was beautiful, and would probably be even more so in the daytime, which, given the tiny crinkles at the corner of his eyes and a mouth that looked ready to grin at a moment's notice, had to be his natural element. The harsh spotlights leeched any hint of warmth from his coloring, but Tate was certain that in the proper light, Jaime was made of lush browns and rich golds. Jaime was made of everything Tate found attractive—and was also exactly the type of man who'd never be caught dead hanging with trash like him.

"Yeah, go on, Tate." Hernandez waved dismissively before turning back to the other cops.

Tate forced himself not to run—with his eye fucked, so was his depth perception. If he'd gone his whole life without knowing what Jaime looked like, without knowing the gentleness of Jaime's touch, he would have been better off.

OUTSIDE OF his apartment building Saturday afternoon, Jaime Escobar fiddled with his phone, shielding it from the glaring sunlight. He'd checked his messages half-a-dozen times in the past ten minutes, but nothing from his cousin Caleb yet. Jaime started pacing again. He and Caleb had long ago figured out that a single vehicle gave them an easy way to escape family functions early, but if Caleb didn't hurry up, Jaime was going to have to drive himself over to his parents' place to avoid being late, and that would suck. Especially given his current mood. His shift on Friday night had proven strangely unsettling, despite the lack of deaths or major disasters, and he'd been out of sorts ever since.

He could pinpoint exactly when and where his universe had been thrown out of whack, but he'd spent the intervening hours shying away from thinking about it.

Oddly, ignoring it was becoming more difficult, rather than less. But today was supposed to be a happy day, and Jaime was determined not to let his foolish emotions get the better of him.

Foolish. Dr. Whitley, his therapist after he returned from active duty, would have berated him for being so dismissive of his own feelings. Nevertheless, Jaime had spent far too many minutes letting his mind wander, and if he wanted to avoid any well-intentioned familial interrogations, he needed to get his shit together. Or at least wrap it up in pretty paper and a bow as a distraction.

Instead of Caleb's work truck, a sturdy four-door vehicle turned down his street. Jaime should have expected it, and yet that small detail only increased his internal turmoil. The car pulled into his driveway and the passenger window rolled down.

"Looking good, Jaime." Raven, Caleb's sexy, ex–porn star boyfriend and owner of the sedate car, gave him a big smile.

Jaime forced himself to smile back. Raven was an awesome guy who was perfect for Caleb and made him deliriously happy, but there were times when Jaime wished it was just him and Caleb against the world. Not too long ago, he and Caleb would ride to family events in Caleb's work truck, him sucking back a giant latte, and talk about their sex lives, or lack thereof in Caleb's case. But at that time, Jaime had been the only family member who knew Caleb was gay, and that secret had begun to damage Caleb in a myriad of ways. This was better, Jaime could easily concede that, but it didn't stop him from wanting the comfort of the familiar.

Jaime slipped into the car behind Raven in the passenger seat. Raven might own the car, but he preferred not to drive on the highway if he could avoid it, and ever since he and Caleb had settled into a relationship several months ago, Caleb usually drove the three of them to family events.

"Here you go, *papi.*" Caleb handed him an enormous paper cup, and this time Jaime's smile was genuine.

"*Gracias.*" Most things in life could be made sweeter with a generous application of latte. Maybe even an afternoon avoiding his mother's disapproving looks.

He belted himself in and relaxed in the backseat, letting Caleb and Raven's conversation wash over him while he sipped at his drink.

"Jaime."

Jaime blinked. Caleb's exasperated tone told him this wasn't the first time he'd tried getting Jaime's attention. Somehow he'd managed to avoid thinking about anything at all with enough doggedness that he'd completely zoned out on Caleb and Raven.

"What?"

"You weren't asleep, were you?" Raven asked.

"No. Just... thinking." Or just the opposite, but it would be too much effort to explain.

"Tough shift?" Caleb knew damn well how bad some of Jaime's shifts could get, and Jaime appreciated his ready sympathy, but his Friday shift had been a breeze. Or it would have been if not for the appearance of one pugnacious, stubborn redhead named Tate.

Jaime swallowed a sigh. "Not really." At least, not in a way he could readily quantify. And certainly not in the way Caleb meant.

"What's wrong, then?"

"Nothing." And everything. "Just tired."

Caleb steered the car to an open parking spot along the verge and turned it off. If they were already there, Jaime had spaced for more than a couple of minutes. If only he could somehow repeat the feat once he was inside.

"Jaime, you work too hard. There's no reason to pick up extra shifts," Caleb admonished. Then he twisted in the seat, looking vaguely horrified. "You... do you need money? You know you can ask me if you need anything."

Bitter laughter welled up in his throat, but Jaime tamped it down. Caleb couldn't give him what he wanted, and was in fact responsible for Jaime coming to the realization he'd never get it. "No, I don't need money. I pick up extra shifts because...." He trailed off. What could he say? He didn't have a boyfriend? He was bored? He had nothing better to do than work? All true, and all had become glaringly obvious since most of Caleb's time was wrapped up in Raven.

He didn't resent Caleb's happiness, but it certainly seemed pathetic that once he had a boyfriend, Jaime noticed how empty his life was.

The last thing he needed was to make Caleb feel bad, or even worse, sic Raven's "matchmaking" tendencies upon himself. He loved Caleb like a brother, and Raven was worming his way into Jaime's heart, but they had zero idea what sort of man he'd be interested in.

"Caleb, it's nothing to worry about. Just a few coworkers needing some extra time off. No big deal. I'm not really picking up that many extra shifts."

No more than he was legally allowed, at any rate. But his newfound need to fill the time meant he'd been taking on an extra shift down in Kissimmee on Friday night instead of searching Grindr for a hookup, or enduring yet another fruitless date, or watching TV in his underwear.

Dwelling on that call behind Area 52 had no point. No matter how often his thoughts turned to Friday night, it didn't help, it didn't make anything better. Which meant the wisest thing to do was to forget about it. He took a deep, calming breath and got out of the car.

Caleb pulled a large box out of the trunk. "Shit. You didn't forget a gift, did you? We can put your name on the card."

With some effort, Jaime kept from rolling his eyes. "I'm tired, yes, but I haven't completely lost my shit." He pulled a small card out of his pocket and waved it. "I'm covered."

Just because he picked up a few extra shifts to fill the time didn't mean he was desperate enough to attempt shopping as a time waster. Cash made the best, most convenient gift he could give.

Time to go in and congratulate the happy couple.

JAIME LEANED back against the wall, letting the muscles in his face relax. He'd been smiling for what felt like hours, and now that Isabel and Alberto were finally opening presents, no one was paying him any attention.

It was official. His baby brother was engaged. His sister, Maribel, was pregnant. In a few short months, she'd present Mama with grandchild number six, three of hers and three belonging to his oldest brother, Miguel. Jaime hadn't even been able to find a man he wanted to spend a week with, never mind the rest of his life.

Of course, until Caleb had come out of the closet last year and introduced Raven to the family, Jaime hadn't really thought there would be any point in having a boyfriend. He'd been out since high school, but there was a difference between his family knowing he was gay and truly accepting him in a relationship with another man. But they'd taken to Raven's presence beautifully, and Caleb's happiness had only served to expose an underlying restlessness. A nebulous desire for more that he'd

successfully buried—or more like, did his best to pretend didn't exist—
for years.

But his mama didn't ever pester him about finding a nice boy.
Getting married. Giving her grandchildren. Despite what everyone
seemed to think of him, it wasn't like he didn't want those things. But
he'd come out years before his mama could start with those particular
guilt trips. Watching her matchmake and pressure and cajole his siblings
emphasized that he was different. Maybe not quite normal in her eyes.
His brothers and sister had hated the pressure until they'd managed
to find someone, but not as much as Jaime hated knowing his mother
wanted all of her kids to find love except for him.

Today Mama was in her element. A wedding to plan, a new
grandbaby to prepare for. She was lording it over her sisters and sisters-
in-law like she'd won the world championship of matchmaking. He
didn't begrudge anyone their happiness, but he was starting to think
he'd rather go to the dentist, even if he had cavities to fill or teeth to be
extracted.

"Jaime, are you feeling all right?"

The sudden and unexpected presence of Caleb's mom, Tía Maria,
made him stiffen. "I'm fine, Tía. How are you?"

She smiled gently. "I'm well. Although if Isabel gets pregnant
within six months of marrying Alberto, there will be just no living with
your mother."

An unwilling laugh escaped Jaime. Tía Maria spoke with affection,
and yet the harsh truth was there.

"Does Raven know any nice boys he can introduce you to?"

Jaime flushed as a number of tumultuous thoughts scrambled his
wits. Raven knew a number of "boys," but most of them wouldn't be
considered "nice" by the general populace. But Tía Maria was well
aware Raven was an ex–porn star and that many of his friends had been
or were in the business.

She was also the only one in the family who fully treated him like
any other unmarried kid in the family, even if in some of his more obstinate
moments, he didn't know why the people of his parents' generation had
to be so invested in everyone else's love lives and procreation.

"Perhaps. I'm not exactly the settling-down type."

Tía Maria shook her head. "Perhaps." Her tone suggested she
didn't quite believe him, but that was fine. Everyone else believed him,

and he wasn't exactly lying. Until Raven showed up and blew Caleb's world apart, Jaime had thought maybe there wasn't any such thing as "the one." More likely everyone just got lonely enough to settle with the first person they didn't think they'd kill after prolonged proximity. But observing Caleb's emotional roller coaster from a courtside seat, he'd started to rethink that supposition.

Still didn't mean there was a "one" for him, and he wasn't about to ask Raven for an assist. Hell, Raven had spent several weeks trying to foist his friend Will on Jaime, and they'd both known early on that they weren't compatible for the long term. A one-night stand might have been fun, but getting laid regularly wasn't Jaime's problem. Figuring out how to get someone he liked to stick around was the big mystery.

The heat in his cheeks flared again as he realized he was thinking about getting laid while his aunt spoke to him at his brother's engagement party. Then again, it kept him from dwelling on the memory of a beguiling redhead at a call he hadn't been able to shake from his brain no matter how hard he tried.

Tía Maria patted him on the cheek. "You're a good boy, Jaime. You'll find what you're looking for. I know it."

Jaime hadn't been looking for much of anything, so he wasn't sure how that would all play out, but he appreciated her words enough to give her what was likely his second genuine smile of the evening.

As soon as the last gifts were unwrapped, he could probably coax Caleb into leaving. Raven enjoyed hanging out with their family since he had none of his own, but he wasn't used to the sheer number of people and the noise that the youngest generation could generate; it would be a simple matter to present the option of taking off as a benefit to Raven, rather than Jaime. Normally his family didn't grate on him—he'd always had fun camping it up just a bit, playing into his family's stereotypical expectations. But he just didn't have the energy today.

Maybe Caleb was right. Maybe he did need to lay off so many extra shifts. He loved his family, warts and all. There was no real reason today of all days should make them so hard to deal with.

He just didn't know how he was going to spend the rest of the evening. Raven and Caleb were being cuddly enough that they were probably going to go right home afterward. Even if they invited him to hang out, he'd just be a third wheel.

He didn't have the energy to deal with Saturday night crowds at a club. After the mass shooting not long ago, going clubbing wasn't nearly as carefree or relaxing as it had been. Jaime hadn't been in town when it happened, and hadn't been a responder, but it had affected him and everyone he knew. Safe spaces had become less so, and every time he went to a club, there was a tiny part of him that had to be coaxed into it.

Hookup apps could replace the getting laid part of clubbing, and he'd had his share of fun using them, but they weren't adequate substitutes for other kinds of social activities, and he didn't use them too often. His mother would kill him if she knew how many men he'd slept with, some of whom he didn't know either their first or last names. The apps only made that easier, and while sex got him out of his own head, over the years that bandage had become less and less effective. Hollow. Surface. Nothing to mitigate the underlying cause, which couldn't be as simple as an overdeveloped libido or pheromone overdose.

Caleb would probably be shocked if Jaime told him he was planning to spend Saturday alone and chaste, but Jaime didn't want to worry about explanations, so he sure as shit wouldn't mention it. Let Caleb and Raven think he was anxious to get out and get some ass.

CHAPTER TWO

"IF YOU'RE in there, you lazy ass, you gotta go to the store."

The screech combined with pounding on his door made Tate bolt out of bed before he realized what a stupid idea that was.

He took a few deep breaths to keep from screaming as his muscles protested the previous evening's treatment, and his mother didn't stop banging on his door.

In moments the spike of pain smoothed down to a more manageable level. "I'll be out in a minute." His reply sounded almost normal.

Fuck. The day after always seemed more painful than the actual beatings. When he got in a fight, he got wired like he was on something, and although the blows stung, he didn't notice them nearly as much as he did the next day. Groaning, he leaned over the stacked plastic tubs that served as his dresser, trying to find something clean and not too ratty. Sometime today he was going to have to start looking for more work. Hitting the laundromat wouldn't be a bad idea either if he was job searching, but during the day on Saturday was the worst time to go. Maybe he could pretend he was going to work later tonight and hang around the laundromat until his mom passed out.

He grabbed jeans and a long-sleeved button-down, both with cuffs that were only a bit frayed, and one of his special job-seeking vests, before turning back to the bed. The pain might be worse, but the wobble in his step wasn't as bad as it had been walking home from Area 52, and he could mostly see out of both eyes. Gingerly he pressed the skin around his left eye. The swelling had gone down substantially, but by now the worst would be the bruising.

Moving like an old man with arthritis—that big fucker had a long reach despite Tate's wooden weapon—Tate dressed. He smoothed the navy-and-teal argyle vest over his shirt. Over the past couple of years, he'd found a few argyle sweaters and vests at thrift shops. He had some good memories associated with argyle, and they were the most respectable pieces of clothing he owned—they made him look reliable, smart, and sedate, even though he was none of those things. Whether he was fooling himself or not, he usually managed to get new jobs before too long, and he credited that success to his argyle sweater-vests. Some people thought he was crazy for wearing them in the Florida heat, but even though the house he'd lived in all his life was shaded by an old grove of trees, it didn't have air-conditioning. Tate could tolerate high temperatures in a way most tourists and many natives couldn't. After he transferred his final pay from last night's pants to today's jeans, he gathered his laundry into a plastic garbage bag, ready for a swift retrieval later on.

He briefly considered a shower, but he'd showered right before his shift last night, and he didn't think his mother would be happy waiting any longer than she had to. After taking care of necessities like pissing and brushing his teeth, he peered around the cracks in the mirror.

God. His face. His eye was still puffy and starting to purple, which meant the most vibrant colors were still to come. There was an angry scrape on his face that he didn't remember getting, and he didn't bother checking out the other bruises on his body. They hurt like a bitch, but he didn't need to see them. At least his knuckles had been spared, since he'd used a piece of wood. As a high school dropout, he wasn't smart enough to do many jobs, and most of the ones he could were a bitch to do with busted knuckles.

Tate turned away from his depressing reflection and headed reluctantly for the kitchen. For a change, it was just his mom slumped at the table, wearing a sad, wrinkled animal print nightie, a half-smoked cigarette dangling from her fingers. Despite the drinking, drugs, and multiple men, his mother was still young and attractive.

Tate didn't know if there was a "boyfriend" asleep in her room or if he'd left last night, and he wasn't in a hurry to find out. Why his mother took pleasure in such skeevy company, Tate didn't know.

If it hadn't been for a couple of sweet but naughty guys at a few of his previous jobs, Tate wouldn't have thought sex was worth the effort.

"There you are." His mother shook herself awake, flicking cigarette ash in the direction of the ashtray, uncaring that she missed. "Jesus, what the fuck happened to you? Try to suck a straight guy's dick?"

Her laugh was rough and broken, and Tate did his best not to flinch. His mother found lots of things funny that Tate did not.

Then she frowned at him. "You better not have gotten into a fight at work. They'll fire you for that shit, and God knows there aren't that many jobs out there for people like you."

Stupid, she meant. Tate kept his mouth shut, though. He could sometimes control his anger, and if he got into a screaming match with his mother, he'd get kicked out for sure. Living with his mother sucked, but it was better than being homeless.

At least she was too tired or hungover to bother giving him a slap or two herself. She stood up and shuffled to the counter where her purse sat and rummaged through it.

Holding up a bill in one hand, she spoke slow and loud, making Tate grit his teeth even harder. "This one is for cigarettes." She lifted her other hand, waving a bill with a slightly different color. "This is for vodka. Don't be an idiot and fuck it up."

Churning began in his gut. His mom didn't usually get up before they started selling alcohol at the local Publix, but he hated going in there in the morning, because he was never quite sure what time it was, and they all stared at him like he was an idiot. There was a time, when he was a kid, that he'd had a watch that wasn't digital, and he'd been sure he was going to figure out the whole time thing. But it broke, his mother replaced it with a digital one like all the other clocks in the house, and he'd been fucking lost ever since.

Instead of asking—his mom hated when he asked if it was too early—he grabbed the bills and shoved them in different back pockets. The last thing he needed was to get them mixed up with his final pay from Burgers Galore. His mom was going to ask for rent soon.

If he was too early, he'd buy an apple or something for breakfast and go back later. He'd like to splurge on a deli sandwich, but he didn't dare until he figured out if he was going to get another job.

It wasn't like there was food in the fridge. His mom picked up a few shifts waitressing at a local bar—more often when she was between boyfriends—and usually got cheap food from there, not that she'd shared with him since he'd been old enough to get a job.

Tate headed out of the house, bypassing a load of scrap in the yard, and emerged from under the canopy of trees into the bright spring sunshine. The house had been his grandparents' before they died, but Tate had lived there all his life. The only good thing about the dank, humid place was that it was fully paid for, which meant the rent his mother charged him wasn't as much as it could be.

It would be amazing if he could get his own place one day, away from his mother. But that wasn't likely to ever happen.

As Tate approached the gleaming white building in front of him, the sun was high enough in the sky that heat radiated off the fresh asphalt in the parking lot. March was a funny month in Florida. Sometimes it could be as hot as summer, and other days it flirted with being cooler, like it was in January and February. One day he'd like to see snow, but he was just as glad he didn't have to live with it. Given how much time he spent outdoors, he'd probably freeze to death.

Today was going to be a scorcher, though, and this was one of the best places to spend a hot day. Doing his mother's shopping first ensured he didn't arrive before the library opened. The police definitely didn't approve of loitering by the library when it was closed, as he'd discovered a couple of times when he got here too early, which was sort of weird since he usually spent the day loitering inside.

As he walked up the steps and through the door, he tried to ignore the tiny bit of fear in his gut, the feeling that he didn't belong in such a nice place and at any moment he'd be barred from entry. Tuesdays and Thursdays were actually his favorite days at the library, but his work schedule didn't always allow him to show up then. But just about any day at the library was better than staying at home.

Before, he used to go to a tiny library in one of the strip malls not too far from his house. It had been showing its age, and he hadn't been terribly surprised when it closed down. Those couple of years had been bad. He'd gotten into a lot more trouble when he had nowhere to go. Old Town hadn't been too bad, although because he'd just been hanging around, a few guys had thought he'd been cruising, and some had been all too happy to try to pick up his underage ass. Tate had no patience for that shit, not when he'd dealt with skeevy assholes in his home for years.

When they'd built the new library in Celebration, it had taken him a long time to get up the nerve to go. Celebration was where a bunch of rich folks lived, and even though libraries were supposed to be for everyone, he figured they'd know he was a brainless piece of trash and kick him out. Or call the cops. But that first day—after getting lost several times—he walked into the shiny new building and immediately saw a friendly face—the same woman who waved to him now.

"Good afternoon, Tate." Mrs. Birenbaum was shorter than Tate, heavy, with a head full of gray curls and a fondness for polka dots. When the old library closed, she'd been an associate librarian reporting to an ancient, cadaverous man. But he retired, and when the new one opened up, she'd returned as head librarian, and Tate couldn't have been more pleased. Mrs. Birenbaum was nicer than his mother and didn't treat him like a moron the way everyone else did.

"Hello, Mrs. Birenbaum."

Tate didn't have much interest in telling anyone about his shit time at school or shit time at home or shit time in the work world, but Mrs. Birenbaum talked a lot. One of her sons had ended up with red hair like his, shocking both her and her husband, who both had dark hair, once upon a time. She often said it was the hair that made her a softy, but Tate suspected she was just a big marshmallow inside, even if he maybe got a bit of special treatment because he reminded her of her son.

Mrs. Birenbaum rummaged under the desk and pulled out a short stack of books. "Which one did you want today?"

Tate walked over and picked up the space opera he'd started at the beginning of the week. "This one, I think."

She smiled and returned the rest of the books to their spot under the desk. Tate had a library card, but he'd learned a long time ago that none of his possessions were off-limits when his mom drank. After having to pay for a couple of ruined books early on, he'd gotten in the habit of reading at the library but never taking anything home. Mrs. Birenbaum had been keeping his reading materials under the desk for years, to keep them from being checked out by another patron. Tate didn't usually keep more than a few books on hold for himself, but the space opera had two sequels, and he had a simpler action thriller for the days when dealing with the space opera was too much.

Fantasy and sci-fi had been the hardest for him to get into because he had enough trouble with regular English words; recognizing made-up words wasn't easy. But he really liked the space opera. The hero was a man who didn't belong anywhere and who no one liked, but somehow he'd ended up as the man needed to save the universe. Tate liked reading about guys like him.

When Tate looked up, he found Mrs. Birenbaum staring at him with a pained expression.

Right. His stupid eye. "It doesn't hurt too bad."

"Are you sure, honey? I could probably rustle up a cold pack for it. Have you seen a doctor?"

Tate shrugged. Did Jaime count as a doctor? "It's fine. I've had worse."

A soft gasp escaped Mrs. Birenbaum's lips before she smiled again. "Will it be a problem at your job?"

Work was the last thing he wanted to talk about. "Got fired last night." He gave her a rueful smile. "I'll be out of your hair soon. Right before dinner is one of the best times to look for a new job."

Cashier, busboy, or dishwasher were about the only jobs he could get without a high school diploma, and he'd long ago figured out that showing up right as people called in sick for a dinner shift was the best way to get hired on the spot. Unfortunately it also made him easy to fire, but there wasn't much he could do about that.

Mrs. Birenbaum had offered to help him job search on one of the library computers, but there wasn't much point. The type of jobs he could easily get didn't usually bother posting ads, and even if he applied online, how were they supposed to get in touch with him? He didn't have a cell phone, and if they called the house… well, if his mother let the call get picked up by the machine, he had a chance of getting the message. More than once, though, he'd been unable to decipher the message when their ancient answering machine played it back.

Mrs. Birenbaum had kindly helped him set up a free e-mail account, but he rarely checked it. Who would want to e-mail him?

"Come see me before you leave. I have some powder in my purse— maybe we can make that shiner a little less noticeable."

"Okay. Thanks." Heat crept into his cheeks. Was wearing a grandmother's makeup more or less embarrassing than being unable to hold a job for more than a couple of months? But he'd submit to the makeover, because he needed another job and Mrs. Birenbaum was probably right about it being harder if he looked like a brawler fresh out of police custody.

He took his book to one of the more comfortable seats by the window, out of sight of the front desk and Mrs. Birenbaum's concerned glances. Sometimes it was hard to find an empty one on a Saturday, but the rest of the week had been packed with programs designed to entertain kids on March break. Today it was like a ghost town. Clearly the neighborhood kids and their parents had had enough of the library for the week.

He opened the book, but he couldn't quite bring himself to focus on it. Instead, he stared out the window, remembering the EMT who'd treated him the night before.

Jaime had been hot—hot enough Tate might have let himself get cruised by him if they'd met anywhere but at the site of one of his fuckups. Depending on when and where he met guys, he could sometimes fool them into thinking he was smarter than he really was. Those were the guys he wished he could figure out how to keep after they met the *real* Tate and realized the woman he lived with more resembled a drunk, screaming landlady than a mother. The guys who just liked his face, or wanted to fuck a redhead, or a twink, or a barely legal, or whatever label they applied to him? Those guys could fuck the hell off, and he told them so, sometimes with his fists.

Tate didn't get a lot of dates. Certainly not dates like people had on TV, or that he saw when he worked in nicer restaurants as a busboy. Nice dates with conversation and someone paying for a meal that had servers to bring food to the table.

What would it be like to date a regular guy like Jaime? More to the point, what would it be like to live a life where a man like Jaime would want to date him? His imagination wasn't up to that task, though. Besides, every scenario he imagined ended up with them kissing, then going to bed. The library was pretty much the worst place in the world to exercise his sexual fantasies. The library was too nice for those sorts of thoughts, aside from the humiliation and inappropriateness of boning up in a public place filled with kids.

JAIME FLUNG himself upright, a shout lingering on his lips, ears still ringing from the explosions. It took a few shattered breaths before he recognized his bedroom, which was half a world away from the desert he'd served in. Sweat dampened his sheets where they'd twisted around his naked body, and he tried to practice yoga breathing while he waited for his heart rate to slow.

As soon as his vitals were mostly back to normal, he glanced at the clock by his bed. Three in the morning, and there was almost no chance he'd be able to get back to sleep. It'd been a long time since he'd had one of those nightmares, but hey, PTSD—the gift that could last a lifetime. He hadn't been hit with it as hard as some of his team or other returning veterans, but in the immediate aftermath of a nightmare, being thankful was a challenge. He was, however, thankful he'd been able to afford adequate and appropriate therapy when he returned.

He scrubbed his face with the sheets that were going straight into the wash and got out of bed to grab a pair of pajama bottoms and a T-shirt, muscles trembling ever so slightly.

First thing he did was head into the kitchen to start a pot of coffee. Drinking coffee in the middle of the night maybe wasn't the smartest thing in the world, but there would be no more good sleep to be had now, and he could nap later. For a change, he had an entire Sunday off.

After he stripped the bed and started the washing machine, the scent of freshly brewed coffee led him back to the kitchen. He had a small box of leftover pastries from Alberto and Isabel's engagement party. Peering in, he decided it wasn't worth dirtying a plate. He simply poured a large mug of coffee, grabbed the box, and settled in his living room in front of the television.

His mama would die if she knew how often he ate crap in front of his television instead of eating properly cooked meals at the kitchen table, but those little family rituals didn't mean much for a single man and made him feel lonely and pathetic whenever he tried. Besides, if he ever really had a craving for *ropa vieja* or *arroz con pollo*, he could just stop by his parents' house. With Alberto still living at home and various grandkids frequently in residence for babysitting, his mama usually had something good already on the stove or in the oven.

He scrolled through the options on his on-demand movie subscription account. He'd tried watching things people had recommended, but even on days when he didn't have nightmares, many of them either included violence too close to reality or reminded him too much of all the things he'd seen. Some of his coworkers didn't have any issue with it, but one of the reasons he got along so well with his semiregular partner, Angelica, was that they both preferred soft and fluffy, or funny, or romantic television and movies to crimes or thrillers or, God forbid, military flicks or stuff with explosions. Oddly enough, he didn't mind horror films, but definitely not after waking with a mind full of blood.

With a contented sigh, he started up a Miss Marple movie. His family would probably laugh their asses off if they ever found out how much he loved Miss Marple, but he'd always had a thing for the underdog, and a little old lady detective was almost the ultimate underdog. Sure, the movies were littered with dead bodies, but it was all sanitized and never bothered him.

The slow setup of the mystery and introduction of the potential subjects only held half his attention, though. Normally his dream was the same—the day he'd lost Mario. Although Don't Ask, Don't Tell had still been in effect when he'd been in the Army, that hadn't been what had kept him and Mario from being lovers. Primarily it was that they liked each other so much. But Mario had just rotated in for a three-year deployment, and Jaime was just finishing his four years of active duty. Their service wasn't going to overlap enough to figure out if a multiyear long-distance relationship would be worth working toward, so they'd contented themselves with being friends. Getting involved with mere weeks left together would only make the parting more difficult. Jaime had clicked with Mario.

Mario had been a scrappy little bastard. He'd squeaked by on all minimum regulations required to get into the Army, and he never backed down, like a stubborn Chihuahua trying to take on a mastiff. Jaime had admired that ballsy, take-no-shit attitude, the strength it had taken to hold his own when it seemed like everything was against him. He'd been determined as fuck to prove himself, and he did. Jaime wasn't the only one in their squadron who'd admired Mario's grit, but he was the first one to recognize it, and probably the only one who wanted to fuck Mario through the floor whenever he got hot-tempered.

Jaime had already intended to stay in touch with Mario and had planned to suggest Mario relocate to Orlando when he came home from Afghanistan—he didn't have a home or close family back in New Jersey—regardless of whether Jaime had been seeing someone.

But Mario died before Jaime left the sands, and coincidentally or not, Jaime had never found anyone who'd suited him as Mario had.

The most unusual thing about his dream, though, was the absence of Mario. Everything else had been the same, but instead of Mario dying in battle, it was a fierce redhead named Tate.

Maybe he shouldn't have been surprised. He'd been prodding the memory of that call on Friday like he would a sore tooth.

He was used to providing medical assistance in the midst of firefights and heavy artillery shelling in Afghanistan, so he didn't usually balk at getting close to the action. No gunfire had been reported—something of a miracle—but he'd been wary just the same.

By the time he and Angelica had arrived on the scene, the first pair of EMTs were in the parking lot, treating a scared young man for shock and possible sexual assault. They'd continued on to find a small cluster of cops, weapons drawn and spotlights shining on the picnic area behind the minigolf administration building.

Jaime's eye had gone first to the guy lying prone in the dirt, their first priority when the police called the all clear. The much larger combatant dropped a switchblade, obeying the shouted instructions, and the smaller man let a broken two-by-four fall at his feet.

For a moment Jaime had been unable to breathe. He could only see the face of one man. Now that he was weaponless, his stance and demeanor reminded Jaime of Mario when he was spoiling for a fight, even though there were few similarities in appearance.

Reddish blond hair gleamed garishly in the spotlights. His shirt was dirty and torn, and blood from his nostrils and split lip streaked starkly against his pale, freckled skin. His left eye had puffed almost entirely shut, but the other whisky amber eye glittered with the fever of adrenaline rush.

It wasn't difficult to tell who had been the underdog in this fight, even if the blond kid at the minigolf entrance hadn't told Dispatch about the red-haired guy who'd waded in to save him.

But the adrenaline would make it difficult to get the guy treated. Which meant Jaime had to leave the unconscious dude for Angelica. He was better at dealing with guys like this, better at preventing a resurgence of violence.

One of the officers cuffed him on the shoulder. "Don't see you down this way too often."

Jaime glanced at the cop long enough to identify him before returning his gaze to his potential patients. "Diego. Long time no see. How are you doing?"

"Same old, same old. Give me a call, we'll go for coffee or something."

Jaime agreed. He'd met Diego Hernandez at one of his favorite haunts, a gay club called Club Gallo. They'd shared a couple of very enjoyable blow jobs in the bathroom on a few occasions, then graduated to dating. They'd gone on two dates, Diego being coy about his day job, although Jaime hadn't realized it at the time. Then he'd come across Diego at the site of a vicious domestic violence call, and that was the end. He understood why Diego hadn't told him the truth about his job, but the evasion, combined with knowing they'd be working together on occasion, just made it too weird. The dates had been enjoyable, but Jaime had already known it was never going to be a long-term thing anyway, and there'd been no hard feelings when it ended. The blow jobs stopped shortly thereafter too, and now they were buds.

Diego allowed him in to do his work, and Jaime headed right for the redhead Diego had called Tate. It took a few minutes to calm him—he was like a skittish colt—but Tate eventually relaxed a bit and let Jaime inspect his injuries.

As he worked, he suspected Tate would be gorgeous without the bruising and swelling—his bone structure was fine and his skin smooth and unblemished. Jaime rather liked freckles, although he'd fucked a few guys who considered them a detriment.

A closer look revealed Tate hadn't broken his nose—not this time. At some point in the past, though, Tate's nose hadn't been set properly. When Jaime suggested the hospital, Tate tensed up again, bordering on pugnacious. Aside from their size, Mario and Tate couldn't be more different in appearance, but that didn't stop a wave of nostalgia and familiarity from sweeping over Jaime.

Not like he could force Tate to do anything he didn't want to do, but it wasn't hard to tell it was the potential cost that kept Tate out of the ambulance. Even the possible threat to his vision hadn't convinced him. Jaime just hoped Tate had enough sense to seek out medical assistance if something went wrong with his eyes. Vision problems tended to scare people like simple pain didn't.

Knowing he'd done the best for Tate under the circumstances didn't change the fact that he wanted to follow up, find out how Tate was doing. Wanted to know Tate's last name and how he'd ended up in that situation. See what he looked like when both eyes were healed and unswollen. Those desires had only intensified after Jaime's unsettling dream, but the odds of seeing Tate again bordered on the impossible, which only increased his mental restlessness.

A woman on-screen screamed, and Jaime blinked. Dead body in the library, and he'd been so lost in thought he didn't know who the suspects or victim were. His coffee was starting to get lukewarm too. Jaime restarted the movie and dug out a pastry, determined to pay attention to a mindless mystery rather than the riddle of the redhead. He didn't even bother getting up to nuke his coffee—he'd drunk far worse during his military service.

For now, his only concern was Miss Marple and the assortment of shady characters populating St. Mary Mead.

CHAPTER THREE

MONDAY NIGHT, on Tate's walk from the library, he decided to detour past Area 52. Dusk was falling, and Tate still faced the dilemma of going home while his mother was awake, or pretending to be at work and finding places to kill time. He'd done a hell of a lot of reading at the library since Saturday.

He suspected Kris would have given his notice Friday night, but just in case, Tate decided it couldn't hurt to see if he was working. See how he was doing.

Instead of sneaking around the back, Tate walked up like any paying customer, not that he'd be spending his dwindling funds on minigolf of all things. But he could pretend for long enough to see who was working the cash. Even though he'd been fired from this job too, he hoped intervening on Kris's behalf wouldn't get him chased off the property.

An older couple stood in front of the cash register, paying for their golf game. Tate shifted to the side so he could see the cashier. Kris's shock of blond hair looked the same as ever, but the face underneath was tired and almost as pale as Tate's natural state.

Once the couple had taken their golf balls and clubs, moving on to the first hole, Kris glanced Tate's way, mouth opening on a halfhearted greeting. Then his eyes widened in recognition.

"Tate! Oh my God, Tate!" He barreled out from behind the counter and flung his arms around Tate's neck.

Unused to such behavior, Tate simply stood there while Kris squeezed and gave him a big fat kiss on the cheek.

"Tate, my hero."

Heat washed up Tate's neck and into his cheeks. He wasn't anyone's fucking hero. "Kris, don't say that."

"I forgot how pink you can get." Kris's smile was wide and genuine, but that didn't change the fact that there was a hardness about him, sharp edges where before he'd been made of cotton candy with puppy-dog eyes.

"I just wanted to…." Obviously Kris wasn't okay. It could have all been worse, but the experience had to have changed Kris. He probably wouldn't be okay for a while. "Check on you. I didn't know if you'd maybe quit."

Kris shrugged. "I thought about it. But I need the job—I took the year off to work before going to college, and I'm headed there in the fall. This is a decent place."

Tate didn't know what else to say, and he couldn't exactly hang out here like a loser. "Well, maybe I'll stop in again."

"Wait, don't go." Kris grabbed his arm. "I'm so glad you came by. I didn't know how to get in touch with you, and I really wanted to thank you."

Tate didn't know what to say to that. But a rumble in his stomach filled the silence between them, and Kris smiled again.

"Come eat dinner with me. Please?"

Tate stared at him for a minute. "Not at the picnic tables?"

Kris paled. "Uh, no. Not ever again, I don't think."

That was more like it. He'd have thought Kris super brave or super crazy if he was ready to eat after dark down at the picnic tables so soon after his ordeal.

"No. Chickie's is just next door. We can eat there. My treat."

How fucking pathetic was it that a pre–college student was going to buy him dinner because he couldn't afford to eat at Chickie's and hadn't eaten since he'd splurged on an egg sandwich for breakfast? Yesterday he'd only eaten half of Mrs. Birenbaum's turkey sandwich, when she insisted she wasn't hungry enough to eat both halves.

But he was too hungry to say no.

"Sure. That would be great."

"Just give me a minute to get Kelly up here to take over on cash." Kris paged Kelly over the intercom and went back to stand behind the cash register.

Kelly still worked here too? Tate never would have guessed.

A group of four giggling teenage girls came in off the last hole while Tate waited, a couple of them giving moon eyes to Kris, who waved at them without much enthusiasm. Kris was a cutie to be sure, but those girls didn't have the right plumbing to interest Kris.

Kelly strode in off the greens behind the group of girls. "Taking dinner now?" she asked Kris before she saw Tate.

"Tate!" She rushed over and gave him a hug too. Tate had never been hugged so much in his life. "I'm so glad you were here Friday night."

At this rate his cheeks would be permanently red. Must make an interesting contrast with the purple and black around his eye.

Kelly joined Kris behind the register. "Don't hurry back, okay? I'll cover for you."

Kris nodded and led Tate back down to the sidewalk.

While they'd been inside, full dark had fallen, and now the katydids sang their nighttime humidity songs.

Tate still didn't know what to say, and Kris didn't seem interested in breaking the silence. Not that walking along the Irlo Bronson Highway was ever silent; cars roared past all times of the day and night.

In a surprisingly short time, they were settled in a pink vinyl booth, their black trays laden with burgers, fries, and soft drinks. Tate hadn't had anything but water in years—soft drinks were wasted money in his opinion, but he didn't mind the treat since Kris insisted.

Partway through their meal, Kris put his burger down and stared so intently at Tate—or rather, Tate's black eye—that he also felt obliged to pause in his dinner. Not a bad thing, really. It was more food at one sitting than he was used to, and his stomach was getting full.

"You must think I'm an idiot."

Tate shook his head. "No, I'd never think that." Kris didn't get fired from every fucking job he had—obviously the kid wasn't an idiot.

"They'd come in earlier that day." Kris dropped his gaze to the table. "I flirted with them both. Invited them to come back for the end of my shift. I thought it would be… sexy. Having a threesome, you know?"

Tate lifted a shoulder. He had a hard enough time finding one guy he could have sex with who he didn't want to punch for being an asshole. Two seemed like too much trouble. "Hey. You don't have to tell me anything."

"I owe you an explanation," Kris whispered to the table.

"You don't owe me anything. I'm glad I was there." Because there was pretty much no way Kris had been getting out of that on his own, not gagged and held down by two larger men.

"I can't believe I was so stupid."

"No. Not stupid. They had no right to take what you weren't willing to give. They're the assholes, not you."

Kris lifted his head, eyes wet and red-rimmed. Poor kid. Once that sunshine and rainbows innocence was gone, it was gone for good.

He sniffed and wiped at his eyes with the back of his hand. "I, uh, never did find out. What were you doing there? Did you hear something?"

Tate shoved a couple of fries in his mouth before he answered. God, he fucking hated having to admit to people how pathetic he was. "Got fired. Couldn't go home that early, and I remembered the picnic area would probably be empty at that time of night, but found you there and… well…."

"You were just going to sit in the dark? For hours?"

Tate shrugged.

Kris pouted. If Tate were another sort of man, he'd probably be attracted, but even if Kris wasn't too young for him, Kris wasn't his type. An image of Jaime flashed in his mind, but he ruthlessly shoved it aside. Even if he ever saw Jaime again, there was zero chance he was gay or that he'd be interested in Tate. But he couldn't deny Jaime seemed much like his ideal man.

Fortunately Kris wasn't attracted to him either, so Tate didn't have to worry about Kris taking this meal or his actions to indicate interest. Which might be why Kris was so comfortable with him now.

"I'm so conflicted."

Uh-oh. Maybe he was wrong about Kris's level of interest. "How so?"

"I want to be upset you got fired, but I can't, because I'm so fucking happy you were there. The right place at the right time."

The tension in Tate's shoulders bled out. "Oh. Well, you know me and jobs. Don't be upset I got fired." Tate got upset enough for both of them. And in this case, he found himself glad as well. First job he'd ever been happy to lose, truth be told.

"Find anything else yet?"

Tate shook his head, then pointed at his bruised eye. "Nah. No one wants to hire someone who looks like they get in fights all the time."

He'd tried two places Saturday before the dinner rush, but not even Mrs. Birenbaum's makeup job had done enough to hide the damage. Tate had pretty much given up on the job search until the bruising faded.

"Hey, maybe you could ask Mr. Singh for your job back. I'm sure he'd be grateful enough to hire you back."

Not likely. Mr. Singh had been a decent enough boss, but Tate didn't think he'd ever be forgiven enough to get hired back. Area 52 hadn't been one of his normal fuckups: messing up money or showing up way late for his shifts. Nope, he'd almost gotten in a fight on the greens, right beside a statue of a gray-faced, wide-eyed alien like they showed in the tabloids.

A couple of drunk college guys had started calling a group of younger guys names—faggot, cocksucker, things like that. The younger boys didn't have any way to retaliate, and they were getting upset. As in, having their evening ruined, one or more of them going to end up in tears kind of upset. Tate hadn't been able to let it go. If Mr. Singh and one of the other employees hadn't rushed out when they did, blows would have been exchanged. Mr. Singh had been regretful when he fired Tate, but he'd also been firm and determined. At least Tate had managed to get those college thugs banned for life, and the younger guys a handful of free passes.

"Don't worry about me, Kris. I'll find something. I always do." Even if each new job search seemed more useless than the one before.

"Let me know if I can help, okay? And…." Kris smiled shyly at him. "Maybe you could come back and keep me company at dinner again sometime. Or we could just hang out and do something."

Tate let himself smile back. "Yeah. Maybe we could do that." Maybe Tate's anger had finally done something useful and given him a friend. Friends weren't easy to come by.

JAIME PLOWED through his week, trying not to think of Mario or Tate, but he ended up having a couple of nightmares, and now he faced the prospect of another lonely weekend. Raven was doing one of his Tartan Candy gigs, where he and his friend Will pranced around looking sexy in kilts and got paid for it. Caleb and Will's new boyfriend, Dallas, were helping out too. Jaime could have invited himself along, but he couldn't picture himself in a kilt, and they didn't need three guys pretending to be bodyguards or administrators or whatever Caleb and Dallas told themselves they were doing besides ogling their boyfriends.

At least he'd had the foresight to text Diego Hernandez earlier in the week to arrange a lunch today, when they both had the day off. Gave him something to do, and hopefully wasn't too date-like.

He wandered into the Italian restaurant and quickly found Diego.

"¡*Hola!*" Diego handed him a menu as Jaime slid along the bench on the opposite side of the booth. Diego had dark hair and eyes, with sunbrowned skin. His eyes were friendly and warm, as they always were, even when he was on the job.

"How are you, Diego?"

"Good, good. Haven't seen you at Club Gallo lately."

Jaime shrugged. "Been busy."

Diego waggled his eyebrows. "Got a *chiquito* keeping you warm at night?"

Jaime laughed. "If only." Diego did love his twinks. Yet another reason they'd never have worked out—Jaime didn't fit the twink mold at all.

"Me too. My mother keeps wondering when I'm going to get married. So much pressure."

"Wait, you told your mom?" Last Jaime knew, none of Diego's family knew.

Diego let loose a belly laugh. "You're hilarious. No, *Mamacita* is still back in Mexico, thinking one day I might find a suitable woman I could bring home." Diego gave him an exaggerated look of disappointment. "It's very hard to find suitable prospects in Orlando."

Jaime laughed. "Too true. At the moment, my mama is too involved in my brother's upcoming wedding to bother with my love life." Which triggered the question: What would Rosa Escobar do once her three other children were safely married, and Isabel pregnant? Would she then turn her attentions to Jaime, or would she consider her motherly duty done, and give Jaime up as a lost cause?

Jaime and Diego ordered lunch and chatted a bit more about their families and work before Jaime casually steered the conversation where he wanted it to go.

"So what happened with those guys a week ago?"

Diego stared at him blankly for a moment, and Jaime was ready to elaborate—Diego might have arrested a dozen or more guys over the past week. But then comprehension lit Diego's expression.

"Oh, that call at Area 52. Yeah, it was a bit of a shock to see you there."

"Yeah, a bit weird. Those guys going to prison?"

The waiter arrived with breadsticks and marinara, and Diego grabbed one, sending the scent of garlic wafting over. Jaime's mouth watered, and he pulled his own out of the basket.

Diego chewed and swallowed his bite before answering Jaime. "Not sure. Probably. As I told that jerk—I don't remember his name—the knife was a mistake. If they hadn't brought that?" Diego shrugged. "Maybe just a slap on the wrist. The kid they assaulted just turned eighteen. A few weeks earlier and they'd have thrown the book at them."

Jaime sucked in air—and a chunk of breadstick. He coughed and Diego watched in silence, presumably to see if Jaime needed the Heimlich. After a moment, the crisis passed, and he drank gratefully from the glass of water.

"You okay?"

"Fine, thanks." Jaime cleared his throat. "Sorry. You just surprised me. I hadn't realized Tate was that young." Just turned eighteen. Jaime was a pervy bastard. Any nebulous plans he'd had about asking Tate out if he should see him again went up in smoke. Younger was one thing, but eighteen? Just over half his age seemed far too young for him. It was one of the reasons he'd never asked Raven for any introductions to the porn stars he knew. Raven had made porn movies until his late twenties, but Jaime knew damn well most of the guys were eighteen and nineteen— maybe younger if they had fake IDs.

Diego smiled knowingly and tapped the side of his nose. "Oh-ho. I should have known. This is all about Tate."

"What? No." Good thing Jaime wasn't prone to blushing. "I was just curious about it. You didn't arrest all three of them, which seemed unusual." If Jaime hadn't been busy hustling the two assailants off to the hospital, he might have asked Diego about it after the incident. Then again, he hadn't realized at the time just how much Tate was going to stick with him.

"Oh, sure. Curiosity." Diego's tone left no uncertainty—he thought Jaime was full of shit, but was willing to play along. Jaime could accept that for now, because he wasn't admitting anything else except under torture.

Jaime waited until Diego finished his breadstick, knowing that if he pushed the matter, Diego would prolong the agony just to fuck with him. Sometimes even the nicest cops had sadistic streaks a mile wide.

"Anyway, the eighteen-year-old I was referring to was the one Tate saved from getting raped. Tate's a few years older, sure, but not by too much. Early twenties. He's had a hard life, and that can age a kid."

The relief that swept through him was greater than Jaime ought to feel. But early twenties didn't sound nearly so unattainable or ridiculous as eighteen.

The tension of the moment broke further with the arrival of steaming plates of pasta. Jaime didn't often eat pasta—too many carbs—but his recent lack of sleep had given him a craving. And Diego never found a carb he didn't like, somehow managing to not gain an ounce.

After the silence stretched on too long, Jaime had to do something. Diego must know more than he'd shared so far. "So you know Tate, then?"

There hadn't been a hint of anything sexual when Diego had spoken to Tate, but then, neither had there been a hint when he'd spoken to Jaime at the scene, and Jaime had had Diego's cock in his mouth. More than once, even.

Diego narrowed his eyes. "Not like that. Tate Buchanan is not my type, especially since I only ever come across him *at work*. And not like you and I come across each other, *¿sí?*"

Odd. A week ago just the knowledge a guy'd had a number of brushes with the law would have sent Jaime running in the other direction. Thing was, he didn't know if Tate was gay or if he'd be interested, or even if Jaime's attraction would last beyond a civil discussion where Tate wasn't high on adrenaline and ready to snap like a cornered animal. But that single spark had ignited an ember that had been slow burning for a week, and it was the most Jaime had felt for any guy since Mario. Fucked if Jaime wasn't going to at least figure out if there was something there aside from the cracks in his brain.

But now he had a last name. The tiny nugget of information made him want more.

"Yeah, okay. So let's agree he's maybe my type. What do you know?" He didn't blame Diego for lifting an eyebrow in derision. Jaime wasn't exactly discriminating when it came to sexual partners.

"He's not gay."

Jaime let his eyes close, those three words almost like a blow. God. He didn't even know this guy, and he was busted up because he was straight? Maybe the PTSD had morphed into some other weird obsessive mental disorder.

"Shit, man, you should see your face. I was just shitting you, I…. Why do you even care?"

Jaime blinked his eyes open, staring at Diego, trying to read the truth on his face. "Honestly, Diego, I don't even know. There was just… a spark. You know?"

Diego shrugged. "Yeah. I know. Not always enough to start picking out china patterns, though."

That wrenched an unwilling laugh out of Jaime. If things ever got that far, he didn't see Tate as the type to pick out china patterns, for fuck's sake. It sure wouldn't be him either. He'd never understood the concept of "good dishes" that required a whole enormous piece of furniture to display them when they weren't in use… and they were never in use.

Diego finally took pity on him. "Okay, so as soon as I heard about the red hair, I sort of suspected Tate would be involved."

Again, that should worry Jaime, but it didn't. His years in the desert hadn't been sweet or soft, and he suspected Tate might have some idea what that meant, even if Tate had never left Florida in his life.

"So he's been arrested? Been to prison?"

"That kid." Diego shook his head. "He's probably been in more fights than he's had hot dinners, but oddly enough, nothing that ever stuck. Been arrested a few times as a juvenile, but no convictions. Most times we don't even bother bringing him in."

"Like Friday?" Jaime still couldn't reconcile one participant in a fight just being let go. He'd witnessed the aftermath of a number of fights— usually bar brawls and the like—and usually everyone got rounded up, zip-tied, and the particulars sorted out at the station.

"Yeah, like Friday." Diego nodded and ate another couple of mouthfuls of baked ziti before he continued. "See, he was a lot more volatile when he was a teenager, but lately every time he's involved, it's in situations like this. I mean, he saved that other kid from a really shitty situation. No one wants to punish him for that."

"He's a vigilante?" Jaime couldn't quite reconcile that notion with the angry, disheveled Tate in his memory.

Diego laughed again. "Oh hell no. If that's what it was, we'd be arresting him for sure. Just seems like he's in the right place at the right time and ends up in self-defense situations. And you saw him. He's never once, that I've seen or heard of, taken on anyone but bigger guys, bullies and criminals. I think he's maybe a little *loco*, because it almost always looks like he takes the worst of the punishment."

Jaime wanted to ask more, like where Tate lived and worked, but that would be pushing Diego's goodwill too far, especially since Jaime had already showed himself to be just ever so slightly obsessed.

They turned their conversation to less volatile topics as they finished their meal. After they paid and wandered out to the parking lot, Diego grabbed his arm and looked him in the eye.

"I only want the best for you, *papi*, believe me. If we'd worked out, I would have told my *mamacita* about you."

Jaime sucked in a breath and opened his mouth to apologize—he had no idea Diego had been so much more invested in their interludes than he was—but Diego waved his hand.

"Water under the bridge, *mi amigo*. I'm glad we're friends. But I don't want to see you get hurt. And I'm not sure pursuing Tate is wise, if that's what you intend. But if you need to talk, let me know."

Breathless from the notion that yes, he probably was going to pursue Tate and that he'd been so obvious about it, Jaime only nodded.

A week ago, if Diego had admitted his feelings, Jaime would have given him a real chance. Would have given in to the loneliness whispering in his ear that he was being too picky, that he just needed to find someone he liked and could get along with to settle down. Diego fit the bill perfectly, but now that Jaime had found a spark, he couldn't ignore it. Not for the safety of a sure thing.

Jaime's life had been full of risks—what was one more?

Chapter Four

Saturday afternoon Jaime stared at the giant UFO poised above him, creating shade over a quarter of the parking lot. It looked a lot less impressive in the daylight, but there was still a certain appeal to the kitschy-ness of it all. When he was a kid, he'd attended a number of birthday parties at minigolf places just like this one, or even gone just as something to do on the weekend with friends, and then, later on, either as a drunken lark or on a date.

He had a lot of fond memories of cheesy minigolf courses, but he'd never been as anxious at one as he was today. Ridiculous, because everyone who knew him would say he had more than his fair share of self-confidence. Or possibly arrogance, depending on who you talked to. His family and friends would never know just how terrified he was at the prospect of going into that small building designed to look like the aluminum-sided RV every alien conspiracist had owned in every UFO flick ever.

Even he wasn't sure if he was more afraid of being rejected or of finding no way to track down Tate Buchanan. He didn't even know the name of the victim from the previous week, and he certainly didn't want to refer to that horrific incident, because that would be in extremely poor taste, but short of haunting Diego's calls in the hopes of finding a single redhead, this was the only place he could start.

Jaime got out of his car. He'd planned his timing carefully, despite the fact that the heart of Kissimmee was way the fuck out of his way. He was expected at a dinner with his friends, so he couldn't linger here long, nor could he dwell on whatever happened now.

He opened the door of the trailer, getting a blast of freezing cold air in his face. His cousin Caleb would have been in heaven, but Caleb's lack of heat tolerance was a source of amusement for the family. Not that temperature control didn't come in handy, but Jaime didn't know how people could stand working in a place cold enough to hang a side of beef.

Flicking off his sunglasses helped, but the dim interior was a sharp contrast to the bright afternoon sun. Unsurprisingly, there were a number of alien- and spacecraft-themed gifts, most of them emblazoned with the Area 52 logo and website, alongside a wall of overpriced snacks and drinks. The true focus, though, was the cashier station where one rented balls and putters.

Jaime grimaced. When he'd decided today would be the best day to inquire after Tate—a decision made partly because of his lunch with Diego and partly because he had other plans this evening to provide a distraction—he had completely failed to consider that Saturday afternoon might be one of the busiest times. A harried mother supervised what appeared to be a birthday party, handing out clubs and balls to kids who'd already indulged in far too much sugar. Five adults stood in two lines for the cashiers, while a couple of other players inspected alien-head mugs and "I was beamed up at Area 52" magnets as they waited for their tee time to be called.

He wasn't about to waste the trip, however. He grabbed a bag of chips and a bottle of lemonade and got in line. He'd chosen the shorter line, but the congestion around the counter and the giant screens in front of the registers prevented him from observing either cashier. All he could say for sure was that neither of them had red hair. One had black hair, the other blond.

Finally he was next in line. As his cashier rang him up, Jaime got out his wallet and cleared his throat. "Do you know if a Tate Buchanan works here?"

Jennifer, if her name tag was to be believed, looked up at him. "Sorry, who?"

"Tate Buchanan."

She shook her head as she took his money. "Nope. Sorry. Don't know a Tate."

The young man at the other register, with a Kris name tag, swiveled toward him. "Can you wait around a few minutes?"

Jaime nodded, trying to ignore the tiny spurt of hope. He took his change and moved out of the way. He cracked open his lemonade and sipped at it, simply for something to do.

Ten minutes later there was a lull in customers and the blond guy left Jennifer in charge of the counter. He inspected Jaime up and down, and there was little doubt in Jaime's mind the guy was gay, even if he was far too fucking young. But then, Jaime didn't get the sense that Kris was interested in a quick romp.

Then Kris glanced around. The line for the cash register had diminished, but there were still a number of people waiting for their turn on the golf course.

"Come outside?"

Jaime agreed. He wasn't interested in airing his personal shit for the tourists any more than Kris seemed to be.

Kris led them around to the opposite side of the building and the canopy that covered a half-dozen picnic benches where customers could eat or serve cake for birthday parties. They moved close to the building to take advantage of the shade, and were out of earshot but not visual range of many of the course's customers.

"You a friend of Tate's?" The speculative look in Kris's eyes was tempered with suspicion. But then again, Kris was just being careful, and Jaime couldn't fault him for that.

Unfortunately, the explanation might not get him on Kris's good side.

"My name is Jaime. Jaime Escobar." He wasn't sure what the most tactful approach would be. He didn't know how much any of the employees knew, and he certainly didn't want to start any gossip about the victim. "Look, uh, there was an incident here, last week? I was the EMT who treated Tate, and I was just hoping to track him down."

"Oh God. Is there some awful medical problem?" Kris's face paled, and his hands flapped a bit like he couldn't figure out if he should run back into the trailer or grab a phone or race to his car.

"Whoa, whoa." Jaime held his hands out and quickly fell into his calming work speech patterns. "Okay, I can't actually discuss specifics of Tate's care outside of approved family members, but please don't worry."

Jaime was still moderately concerned about the blow Tate had taken to the eye, but that was another issue entirely.

Kris heaved in a breath and settled. "Oh good. I saw him just a few days ago, and he seemed fine."

"So you know how to get in touch with him?" Jaime sounded far too eager, judging by the renewal of Kris's speculative look.

Oh shit. Maybe Kris was his boyfriend? Jaime had to tread carefully.

"Uh, I mean, I'm glad to hear he's doing well. That's good." Or he was going to tread so carefully he chickened right the shit out.

Kris nodded, the beginnings of a smug smile starting.

Fuck it. He was here, he might as well say something now, because he sure as shit wasn't going to be able to do this again. Besides, what was the worst that could happen?

"So, could I leave my number with you to pass on to him?"

"Ha. I knew it."

"Knew what?"

"You like him."

Jaime barely refrained from rolling his eyes. Kris might still be in high school, but Jaime wasn't. But he couldn't exactly refute the statement. He also didn't much want to discuss it with a stranger, but he didn't know how to say that without sounding like a complete dick, especially when he wanted Kris to do him a favor.

Kris rolled his eyes. "Don't give me that look."

"What look?"

"All puckered up like you've eaten a bucket of sour lemonheads."

"What?" What the fuck were lemonheads? But he did his best to unpucker and look nonchalant.

Suddenly all the mirth fell out of Kris's face, and before he even spoke, Jaime knew what he was going to say.

"I was the guy Tate saved. During the incident." Kris grabbed his forearm and squeezed. "So whatever you did to make sure he's healthy, I'm so grateful for. Because I know how bad it could have been if he hadn't come along."

Shit. This kid was too fucking sweet and young to have had to deal with shit like this. With those words, Jaime's personal stuff went on the back burner. "Have your parents gotten you a therapist? If not, I can recommend a good one."

Horror streaked across Kris's face. "My parents? Thank holy fuck I'm eighteen. They don't know any of this happened."

Jaime wanted to protest, but all too often parents didn't support their LGBT kids, and it was especially tough for male victims of sexual assault, who'd as often as not be denigrated as weak or less masculine. Faced with Kris in the flesh, though, he'd completely forgotten he was an adult in the eyes of the law.

"Okay, but… something like this can have lasting effects. If you're able to, if your health insurance covers it…." Jaime pulled a business card out of his wallet. "Give him a call. Please."

Kris stared at the card as though it were coated in poison. "What, this guy hands his cards out to EMTs to drum up business for him?"

Maybe the kid wasn't quite as innocent as he appeared, but that could be good. If looks *weren't* deceiving, this world would eat Kris for breakfast and spit out the bones.

"No." Jaime was a big believer in privacy in health care, especially when it concerned his patients, but more than once he'd had to open up his own personal traumas in exchange for trust. "But he's treated me for PTSD since I got back from Afghanistan. He's helped me tremendously."

Kris's gaze flicked sharply upward and once again subjected Jaime to a laser-like inspection. "Oh. Thanks." He tucked the card in his pocket, which was the first step, as far as Jaime was concerned. If Kris was lucky, he wouldn't have any lingering psychological issues, but Jaime wouldn't be surprised if the trauma had laid a booby trap or two for the next time Kris tried to have sex.

"You take care, now, Kris." Jaime patted his shoulder and turned to go.

"Wait. What about your number for Tate?"

Once again Jaime was thankful he didn't really blush, because talking to Kris had completely distracted him from his original purpose. "Oh. Right."

Kris smiled and pulled out his phone. "Tate doesn't have a phone or anything. If he's got e-mail, he's never shared that either, but he did say he'd drop by sometime soon. I'll make sure he gets your number next time I see him."

Tate didn't have a phone. That made Jaime sick on so many levels. Phones were almost surgically attached to the hands of everyone he knew. He assumed Tate didn't have enough spare funds to afford a phone, which was sad in itself, but the prevalence of cell phones meant a radical decrease in public pay phones, and if Tate ended up in trouble, he'd have a hard time getting help.

But Jaime didn't bother saying anything. Not like there was anything either of them could do about it. He took Kris's phone and typed in his number.

"Thank you. I appreciate it."

Kris smiled a little sadly. "You seem like a good guy, Jaime Escobar. And I think Tate could use a little good in his life."

Jaime returned the smile before turning away to really leave this time. If he hit any traffic on the 4, he was going to be late, and Raven hated when people were late. Jaime would never hear the end of it.

JAIME APPROACHED the booth where Caleb, Raven, Will, and Dallas were already viewing menus, and tried to tamp down his irritation yet again that he was the third wheel squared. He knew he was just being more sensitive than he should be, but it sucked so hard. He'd been so happy Caleb had found Raven, even if it meant Jaime was at loose ends more often than ever. And now Raven's best friend Will had gotten together with his coworker, Dallas. Jaime loved them all, but the rampant couplehood grated like sandpaper over a sunburn. More so in the past week.

And here he was, pretending everything was normal and pretending it didn't bother him. Because these men had rapidly become a second family... well, Caleb already was, but whatever. He didn't want them to think he wasn't happy for them, but he wanted a slice of that pie for himself.

"Hello, all! Always a pleasure to be in the company of such gorgeous men." Jaime pasted on a big smile as he slid into the booth beside Raven and kissed his cheek before leaning over the table to cup Dallas's cheek. "Looking good, Dallas. I guess Will isn't working you too hard."

Dallas turned a pretty shade of pink, and Jaime winked while Will grumbled under his breath. He did so enjoy poking Will's temper, although Will had mellowed enormously as he'd settled into a stable relationship with Dallas.

An attentive waiter came by and took his drink order. They'd all discovered a number of inventive nonalcoholic drinks, since both he and Raven had bad stories about drunk driving, but there were times, like today, that he wished he hadn't driven, because a bit of buzz wouldn't go amiss.

Jaime picked up the menu, even though he knew what he was going to order. "So, Raven, I'm surprised we're doing this on a Saturday. No Tartan Candy events this weekend?"

Raven laughed. "Amazing, isn't it? With spring break on different weeks all over the country, we've been booked solid every weekend since the beginning of February, but this weekend ended up free."

On the other side of Raven, Caleb snorted. "Unfortunately, it's given him time to scheme."

"Scheme? That sounds intriguing."

The waiter returned with his drink, and Jaime sipped at it, pretending his strawberry piña colada was swimming in 150-proof rum. He let Raven's chatter wash over him, adding in a few noncommittal affirmative statements when it seemed as though people were waiting for him to respond.

ONCE THEY'D paid up, the five of them stood outside the restaurant.

"You coming with us to the club?" Caleb looked pointedly at Jaime. It had taken some time after the club shooting for any of them to want to go out, and there was a hint of defiance in Caleb's tone, that they were going to go out and be themselves in spite of the fear. Hopefully over time some of that fear would ease, but Jaime didn't think it would ever be erased.

The past couple of times they'd gotten together, it had been Jaime begging off, rather than Caleb, for completely different reasons. A one-eighty from the innumerable times he'd coaxed and coerced Caleb to go to the clubs with him, trying to get him to loosen up and get laid. Funny how it had taken everyone he knew diving into the relationship pool for him to realize just how unsatisfying he found his nameless encounters. He wasn't ashamed of them, but he didn't want to continue on the way he had been. After all, he'd never found a spark in the bars. It took a chance encounter with a near criminal to do that.

"I don't know. I'm a little tired."

Caleb raised an eyebrow. "Then you shouldn't be working all those extra shifts. Your mama is starting to call my mama, and she's asking why Tía Rosa never sees you anymore."

Jaime raised an eyebrow right back. "I'm sorry, this is how you're convincing me to go to a club?"

Raven laughed. "He tries, but he doesn't really have either of your mothers' skills with the guilt trips."

"C'mon, Jaime. It'll be fun." Dallas added his input.

No, it probably wouldn't, but it would be better than sitting at home checking his phone every two minutes. It could be days or weeks before Kris saw Tate to pass on Jaime's number, and even then, he might not be interested in calling.

"Fine. Yes, I'll go." Fortunately his clothes were close enough to suitable for clubbing, although he usually went commando. Then again, he wasn't planning on any back-alley blow jobs or one-night stands, so ease of access wasn't an issue.

"Good." Caleb clapped him on the back. "I'll go in your car."

Jaime blinked. "Why don't you just drive with Raven?"

"First of all, Dallas drove all of us here—he's our designated driver. And secondly, we haven't had much time to chat, just you and me."

Jaime bit back a bitter remark about how that wasn't his fault. It was no one's fault, and it was perfectly normal, even if Jaime didn't like it. He got out his keys and let Caleb follow him to the car.

"I assume we're going to Club Gallo?"

"Of course," Caleb answered.

As soon as Jaime got them on the highway, Caleb pounced. "Tell me what the fuck is wrong, Jaime."

What? He'd tried so fucking hard to pretend like everything was normal. "Nothing's wrong."

"Bullshit. I've known you since birth. You've been out of sorts for weeks now, and you're getting worse. Dinner just confirmed it."

"What are you talking about?"

Caleb laughed, but it had an angry edge to it. "You agreed to be one of Raven's models for Tartan Candy's kilted men calendar."

"Shut up. I did not." Raven had been trying to come up with ways to make Tartan Candy a viable business beyond him and Will in kilts at events, and his newest brainchild had been sexy calendars. He wanted to start the shoot soon so he could have product ready for distribution for the fall, when people started thinking about the next calendar year. He'd asked more than once if Jaime would model, but Jaime had always declined because he thought he'd look ridiculous in a kilt. Who put a full-blooded Cuban American in a fucking kilt? Aside from his cousin's odd boyfriend, who thought everyone ought to be in kilts.

"You sure did, and if you back out now, there might be tears." There was also an underlying hint of menace in Caleb's tone, which Jaime inferred to mean Jaime better not upset the love of Caleb's life.

"I guess I don't have a choice. But see if you can postpone it or change his mind, please?" Any number of EMTs he knew would never let him hear the end of it, and a number of cops would tease the shit out of him too.

Jaime pointedly stopped talking and changed the radio station, hoping Caleb would let it drop, but Caleb could be bullheaded.

Out of the corner of his eye, he saw Caleb shrug. Fuck. Jaime was going to end up wearing that damned kilt, if only so Caleb could add to his already extensive blackmail file.

Caleb only gave him a few minutes' reprieve, which he spent regretting the fact he hadn't paid more attention to the guys at dinner.

"Seriously, *papi*, what's going on?"

The fates hung in the balance while Jaime nearly gave in to the urge to tell Caleb he'd met someone. Then sanity reasserted itself, because he hadn't really, had he? Hell, Tate hadn't even introduced himself. If it weren't for Diego, Jaime wouldn't even have a name to hang on the redhead. He certainly didn't need to endure any amount of teasing for becoming obsessed and moony over a guy he'd crossed paths with at work.

"Seriously, nothing really. Just a… weird week at work." Not precisely a lie, since just about every call he'd been on since meeting Tate, he'd looked over any bystanders for a lithe, compact red-haired man.

But he didn't like lying to Caleb. Most of his life was an open book to his cousin, with the exception of some of the ugliest, most painful parts of his military service and the lingering aftereffects. Neither was Jaime interested in dealing with Caleb's incredulity over Jaime wanting to settle down, all appearances to the contrary. Perhaps it would be different if Jaime hadn't kept Mario a secret….

If something came of his little excursion to Area 52, there'd be plenty of opportunity to tell Caleb. But there was a lot of ground to traverse before Jaime would be in a position to be introducing anyone to the family. He probably had a better chance of getting hit by lightning—no, this was Florida; the chance of that was damned good. A better chance of winning the lottery than he had of even getting Tate to call him back, never mind a fairy-tale happy-ever-after.

"Sorry, Jaime. Did you want to stay at Raven's place tonight?"

Jaime rolled his eyes. Caleb spent almost all his spare time in Raven's large, airy condo, and Jaime had stayed over in Raven's spare room more than once, but mostly when he was drunk enough not to hear or care if he heard them going at it like lust-addled rabbits. Drinking wouldn't fix the shit in his head, and he knew better than to try to use it as a panacea, so sober he was going to have to be tonight. It was like the universe was determined to poke him in the eye as many times as it could.

"Thanks, but I'll be fine. Getting some exercise in the form of dancing will help."

"Oh, right." Caleb leered. "*Exercise*. Got it."

Jaime sighed quietly. He'd just have to dance his bad mood away and hope he hadn't turned into a giant walking cliché, an old fart with a pathetic hard-on for a twink. He curled his lip. He wasn't exactly fond of labels, whether they were applied to his ethnicity or his sexuality. There was something too confining about them, and no matter what Tate might look like uninjured, there was no way he was a stereotypical twink. Maybe Jaime wasn't completely hopeless.

WITHIN A few minutes, he pulled into the parking lot behind Will's car. Smart. He'd seen Dallas's rusted-out piece-of-shit mobile, and Jaime wouldn't want to trust it to make it down the block, never mind to Club Gallo and home again.

He followed the guys into the club with a friendly wave to the doorman, Lyle. Lyle clutched at his heart in exaggerated mock surprise. Yeah, it had been a while since Jaime had shown up. He was a regular, but not a regular drinker, so it wasn't as though Club Gallo would notice a dip in its revenue.

Partway to the area with the tables where Will and Caleb preferred to hang out while the rest of them danced, Jaime rocked to a sudden stop.

Was that a glint of red hair on the dance floor? Jaime detoured to get a closer look at the writhing bodies. With a wash of colored lights—red, then blue, then purple—he couldn't discern anyone's hair color, but then the colors disappeared and he caught sight of the redhead. Craning his neck, he tried to see the guy's face. The guy leaned over to one of his companions and latched on to him for a thorough tongue exploration, making Jaime's heart race. He felt breathless, like he'd taken a gut punch. With only the guy's left profile in view, he couldn't even say with certainty whether it was Tate.

His companion broke the kiss and shifted them so they were dancing back to front, the bigger man's arms wrapped firmly around the redhead's waist, mouth pressed against his neck.

Another shift in time to the music and Jaime's spine lost its stiffness. Not Tate. What he'd learned from Diego made it seem unlikely that Tate spent a lot of time at clubs, but he couldn't help looking. Like he'd looked everywhere this week.

He was an idiot.

He spun around and wove his way back to the table the guys had appropriated.

"Anything wrong?" Caleb frowned at him, no doubt wondering whether Jaime had been lying his ass off in the car.

"Nope. Just thought I saw a friend on the dance floor. I was wrong."

Caleb accepted his explanation, for now. But Jaime's fascination with Tate—and the memories he stirred of Mario—was unexpectedly affecting. If he caved to the strong urge to tell Caleb about it all, he'd have to defend his decision to keep it all secret, and he wasn't ready for that, especially since he suspected Caleb wouldn't understand. Not when it had been years since Mario died and Jaime had never told anyone about him or the PTSD.

What he'd seen over in the desert were things that no one needed to know, including how Mario died bleeding out on the sand. Jaime's nightmares were bad enough, and the time after his stint in the Army had been dark. Keeping that darkness from throwing shadows on his family had been a real struggle. Caleb would have been supportive, Jaime's parents and siblings maybe would as well, but he hadn't wanted to bring his ugliness into their lives.

One thing was for certain. He needed to make sure his fascination with Tate wasn't just his overdeveloped altruism muscle taking over—or another body part that hadn't been getting nearly enough exercise lately.

Jaime sprang to his feet. "I'm going to go dance. Grab me a cranberry and soda, please."

Caleb waggled his eyebrows, but at least on the dance floor, Jaime would probably be able to hide the fact that he wasn't leaving with a random guy. His heart just wasn't into the random hookup scene anymore, Tate or no Tate.

CHAPTER FIVE

TATE SLIPPED into Area 52, hoping Kris was working tonight. His mom had been haunting the house, so he didn't dare use the phone there to call and check—he always fucked up phone numbers, and having his mother watching, waiting for him to slip up so she could make fun of him, only made him that much more likely to dial wrong. But Area 52 wasn't out of his way, and he didn't have anywhere to be yet, so it was hardly a waste of time. He had more than enough to waste.

He and Kris saw each other at the same time, and Kris smiled, bouncing a bit behind the counter. He finished with his customer—the only one not on the course—and came around to hug Tate.

Tate still wasn't sure what to do about the hugging.

"I'm so glad you showed up! I was wondering how long it would be before I'd see you again." Kris gave him a quick kiss on the cheek and let him go. "How's the job search going?"

Tate hadn't been sure how often was acceptable for a friend to show up—these were rules he didn't know—but honestly, he hadn't wanted to be a charity case, hanging around Kris hoping a kid saving up for college could buy him another meal. That was the definition of pathetic. Worse than pathetic, even. That was full-on asshole territory. He'd even purposely showed up tonight after dark in the hopes that Kris had already eaten.

"Good." As good as it ever got for him, anyway. Between his black eye fading enough that another application of Mrs. Birenbaum's powder covered the bruise, and his lucky sweater, he had another job. "I'm bussing tables at the Flying Pizza Pie. I started last night." His normal plan had worked to perfection, and none too soon. His mother had taken the last of his final pay yesterday, so all he had right now was his portion of the tips from last night.

Kris clapped. "Yay! I'm so glad you found something. Are you working tonight?"

Tate shook his head. "I have Sunday and Monday off."

"Awesome. Then you can have dinner with me again. We can celebrate."

"Oh. Uh. You didn't eat already?"

"Nope. There was a big rush right when I normally go eat. It just slowed down about fifteen minutes ago. I'm going to get Jennifer up here to cover, and then we can go."

Tate had to come right out and say it. "I don't think I can afford to buy anything." He wasn't about to pull out the money in his pocket and ask Kris if he had enough. Losing the first friend he'd had in forever in a matter of days because he wasn't smart enough to figure that out would suck so hard.

"That's okay. I'll cover. We're celebrating your new job, remember? You shouldn't pay for your own celebration."

More rules he flat-out didn't know. When had he ever celebrated anything? If he was smart, he would just leave, or tell Kris no. But time and again he'd proven he wasn't smart, hadn't he?

"Besides, I might have some more good news for you." Kris almost sparkled with excitement, but unless he had somehow figured out how to grow a money tree and was willing to share that secret with Tate, Tate couldn't think of a damn thing Kris could tell him that would be good or bad news for him.

Kris called Jennifer; then another couple of customers came in. While Kris helped them, the manager's door at the back opened. Mr. Singh walked out, and Tate scanned the place, looking for somewhere to hide. When Tate had worked there, Mr. Singh had never stayed past dusk. There wasn't anywhere for Tate to go, and he froze, hoping maybe Mr. Singh didn't remember him. Mr. Singh was a grandfather—they weren't supposed to have good memories, right?

"Mr. Tate." Wrong.

Tate mustered up a tiny smile. He'd sort of missed the way Mr. Singh addressed his employees. He was Mr. Tate, Kris was Mr. Kris, and whether or not she was married, Jennifer would be Miss Jennifer.

"Uh. Hi, Mr. Singh. I was just meeting Kris for his dinner break."

Mr. Singh approached and patted him on the cheek. If Mr. Singh weren't old and cute, Tate would never put up with shit like that. "That's fine. I don't mind you being here, as long as you don't distract Mr. Kris from his work or yell at my customers." He lifted one white eyebrow, but as when Tate had gotten fired, Tate didn't sense any real anger.

"You don't?" That didn't sound like the Mr. Singh he remembered.

"You're a good boy, Mr. Tate, and you did a good thing." He lowered his voice to a whisper. "I think Mr. Kris will be less nervous when you're here."

Tate's ears and cheeks heated up. He hadn't done anything to be thanked for—he'd just lost his temper, but this time he saved Kris and didn't get fired because of it. But he ignored Mr. Singh's praise and focused on the other thing he'd said.

"Maybe he could work the day shift for a bit?"

Mr. Singh shifted his eyes upward as though asking for divine intervention. "I tried. There were a few people willing to switch, at least for a few weeks, but he said his parents would ask questions, and they did not know what happened."

Tate shrugged. Certainly wouldn't be information he'd be in any rush to share with his own mother, so he sort of sympathized.

"Mr. Tate, if I could hire you back, I would."

Tate blinked. Although getting fired by Mr. Singh had been about the best experience he'd had getting fired, he certainly hadn't expected any expression of regret.

"That's okay, Mr. Singh. I've got a new job." Thank fuck. "I'm doing fine."

Those words prompted a familiar expression—disbelief. Mrs. Birenbaum wore it all the time. Things could always be worse. He wasn't homeless, and he ate almost every day. With a new job, eating would get a little more regular too. As long as he managed to keep this job for longer than the last one.

"Mr. Tate, you're welcome to stay here with Mr. Kris. If, as I said, you don't interfere with his work and don't yell at my customers."

It wasn't as though Tate ever wanted to get angry. But he couldn't always help himself.

As though Mr. Singh could read his thoughts, he sighed and patted Tate on the cheek again. "Do your best, okay?"

"Okay." It was nice of Mr. Singh to let Kris have company, though, and Tate might actually take him up on the offer. It wouldn't hurt to have somewhere else to hang out—somewhere free—especially after the library closed.

Kris switched off with Jennifer and came over to them, a curious look on his face. "Ready to go?"

Mr. Singh opened his mouth to say something, but he clearly changed his mind about saying it. "Have a good dinner. I will probably be gone by the time you get back, Mr. Kris."

"Sure thing, Mr. Singh. Jennifer and Layton said they'd close up tonight."

"You're a good boy too, Mr. Kris." Kris got the same cheek pat before Mr. Singh made his way back to the manager's office and Kris dragged Tate out of the building.

"Okay, I want to know what that was all about, but first, I have to tell you something. I thought I was just gonna burst when I saw you come in."

Tate didn't even care what Kris wanted to tell him. He knew Kris couldn't possibly have gotten over his assault this quickly, but whatever was on Kris's mind had turned him back into cotton candy and rainbows without any shadows, exactly how a guy like Kris should be.

A guy the size of a quarterback strode in from the parking lot with a giggling girl hanging on his arm, and Kris grabbed Tate's hand and pulled him over to the picnic tables. After dark on a Sunday it was deserted—and yet still well lit.

Kris waited until the couple went through the door, bouncing on the balls of his feet. Tate nearly started laughing. He'd forgotten how excitable Kris could get.

"Okay, they're gone. What is with you?" Having a friend was kind of cool.

"You have an admirer."

Tate didn't know what to do with those words, and he stared at Kris, who stared back, an expectant expression on his face, like when someone told a joke Tate didn't get.

Much like those jokes, he was going to need an explanation. "I don't understand."

"Someone liiiiiiiikes you. Thinks you're sexy."

"What the fuck have you been smoking?" Tate bit his lip. He hadn't meant his utter disbelief to sound mean, but this was too weird.

"No, I'm serious."

"Someone came and told you I was sexy?" Maybe Tate had accidentally dosed himself on one of his mother's "medications," because who would do that? Why would they do that? Even if someone had thought Tate was sexy, why would they even think to approach Kris about it? The guy would have to be stupider than Tate was.

"No, of course no one did that. That would be weird. But it was obvious he thought so."

Well, that cleared things right the fuck up. Tate rolled his eyes. He wanted to tell Kris they should go to dinner, but that seemed a little rude since Kris had offered to buy again. Tate was just going to have to wait until Kris got this out, whatever it was that was making him squirrelly.

Kris huffed out a dramatic sigh. "I don't suppose you remember a super-hot Latino EMT? I mean, you only met him like over a week ago. He's too old for me, but if you don't mind an older guy, he's probably fine for you."

There was only one super hot EMT Tate had come across, ever. "Jaime?"

Kris clapped his hands and bounced even harder. "I knew it! It's like fate. Or destiny."

God. Tate was still fucking lost. But at least he had a tiny breadcrumb to follow. "Jaime showed up here?"

If it had been one of the cops, Tate would have freaked out, because that would probably mean they hadn't been able to find him at home and he was about to get arrested for something. But he'd never had an EMT track him down afterward. Hoping for anything was just too terrifying, though.

"Yes. He left his phone number for you." Kris pulled out his phone to show Tate.

Joy and terror collided, making his stomach swoop. Tate got phone numbers from people on occasion. Usually rudely shoved into his pockets when his hands were full, and he was never inclined to contact any of those people. Jaime was a different story.

"I don't... I don't do well with phones." Understatement. "I always dial numbers wrong and stuff."

Kris stared at him, bouncy excitement coming to a screeching halt. "I don't... I mean... he's too old for me, but he was hot, and sweet, and really into you. I could tell. Did you not... are you not interested?"

Almost spraining something, Tate managed to not roll his eyes. He wasn't about to take Kris's word for it that Jaime was "into" him. But Kris's question... he didn't want to lie. If Kris had asked if Tate wanted to call Jaime, the answer would have been a swift no. But Kris had worded it in such a way that Tate would be lying if he said no.

"I don't know if it's a good idea."

"I could text it to you, if you only had a cell phone."

Tate laughed even though he hated how Kris sounded like such a thing wasn't possible. "No, I don't have a cell. God. I barely have a job most days. I can't afford a phone."

Kris's cheeks went a little pink—a gentle color, not the profusion of red that Tate's went when he was embarrassed. Some people had all the luck. "I'm sorry. I could write it down for you. You could call him from home or something?"

Fuck no. Not a chance. Not when he couldn't ever tell when his mom would be at home. She'd arrived unexpectedly more than once, and he wasn't opening himself up to that sort of scrutiny.

"Don't worry about it. I'm really not good with the phone." But he couldn't deny he was curious. He didn't think Jaime was too old for him, and looking at Jaime out of his one good eye had been the best part of getting into that fight, aside from making sure Kris didn't get hurt worse.

For a moment Kris looked like Tate had told him Santa Claus wasn't real, but then he bounced and glittery unicorns danced in his eyes.

Tate let out a quiet groan. He wasn't going to like this.

Kris stabbed at his phone.

"What are you doing?"

Kris waved at him like he was an annoying insect, and focused on his phone call. "Hi, this is Kris."

There was a pause; then Kris continued. "He doesn't have a cell phone, but he's here right now. Did you want to talk to him?"

There was no other word for the sound that came out of Tate but *squawk*. Kris didn't seriously just call Jaime this very second, did he?

Tate's heart rate increased and nervous sweat sprang up under his arms, and far before he was ready, Kris handed him the phone. He took it like it was a poisonous snake or a ticking bomb. How the hell had this happened?

He cleared his throat, hoping to swallow down the panic, but he didn't succeed. "Hello?"

"Tate? This is Jaime. Uh. Jaime Escobar. I was the EMT who treated you last week." Jaime's voice was deep and rumbly and vibrated in Tate's belly. He'd noticed before that Jaime's voice had been smooth and soothing, but this was something different.

"Kris mentioned that."

There was a pause. The sound of a TV or maybe a restaurant filtered through the phone, so Tate didn't think the call had dropped, but Jaime wasn't saying anything and, well, this conversation was all his fault, so he could figure out how to continue it.

Kris had stepped away, but given how he held himself, it wasn't exactly to give Tate privacy.

"How's your eye doing? Did the swelling come down? Vision okay?"

Oh. Jaime had wanted him to go to the hospital. The panic receded, leaving him unsettled in a different way.

"Yes. Fine." Disappointment made him terse. Following up because he'd been worried about Tate's health was nice. He supposed. Jaime would be the first EMT to do so. Figures he was also the hottest one, and Kris had gotten him wondering... well, about things he never would have. "Overdeveloped work ethic?"

Jaime let out a strangled laugh. "What?"

"You went to a lot of trouble to track me down for a follow-up." He did his best to sound uncaring, because he didn't want either Kris or Jaime to think he'd hoped for anything more. And damn Kris for putting ideas in his head. He was too stupid for a man smart enough to become an EMT.

"God. I'm fucking this up, but I didn't expect Kris to call back so soon, never mind just put you on with no warning."

The self-recrimination in Jaime's words confused Tate.

"I mean, I want to know how well you healed up, sure. That eye looked bad. But I, uh, wouldn't have tracked you down for that. I was... just trying to ease into what I wanted to say."

Something like fear, but warmer and more pleasant, fluttered in Tate's belly. "What did you want to say?"

Jaime let out another little laugh. "You're direct, aren't you? I can work with that."

Tate waited and heard Jaime suck in a breath.

"Would you have dinner with me sometime? Or maybe catch a movie?"

Kris was right. Jaime was interested in him. But Tate was having difficulty processing getting asked on a date. A real date, not just an offer to maybe feed him if he showed up for sex. Once he'd been offered cold leftover noodles from the fridge. He'd been too hungry to turn it down, but he'd seen people have dates, and he'd not had one.

"Tate?"

He started, realizing Jaime was waiting for an answer. This might be the stupidest thing he'd ever done. "Okay. Yes." Tate smiled. "That sounds nice."

Jaime blew out a breath. "Oh, good." He laughed, a much merrier sound than Tate had heard so far. "My schedule is always a little weird. If Mondays are okay for you, we could go tomorrow. Wednesday would work for me too; otherwise we'll have to go next week. Or, uh, I could maybe manage lunch any day this week?"

Tate's smile got bigger. For the first time, he heard the nervousness in Jaime's voice. It helped to know Tate wasn't the only one on unfamiliar ground.

"Tomorrow is good. I don't work Mondays."

"Monday it is. I just need your address, and then I could pick you up at, say, six?"

Tate's smile disappeared, and he pulled the phone away to stare at it for a moment. He hadn't thought that far ahead. A nice guy like Jaime, with a good job and all, would not be impressed by his mother's house.

He put the phone back to his ear. "Maybe you could just pick me up at Area 52. That would be better."

Kris nodded and grinned, giving up pretending he wasn't listening avidly to Tate's side of the conversation.

"Sure. I can do that. See you tomorrow at six."

"See you tomorrow."

Tate handed the phone back to Kris, not bothering to figure out how to disconnect the call. Kris stabbed at something, stuck the phone in his pocket, and then squealed before wrapping Tate in yet another hug.

"See? I told you. Good news. Let's go eat and you can tell me everything."

Everything? He'd been standing right there for Tate's half of the conversation. There was hardly much else to tell.

"Are you working tomorrow?"

"I am. But even if I wasn't, I'd change shifts just so I could be here when he picks you up. This is so exciting."

It was exciting, and Tate wasn't quite sure how to deal with that. At least Mr. Singh's generous offer meant he could arrive early and kill some time hanging out with Kris without worrying about being late. His inability to arrive anywhere on time had gotten him fired more than once. Probably dates wouldn't be any happier about it than bosses were.

CHAPTER SIX

JAIME STOOD by the door of the trailer, practicing deep breathing. Who knew it could come in handy for so many different situations? He couldn't remember the last time he'd been this nervous about a guy. The worst that could happen was they didn't hit it off, but that didn't make him feel any better.

He'd spent the day in a frenzy of cleaning his apartment, mostly to distract himself from running different possible date scenarios in his head, twisting up his mind even more. A tiny part of him had wondered if he had cleaned because he was hoping the date might end up back in his bed, but he ruthlessly tamped that notion down. His apartment was about a twenty-minute drive from Area 52, and the restaurant he wanted to take Tate to—as long as Tate liked Italian food—was about halfway there. But he assumed Tate lived around Area 52 and might not want to go so far away from his home turf to end up at a stranger's place.

A couple of teenagers nearly knocked him over as they left the trailer, and Jaime realized he'd been standing in front of the door like a twit. He rubbed damp palms on his pants.

Being nervous was ridiculous. He was a grown man, and it wasn't like he'd never experienced rejection before. Tate had agreed to the date, so he was already ahead.

Another deep breath before he opened the door and walked through.

It took next to no time to spot Tate slouched against the wall near the counter, talking to Kris. Jaime didn't know if he'd chosen that spot on purpose, but it was like he was in a spotlight, on display.

Jaime bit back a groan. Tate was even better-looking than he'd imagined. His hair was brighter than he'd remembered, and it would probably gleam like copper in the sunlight. He had a wide mouth with full lips that flirted with being pouty. The slight crook in Tate's nose from a previous break did nothing to detract from his appeal. A faint hint of bruise tinted one sharp cheekbone, his skin pale and creamy with a spattering of freckles… everywhere, including over the prominent collarbones visible in the V of Tate's neckline. The freckles might have made him look young, but those whisky amber eyes held too much wariness, too much knowledge of the worst life had to offer. No one paying attention would assume Tate to be naive. Diego had told Jaime there were only a few years separating Kris and Tate, but Tate's soul was old before its time, and he obviously had decades more life experience than Kris. Like Jaime did.

Kris tilted his head Jaime's way, and Tate turned. The second Tate saw him, recognized him, gave him hope. Because for a moment, when Tate's pupils dilated and his jawline softened, that spark Jaime worried he'd imagined was reflected back.

If Jaime hadn't been drinking in every aspect of Tate, he might have missed it, because once Tate mastered his surprise, he was every inch the wary wildcat Jaime had treated a week and a half ago, waiting for someone to kick him but ready to fight back if they did. That sliver of attitude still reminded Jaime of Mario, but nothing else was the same. Relief swept through him. He wasn't trying to resurrect a ghost. Tate was clearly his own person, not a Mario copy, but there wasn't anything wrong in having a type. Jaime's just didn't have anything to do with looks.

This date wasn't going to be like any of his others.

A big smile stretched Jaime's face. Despite the potential for disaster, Jaime was happier than he'd been in days.

He strode toward Tate but stopped when he got close, again a little unsure. Most of the men he dated—even if it was a first date or a date following a successful blow job in a club bathroom—were openly out, and he'd have greeted them with a kiss on the cheek.

Then again, Diego had known Tate was gay, and there wasn't anyone else in the store besides him, Tate, and Kris. And Jaime often greeted family members and friends with a kiss on the cheek as well.

If things ever got to the point of Tate meeting his family—which he shouldn't be thinking of this early on—he'd have to get used to it, because his family did a lot of hugging and kissing.

"Good to see you, Tate." He leaned in and tilted his head to give Tate a kiss on the cheek. It wasn't the kiss he'd longed to give Tate since getting a good look at his lips, but he didn't want to freak Tate out, and the Area 52 gift shop was a little more public than was prudent for the type of kissing he wanted.

As it was, Tate was visibly startled by the affectionate greeting, but he rallied. "Good to see you too." He paused. "Jaime."

A shiver raced down Jaime's back and settled in his balls. Tate's voice was so much deeper than he'd expect for his small frame—not that Tate was tiny, but he was shorter and slimmer than Jaime. Jaime would bet a lot of people underestimated Tate's strength because all they saw was his size.

He made no attempt to kiss Jaime back, but that was okay.

"Ready to go?"

Tate shrugged and nodded. An urge to grab Tate's hand struck Jaime, but he ignored it. For now.

Jaime glanced at Kris. "Thanks. I appreciate it."

Kris beamed like a matchmaking mama and shooed them out.

Jaime had to admit, this might be the weirdest date he'd ever had.

They got settled in the car, and Jaime turned down the radio. He hadn't made actual reservations because he didn't know anything about Tate's likes and dislikes, but there were a number of restaurants he could take Tate to, all of them in the same general area.

"Anything in particular you'd like to eat? I know of a great Italian place, but if you'd prefer Thai, steak, Indian, or Chinese, we can do that instead. Maybe Mexican?" He wasn't going to offer Cuban. Jaime might not spend a lot of time cooking, but he knew how to make a few dishes that were almost worthy of his mother. No sense taking Tate to a restaurant for that when he could—hopefully—use some of his family's traditional dishes to woo Tate in a more intimate setting.

Jaime gave himself a mental slap. Their date had lasted mere minutes, and already Jaime was planning seductive suppers.

A loud grumble came from the direction of Tate's belly, and Jaime grinned. At least he was hungry. When Jaime glanced over, he almost groaned. A flush had reddened Tate's cheeks and throat. Jaime rarely blushed, and his skin was brown enough that it was hardly visible, but he hadn't realized how adorable it looked. Even when he'd hooked up with fair-skinned blonds or sandy-haired guys, the only time he'd seen their skin pink up like this was in bed, and it had never been so stark.

His cock thickened just a bit as he imagined Tate spread out on his sheets, skin pink all over, ready for him. Another shiver snaked along his spine, more intense than before. But he was getting way, way ahead of himself. This date, this man, was different from the hordes of others he'd had, and he didn't want to fuck it up by acting like he had no self-control.

Tate gave him a look that said he'd be wise not to say anything, and Jaime wouldn't. Not until he got Tate used to being teased. He wanted them both to have fun, not to put Tate in a bad mood.

"One of those sound better than the others?" Jaime did his best to sound as though he hadn't noticed either the belly rumbles or the exotic blushing.

Tate's ears went red under Jaime's scrutiny, and his gaze flickered away from Jaime's face.

"Um. Italian? Italian is fine."

"Italian it is." Jaime guided the car out of the parking lot.

BY THE time they got to the Italian restaurant Jaime felt was worthy of a first date, he was sweating despite the air-conditioning. Much of his normal small talk had not gone over well. Tate answered his questions in as few words as possible, without asking any questions. Jaime gave up waiting for a return conversational serve and just volunteered information. He'd found out Tate was twenty-two, worked as a busboy at a place called the Flying Pizza Pie, and lived at home with his mother. Getting to know Tate was an uphill battle, but he seemed to listen eagerly when Jaime spoke about himself, and it felt like the ice between them had thawed ever so slightly.

"What about school? Where did you go to school?" Jaime asked.

A sudden chill descended.

Jaime floundered, wondering if he should ask another question, but his mind was utterly blank.

"I never finished high school."

Jaime cleared his throat. "Oh. Well, that's okay." *That's okay?* Like Tate needed his permission? Any other things he could think of to say sounded equally awful, but he truly didn't care how much or how little schooling Tate had. Education was… important, but it wasn't make or break.

Tate's ears reddened, and Jaime didn't think it was a good flush. *Shit.*

That last question about Tate's schooling had pretty much destroyed whatever progress Jaime imagined he'd made.

He half expected Tate to open the door and bolt when Jaime turned off the car, but instead he just sat and waited.

Jaime should have known better. If nothing else, his discussion with Diego should have made him realize he couldn't approach Tate like he approached dates with guys he met in the clubs. Many of them were just like him—thirtyish professionals looking for sex or maybe companionship. Some of the younger guys were looking for the same thing, or maybe trying to find a sugar daddy. Those guys looking for free rides weren't to Jaime's taste at all—he didn't appreciate the phony flattery hiding the mercenary heart beneath. But perhaps he'd been too judgmental; maybe finding a well-off older man was the only way out of a bad situation for some of those guys.

Tate sat hunched over himself, looking very much like he regretted saying yes to Jaime.

Jaime unbuckled his belt and twisted in his seat so he could look at Tate, who stared at his lap.

"I don't care that you didn't finish high school, you know. All I want to do is get to know you, and the only way I know how to do that is to ask questions. If some of them make you uncomfortable, you can just tell me that."

Jaime remembered Diego saying Tate had been arrested a number of times. "It's not an interrogation. I'm just interested in a simple exchange of information. There's no judgment here, I promise." But if Tate didn't dump his ass immediately, maybe Jaime could help with some of the things that obviously bothered Tate.

"Why?"

What? Why was there no judgment? Jaime was lost. "I don't know what you mean. Why what?"

"Why do you want to get to know me? It's obvious we're different. You're smart, employed, live on your own. Why do you even care about me? If you just want sex, say so."

Tate's jaw firmed up, making him look even more mulish than when Jaime had tried to get him to go to the hospital. As much as Jaime wanted to sleep with Tate, he'd never been more certain of anything in his life that Tate wasn't that easy. And that wasn't the only thing he wanted, however foolish he might be.

His pulse picked up because he was going to have to be more forthright than he'd been since he and Mario had decided not to risk a relationship. He never could have imagined laying all his shit out there for any other first date to see, but he didn't know how else to convince Tate.

Reaching out, he traced Tate's jawline. His finger scraped along short stubble that was too light to see, and Tate sucked in a breath even as goose bumps appeared on his neck.

Jaime hooked a finger under Tate's chin and tugged gently, coaxing Tate to look at him. Staring deep in those amber eyes, he opened himself up for Tate's scrutiny.

"That little zing? The one you felt just now?"

Tate nodded slightly.

"Yeah, I felt that the first night. Before I even got my hands on you." Which sounded a bit filthy but was the truth nonetheless. "You... were obviously the underdog in that fight, but you weren't ready to give up. You were so determined. And you did a good thing. Many people would have walked on, left Kris to his fate."

Jaime brushed a finger over the hint of bruise that shadowed Tate's left eye. "I couldn't even tell then how gorgeous you were. It didn't matter, actually. You intrigued me. I've never tracked down a patient before in my life, but I couldn't stop thinking about you. I want to know everything about you, good and bad, because... because...."

Jaime closed his eyes. It sounded ludicrous to say it aloud, which was why he hadn't told Caleb about Tate.

"Why?" Tate's voice was low, without any antagonism, but it held a genuine note of pleading.

Jaime suspected he'd do just about anything if Tate asked him in that tone. He opened his eyes again. "Because I like you, Tate. And I think I'd like to see if we can make something work between us. Something more than sex."

Tate bit his bottom lip as he stared at Jaime, considering. "There's more bad than good. A lot."

"Let me decide that for myself, if you don't mind."

"I didn't really do anything that night. Just got angry. It's never been a good thing." A hint of shame appeared in those amber eyes. Jaime wanted to erase it. Tate might not have seen it as a good thing, but Jaime thought Kris would vehemently disagree.

For a brief moment, Jaime wondered if Tate had some sort of anger management problem. Given his frequent brushes with the law, it was possible. But Diego's leniency assured him that Tate had at least channeled his anger into something relatively productive. If they got to where Jaime hoped, maybe Jaime could make a case for Tate to get help, but that was an issue for down the road.

"If you aren't feeling it or don't want to give this a shot, let me know. We can still have dinner, but then I'll take you home and never bother you again." It killed him to say it, but Jaime didn't think he could handle "just friends." Not again. It had to be all or nothing… or, at least, a concerted effort at "all."

Tate nibbled at his bottom lip again, the silence stretching out so long Jaime wondered if he'd scream just to break the tension. Then Tate nodded decisively. "Okay. We can try. As long as you promise me one thing."

Jaime nearly said "anything," but that was a dangerous word to throw around at this early stage. "What's that?"

"Don't…." Tate faltered, eyes going bright. "When it ends, promise me you won't call me mean names."

Anger boiled up in Jaime's chest, and it took every bit of his willpower to hide it. He sensed Tate was being as open and forthright as Jaime had tried to be, and just knowing someone had broken things off with Tate in the past, calling him something painful enough to leave scars, made him want to punch someone. And as a rule, Jaime abhorred violence. He was a medic, for fuck's sake.

"Done. If it ends, I promise you I won't be an asshole about doing so." He was careful to emphasis the word *if*, because he was hopeful, and he wanted Tate to share that hope.

Jaime reached over and grabbed Tate's ice-cold hands, and held them. His own weren't precisely warm either, but they were in better shape than Tate's. He gave Tate a playful grin.

"But I should probably mention… I am also interested in sex."

This time the blush that colored Tate's face looked sweet, not shameful, and Jaime thought he might have fun teasing Tate once he figured out what the boundaries were. In spite of Tate's world-weary, street-smart toughness, his request told Jaime he'd have to take a gentler touch than he did with Caleb or his other friends. The last thing he wanted to do was inadvertently open hidden wounds.

"Want some dinner now?"

Tate smiled and nodded.

They walked past the windows on the way in, and Jaime scoped out the diners. There were several tables available, which was good because

Jaime hadn't made a reservation. Maybe next time he would, if he had a way to discuss a proper plan beforehand with Tate. Jaime hadn't had a mobile phone when he was young, like kids today all seemed to, but now he'd feel lost if he didn't have it with him.

He turned to Tate to say something, but Tate wasn't beside him. Jaime twisted around only to find Tate staring at something in his hand, face whiter than any conscious, living person Jaime had ever seen.

"What's wrong?" Jaime's first thought was maybe dizziness or blood sugar or something.

"It's awfully nice in there."

Jaime narrowed his eyes. "Sure, I guess." He liked it, but Tate didn't sound particularly thrilled. "We can go somewhere else if you'd prefer."

Tate opened his fist, revealing some crumpled bills. He looked up at Jaime, expression absolutely terrified.

"Jesus, Tate, what's wrong?" Because Jaime wanted—needed—to fix it. Those wide amber eyes would have him getting fitted for sword and shield to slay whatever dragons threatened Tate. What would he be like once he'd gotten to know Tate? What magic did Tate have that tied him up in knots like this?

Tate's pained, lost look disappeared in a flash, and he shoved the money back in his pocket. Then his jaw squared up, and Jaime braced himself. He'd never met anyone whose skin betrayed changes in their emotional state so clearly, and he already knew—even after this short acquaintance—that Tate was going to be stubborn about something.

Anyone else might get pissed off about it, but Jaime loved it, even more knowing Tate had some emotional scars. It meant he was willing to stand up for himself. If Jaime had wanted a doormat for a boyfriend, he would have gone to the store and bought one.

"I don't think I have enough money to eat here."

Damn it. Jaime hadn't even thought of that. "I asked you on a date. I'm paying for it."

"Isn't it too expensive?"

Bam. Tate flung down the gauntlet, almost daring Jaime to pick it up. Money could cause a lot of trouble, and he didn't want to trample on Tate's pride, nor did he want to minimize Tate's concerns, not if they made him whiten like a sheet of paper. He also wasn't sure standing in front of the restaurant was the best place to discuss this.

Tate's stomach growled again, and he pressed a fist against his middle as though to silence it.

"We still don't know each other well, and I'd like to talk about it some more, preferably over dinner. This is our first date, and I wanted to take you someplace nice. One of the things we can talk about is what sort of dates we'll have going forward. Does that sound reasonable? I'm happy to pay for dinner. I was expecting to."

Tate stared at him, and it felt like he was being weighed and assessed for his truthfulness and trustworthiness.

"Thank you." Tate's skin slowly returned to its normal color.

"C'mon. Let's go." Again, the temptation to take Tate's hand was strong, but those were boundaries he wasn't willing to cross just yet.

This time Tate stayed by his side until they were seated across from each other at a tiny table near a fake fireplace. The wooden beams and stone facing on the walls had a lot of character, and it was one of Jaime's favorite Italian places, although it did tend to be a little pricier than most places he ate.

"Let's order first, and then we can talk some more."

Tate nodded and bent his attention to the menu.

"Do you want to share a bottle of wine or something?"

"I don't drink." Tate didn't even look up as he answered, but his curt tone had returned. Without being able to look Tate in the eye, Jaime didn't know if he'd just reverted to his abrupt speech patterns or if he had a reason for not drinking, like Raven did. But if Tate wasn't going to drink, neither was Jaime. Something told him he'd need his wits about him.

TATE DID not know what to make of the man sitting across the table from him. God, when Jaime had walked into Area 52's gift shop, Tate had just about swallowed his tongue. Dark, shiny black hair that matched his thick, curly lashes. Deep brown eyes with faint crinkles at the sides that Tate associated with a sunny nature and good humor. Tanned skin that probably never burned like his own. Jaime was taller than Tate, wider, and more muscular—he looked fit but not like a serious gym-goer. Everything about him screamed sex and security and happiness. Tate supposed he could be forgiven for not realizing how hot Jaime was right after his fight, but he still didn't understand why Jaime wanted to take him out on a date.

He couldn't deny there was a zing between them, as Jaime had demonstrated in the car. Tate had been afraid he was going to throw wood right then and there. From a touch to his fucking cheek. The same one Jaime had kissed—kissed!

But all the other stuff Jaime had said? Tate didn't doubt that Jaime believed it, but he knew it wouldn't last. Jaime didn't know how much shit was in Tate's life, and when he figured that out, he'd be gone as quick as anyone else.

If Tate was smart, he'd end this crazy thing now, but no one had ever accused him of that before. And no matter how much it would hurt when everything ended, Tate really wanted a little bit of something for himself.

He was already on his first real date and eating at a proper sit-down restaurant—that had to count for something. The best he could hope for was to make a few good memories to hold on to when he was alone again.

Doing his best to ignore the prices on the menu because they'd only confuse him, he inspected the entrées. Most of the items were things he'd never eaten before—if they didn't serve them at the pizza buffet, then he'd have had no hope of trying them. At least the menu items weren't written in Italian or anything.

The waiter smiled down at them like Tate wasn't an impostor who should be wearing a black apron and carrying a plastic tub. Who was he kidding? A place this nice wouldn't hire him even for dishwashing.

He tried to let Jaime order first, but Jaime smiled and shook his head. Finally Tate ordered the spaghetti and meatballs. That had to be fairly cheap; otherwise his mother wouldn't have made it so often when he was a kid.

Jaime tilted his head and pursed his lips before ordering… a whole lot of food. Jaime spoke fast, and the waiter whisked away their menus so Tate couldn't even use them to figure out what Jaime had ordered.

He'd wait until the food came. Anything he didn't recognize, he'd ask about then.

After the waiter had brought a basket of bread and, weirdly, a small plate of oil with pepper floating on it, Jaime leaned forward.

"Have some bread."

Right. He wasn't going to fill up on bread. Assuming he got up the nerve, he was going to ask to take it to go. Bread was filling, portable, and didn't go bad if he carried it around in his knapsack in the heat. It was nice bread too. Not just a regular loaf, but warm with a crusty exterior brushed with flour or something.

Jaime took a slice and dipped it in the oil before eating it.

Well, Tate certainly couldn't take the oil with him, but he wanted to try, see why anyone would do that.

Tate imitated Jaime's lead, although he almost dripped oil on his shirt.

"Oh, that's good." Richer, saltier, and more flavorful than butter. "What is that?"

"Olive oil." Jaime's gaze was intent and maybe just a little heated, although Tate wasn't sure why.

"That's it? Just olive oil?" Not that he'd ever tried olive oil on regular white bread, but he suspected the bread itself added to the delicious flavor.

"Yes. Olive oil and pepper. Simple, but it works."

Yeah, it did. Tate had to sit on his hands to keep from taking more. Getting greedy only meant he wouldn't have lovely bread to eat tomorrow and maybe the next day.

Jaime sipped at his water; then he leaned forward. "Look, I get that I make more money than you."

Oh, back to that conversation. "Um, yeah." The sarcasm came out automatically.

Jaime rolled his eyes but didn't seem upset. "Okay, okay. But here's the thing. Most relationships aren't made up of people who have completely even income and job status and… whatever else. Family or friends or material goods. There's always going to be some sort of inequality or difference. Unless I go out and find another gay EMT who is my age, Cuban descent, spent a few years in the Army, never been married, no kids, works too many hours. But I wouldn't, because I don't want to date a carbon copy of myself. I don't want to…." Jaime trailed off and laughed ruefully.

"I really, really don't want to scare you off. I think this is the equivalent of a man and a woman on a first date and the woman asking how many children he wants."

Tate shrugged. Obviously he didn't know how things worked between straight people any more than he knew how dating worked between two men. "I'd rather hear the truth than lies." Everyone fucking lied to him. He could always see it in their eyes. Except for Kris, Mrs. Birenbaum, Mr. Singh, and, so far, Jaime.

Jaime's eyes widened. "I wasn't going to lie to you." Huh. That seemed true. "But I think I need to keep some stuff to myself. For now."

That seemed reasonable. Tate wasn't about to start spouting off about his arrests and how many times he'd narrowly escaped the fate he'd saved Kris from, in his own home. His mother's drinking and drugs… yeah, Tate could understand that there was a line between truth and lies, especially with a near stranger. And on a first date.

That didn't completely erase his concerns, though. "But we're really, really different."

"I get that. I mean, I don't normally eat in places like this, but I eat out a lot. I don't cook much. And springing for an additional person to eat? I don't want to sound boastful, but it's really not going to make me broke. I've been on my own and working for a long time. I want to take you out and spend time with you. I'm happy to discuss options with you, and we can find things to do that don't cost a lot, but please believe me. If I suggest something, it's because I'm willing and able to pay for both of us to do that activity."

The weird thing was that he didn't get a skeevy vibe from Jaime at all, and he'd had other guys offer to pay his way for stuff in exchange for sex. Maybe it was because Jaime hadn't set that up as an expectation at all. Not that sex with Jaime would be any sort of hardship. Tate had had thoughts about it ever since he'd met Jaime, but every time Jaime spoke, he only wanted it more.

"That seems fair."

Jaime smiled, almost verging into Kris's bouncing territory. Who knew such a simple thing would make Jaime happy?

The waiter returned with Jaime's lemonade and three plates of food he arranged between them on the table. None of which were spaghetti and meatballs.

"What's this?"

Jaime looked guilty, of all things, but Tate waited out the explanation. So far Jaime had been… exactly what he'd needed. Tate was well on the way to trusting him, and Tate didn't trust anybody.

"Just a few appetizers. I mean, the spaghetti here is great, but you can't come to Vincenzo's and not try a few other things."

If Tate were a whore, he'd be a cheap one, had for the price of a good meal. And this was shaping up to be the best meal he'd ever eaten. After the bread, though, he wasn't going to say no, even if Jaime had been a bit sneaky about it. Tate found he could forgive this kind of sneaky, since Jaime had been almost painfully honest the rest of the time.

"What is all this?" Most of it he could sort of guess. One wooden cutting board had an array of meats looking a bit like salami or pepperoni, chunks of cheese, and fat green olives. Another plate had small pieces of bread covered with chopped tomatoes. The final offering was a giant ravioli, although aside from the shape, it bore no resemblance to the kind he got in the can.

Jaime explained the antipasti, bruschetta, and butternut squash ravioli, and Tate tried all of it. Some of the cheeses were too strong, and despite his newfound love of olive oil and bread, he did not like actual olives. The ravioli was the best surprise, as he hadn't expected to like it but instead it might have ruined him for canned ravioli.

They talked while they ate, and it gradually stopped feeling awkward.

"So, uh, do you have any brothers? Sisters?" Although Tate wouldn't wish anyone else in his situation, a sibling to share the misery with might have made his life more bearable.

Jaime nodded but waited until he'd finished chewing before replying. "Yes. Two brothers, one sister."

"What was that like, growing up?" Like a storybook, probably.

"Funny. There were times growing up when I hated having siblings. Alberto, the baby of the family, would steal my toys, break them, and I was just supposed to let him. My sister, Maribel, was an absolute horror when she went through puberty. The oldest, Miguel, would pull all kinds of stupid pranks." Jaime chuckled. "So many times as a kid I wished to be an only child, and now I wouldn't trade them for the world."

Tate focused on the less emotional part of Jaime's words. "What kind of pranks?" He'd been "pranked" a number of times in school, but they weren't good memories at all. Maybe he just didn't understand.

Jaime stared up at the ceiling for a moment. "Mostly it was stupid stuff like salt in the sugar bowl, or hiding sandwiches in our rooms until they started to stink. Although there was this one time he got my sister good. He put food coloring in the showerhead."

Tate blinked for a minute. "What color did the water end up?"

"Green."

"That's hilarious." Tate didn't think red water, which might be mistaken for blood, would be at all nice, but green was funny.

"Oh, that's not all. After she got finished screaming and the water finally ran clear, she got back into the shower. Where Miguel had replaced her shampoo with colored gelatin. He'd expected it to just set in the bottle and not come out, but the heat of the shower must have melted it, and she'd lathered up all her hair with sugary strawberry goop."

An unexpected laugh escaped from Tate.

Jaime grinned at him. "So siblings could be fun, especially when they weren't pranking you. What about you? Got any good stories?"

Tate almost rolled his eyes. After all, most of his stories weren't nearly so lighthearted. Oh. Except…. "There was that one time I was bussing tables and a guy tried to pick me up."

Jaime lifted an eyebrow. "I would think that happens to you a lot."

Sometimes, although he had perfected an air of *don't fuck with me.* "Sure, but he used a sock puppet to try and chat me up."

It took a second for Jaime to fully comprehend that, but a big, cheerful laugh burst forth from him. Tate tried not to feel proud of that accomplishment, but he couldn't help it.

"A sock puppet. No way. I thought I'd had some dating horror stories."

Tate didn't think he much wanted to hear about Jaime's dating history, so he frantically searched his memory for an unrelated story.

"Um, there was this other time. I was working at a Tex-Mex place, and just as we were closing up one night, an elderly lady came by, said she'd had dinner there earlier in the evening. And she'd, uh, apparently had a problem with her dentures. Which she accidentally left wrapped up in a napkin on the table."

"Oh shit. I think I see where this is going."

Tate gave him a wry smile. "Yeah. I spent over an hour in the dumpster searching for teeth."

Jaime shuddered. "Yuck. They'd need nuclear-level disinfection before I'd want to put them in my mouth after that."

"Uh, yeah, agreed. It fucking reeked. And was slimy. Things rot quick in the heat. Eventually she realized, though, that she had them in her jacket pocket."

Again, silence hung for a short moment while Jaime processed, but then his laugh was louder and more uncontrolled than before. This time

Tate couldn't stop a tiny smug smile from stretching his lips. It felt so damned good to make someone like Jaime laugh. Tate still didn't know if this would last, but in addition to the intense heat lurking in Jaime's eyes, hidden behind happiness, it made a good start. There were still more memories to be made.

Tate sat back in his chair as the waiter cleared away their dishes. He was so fucking full, and it was awesome.

Then the waiter returned and placed a giant steaming plate in front of each of them.

He looked up at Jaime. "Oh my God. I forgot we hadn't eaten the meal yet."

Jaime snort-laughed. "Really? Because I have dreams about this chicken cacciatore."

"You dream about chicken cacciatore? Maybe you do need someone like me around. There are better things to dream about." He winked, and the heat in Jaime's eyes intensified, flustering Tate just a bit. He hadn't meant to flirt like that, but he was enjoying Jaime's company, and he'd told the truth.

"I'll hold you to that." Jaime's voice was low and raspy, rubbing over Tate in all the best ways.

"Seriously, though, I can't eat this. I'm stuffed." Tate stared remorsefully at his plate. It also looked like it would ruin him for spaghetti.

"So take it home with you. It's cool enough tonight that it will be all right in the car during the movie."

Tate nearly wiggled in his chair. If he could hide it from his mom and her boyfriends, he'd be eating like a king for the next couple of days. And there was still a movie to come—something else he'd forgotten about. When he was little, his mom would sometimes drop him off at the movie theater. It was great fun, but it had been a long time. "Okay, thanks."

"At least try it, and a bite of my cacciatore. Get a proper sense of how it tastes fresh out of the kitchen."

Before Tate could pick up a fork to taste test his spaghetti, Jaime handed over his fork, laden with what looked like a sample of everything on his plate.

Tate took it and put it in his mouth, his cheeks heating slightly at the intimacy. Then he groaned. "Oh fuck, that is good."

His eyes widened as he realized what he'd said, and he glanced around to see if anyone had heard him. His mother had never cared about his language, but Mrs. Birenbaum and his many, many bosses did.

Jaime just laughed. "No kids about, no worries. And I don't care. When I was in the Army, I'd drop the f-bomb about every other word. Hardest thing when I came home was curbing my mouth around the nieces and nephews."

Tate pushed away the jealousy. There would be no cousins or nephews or aunts or uncles for him. There was just him and his mom. Hell, he was even a bit envious that Jaime had gotten into the Army. Tate had tried as soon as he was old enough, hoping to find a way to make something better of his life, but he hadn't been able to pass the tests.

He might be stupid about tests, but he'd qualify for a doctorate in recognizing lies. The hardest thing Jaime had to deal with in the military hadn't been *language*. The tightening of his mouth and the hardness in his eyes were enough to tell Tate that whatever he'd dealt with hadn't been good, so Tate let the lie stand. He wasn't about to pry. Everyone had their shit, and if Jaime wanted him to know or if Tate could help, then Jaime would have to tell him.

Instead, he handed Jaime's fork back and picked up his own to sample his spaghetti. "Oh my God. This isn't fair. I've never had spaghetti this good." The meatballs were even better. Giant, juicy, and full of flavor.

"Really? Never?"

Tate shrugged. "Never eaten at a restaurant where waiters served me." Might as well get that out early. Nothing had fazed Jaime so far.

Aside from a widening of his eyes, Jaime didn't make a big deal of his shock. Maybe Jaime was as laid-back about their differences as he'd said. Tate knew well enough that it was one thing to say it and quite another to do it. But Jaime was passing all of Tate's tests with ease, and Tate already felt like he'd known Jaime for a long time.

They chatted while Jaime ate about half of his meal, got the leftovers boxed to go, and then Jaime paid without any fanfare. It might take a while for Tate to get used to Jaime paying for things, but what he said made sense. No two people could ever be exactly the same. Tate was content to see where things went, even though he didn't think it would end up like Jaime said. At some point Jaime would realize he was slumming with a dumb kid, and he'd be on his way.

Tate would deal with that when the time came.

"WHAT DID you want to see?" Jaime stared up at the LED screen. Tate looked up too, and it was so fucking precious that Jaime thought he had a clue what any of these movies were. Sometimes he saw movie trailers if his mom was watching TV and in a good enough mood that she didn't mind if he watched it too, but those days were rare. He tried to stay out of her way except when she wanted him to buy booze and cigarettes, or on rent days, because he was afraid if he was around too much, she'd kick him out, as she often threatened to do.

Even if he saw a movie trailer that looked interesting, it would be years before it showed up on regular TV channels.

"I'll watch anything. What did you want to see?"

Jaime turned his attention away from the movie listings. "Anything? No preferences at all?"

"No. I haven't been to the movies since I was a kid. I don't pay attention to what's playing." He was aware that every time he exposed another of their glaring differences, he was almost daring Jaime to get pissed off or call him a liar or just plain tell him to go to hell. But it had been one day. One date. It was huge that Tate was inclined to trust him, but he wasn't there yet.

"Oh. I see. But... no ideas at all?"

Tate shrugged. "The closest I've come to a movie are nature documentaries. There's a small multimedia room at the library, but Mrs. Birenbaum—she's the head librarian—won't allow any of the regular movies they have on loan to be played there. Only educational stuff. So, nope. No preference. Anything that's not a nature documentary."

Jaime smirked. "Damn. Now you've gone and spoiled everything."

Tate laughed and rolled his eyes. "Pick a damn movie."

Jaime didn't stand in line for the wicket but went to the automated machine, so Tate didn't even know what he ended up choosing. Not that the title would help Tate figure out what they were seeing anyway.

Inside the theater, Jaime lined up at the concession stand.

"Not more food, surely." Tate thought he might be waddling, he'd eaten so much.

"There's always room for popcorn."

"I think you're nuts."

"I can get you nuts if you want."

Tate groaned. "No. No nuts." The popcorn did smell good, though. He sniffed.

"You can share my popcorn."

Oh. That would be awesome. So far Tate was loving the way Jaime shared.

"I hope you don't mind. I chose a romantic comedy." Jaime wouldn't quite meet his eyes, but Tate didn't know why.

"Why would I mind?" He hadn't been kidding about the nature documentaries. They were fine in small doses, and he always learned something really cool, but he was also looking forward to seeing a movie that was less than five years old.

Jaime shrugged. "Most guys like explosions, but I… ever since I got back from Afghanistan, I have a hard time with them. I don't freak out or anything, but they make me tense, and so I avoid them."

God. At first glance, no one would ever think Jaime could be afraid of anything. Tate hated that Jaime had obviously gone through a horrible experience, but knowing Jaime wasn't perfect made Tate feel a little more hopeful that whatever they were doing wouldn't crash and burn too quickly.

"It's fine. I don't mind." Tate wasn't used to explaining himself, but he hoped Jaime understood Tate meant about all of that, not just the movie.

Jaime quickly shook off his dejection and led them into the darkened theater, right at the back.

THIS MIGHT be the best date of Jaime's life. Tate had loosened up over dinner, even to the point of making jokes and laughing, although his words were still sparse. He'd gotten right into the movie, staring avidly at the screen and laughing in all the right places. Jaime had almost spent more time staring at Tate than watching the movie. Tate wasn't wrong about them being different. It was like Tate had come from a different country or something. Jaime didn't go to a ton of movies, but he couldn't imagine going years without hitting up a theater.

Best of all, after the popcorn was gone, Jaime had reached over and threaded their fingers together. Tate had smiled and left his hand in Jaime's. He felt as giddy as a teenager.

They'd parked in a fairly secluded section of the lot, conveniently out of the direct overhead security lights. Instead of getting right into the car, Jaime pulled Tate into the shadows and faced him.

"I had a great time tonight," Jaime whispered.

"Me too," Tate whispered back, bright cat eyes gleaming.

Jaime slid a hand around Tate's neck and tugged, bringing their mouths into contact.

Tate froze for a moment but opened readily when Jaime licked at his lips. Jaime deepened the kiss, tasting a faint hint of salt from their popcorn.

When Tate wrapped his arms around Jaime's waist, Jaime pressed them up against the side of the car, giving him full body contact and support to devour Tate's mouth.

At first Tate clumsily followed Jaime's tongue, but he quickly got into the groove, and Jaime fitted his leg between Tate's, providing pressure for their hard lengths.

Jaime clutched at Tate's shoulders, determined not to seek out skin, but it was so fucking hard. He wanted to taste Tate all over, but he didn't want to give up the pleasure of Tate's mouth. Tate's breathy moans and grasping hands only threw gasoline on the blaze.

A car honking made them spring apart. Jaime glanced around, but the car in question wasn't anywhere near them.

Tate stared at him, hungry, pupils blown, lips plumped. Jaime brushed a thumb over Tate's lower lip. "C'mon. This isn't the best place to be doing this."

Florida could be weird, and he didn't need any homophobes fucking up a spectacular evening.

Jaime took in a few shuddering breaths and adjusted his cock, which protested its tight confines, but Jaime gave it a thump. It wasn't making any new friends tonight, and it was just going to have to deal.

"Right. Yeah." Tate shook himself and got in the car.

Ten minutes later they were back in the almost deserted Area 52 parking lot.

Tate frowned at him. "What are we doing here?"

"Don't you need to get your car?"

"Yeah. No car either. I don't drive."

Holy shit. Tate really was from a different country. Or maybe a whole different planet. "Oh. Um, well, I could drive you home."

"Nah. It's not a far walk. But...." Tate was clearly confused.

Jaime didn't know if it would be better to just tell him to spit it out or if he should let Tate get to it in his own time.

"Did you want a blow job?"

Jaime let his head drop back against the headrest. Tate was determined to test his self-control. "God, that sounds fantastic."

Tate's hand immediately went to his zipper, caressing his cock, which hadn't fully deflated from their heated kiss. Jaime grabbed Tate's wrist.

"What's wrong?"

Making sure to smile, he placed Tate's hand back on his side of the car. "Believe me, I'd love a blow job. But not today. Today was us getting to know each other, and I don't want you to think I'm going to expect sex whenever I take you out. That's not what this is." He frowned. "Well, that's not what all of it is. Anyway, what I would like to do is make a second date."

Tate still seemed slightly unsure about what had happened, but he nodded. "I'd like that. I work the evening shift, though, and I'm not off again until Sunday."

Waiting that long to see Tate again might just kill him dead.

"I'm off Sunday too, but I don't want to wait that long to see you. Maybe we could get together for lunch on Wednesday? I don't have to work Wednesday, but I can drop you off at work."

Watching Tate smile made Jaime want to kiss him some more—he wasn't finished exploring all that mouth had to offer, but he was trying desperately to prove he was a good guy, not a horny asshole.

"Yes, okay."

"And you've got my phone number in case you need to get in touch with me. Is there some way I can call you?" He hated the fact that he didn't know where Tate lived or how to call him whenever he wanted.

"Um. I'm not really good with phone numbers."

Jaime almost snorted. Who was these days? He didn't know anyone's actual phone number except for his own. If Tate didn't have access to a phone, he probably didn't have a little black book in his backpack.

"I have an e-mail address, but I have to go to the library to check it."

"If you don't mind giving me that, then. But how often are you at the library?" Jaime didn't remember the last time he'd gone to a public library. Probably he'd still been in high school. He did like to read, although he mostly read e-books on his phone these days.

"I try to go most days. I like reading, and it's a nice place to hang out."

If Tate hadn't already told him he lived with his mother, Jaime might have suspected he was homeless. Tate hadn't been happy about admitting that, but neither had Jaime sensed any guile. Reading body language had become almost second nature to him, since many of his patients had trouble articulating what was wrong, but he'd be the first to admit that his unexpectedly deep and swift emotional investment in Tate might be messing up all his senses.

Regardless, he was thrilled that Tate liked reading; he was amazed it hadn't come up over dinner, even though Tate had mentioned the library briefly. They'd have to delve deeper into that, figure out if they liked any of the same things. He was also relieved Tate had someplace nice to hang out if he didn't want to be at home.

Jaime punched Tate's e-mail address into his phone and sent off a quick "hello" message so Tate would have his.

"Should I pick you up here or somewhere else on Wednesday? Say, eleven?" Meant waking up earlier than he liked to when he was working nights, but he wanted to make sure they had a few hours before Tate had to start work.

"Here is good."

"See you later, Tate." Jaime couldn't resist taking one last kiss, but he broke it off all too soon, much to his cock's distress.

Tate just touched his lips, grabbed his bag of leftovers, and got out of the car.

CHAPTER SEVEN

AREA 52 was still open, and Tate thought Kris was supposed to close, so he walked over to the gift shop instead of going somewhere else. It was too early to head home.

As he approached, he saw some of the greens were in use, but unsurprisingly, it wasn't crowded. Mondays had never been busy when he worked here. Inside the shop, there was no one but Kris, who lit up when he saw Tate.

"How did it go? What did you do? I mean, not the naughty stuff." He frowned. "No, tell me the naughty stuff too!"

Tate shrugged. "I don't know how it went."

Kris came around the counter holding a couple of folding chairs, which he set up in the corner by the manager's office. "Mr. Singh brought these for when you want to hang out here with me."

Tate hadn't done anything worth this special attention, but it was nice to have someplace he could wait for Jaime to pick him up. There was the library too, but he didn't think he could call Mrs. Birenbaum a friend, and having a friend in Kris was a novel experience he wanted more of, even if Kris's curiosity was a little overdeveloped.

After the chairs were arranged to Kris's satisfaction—he still needed a clear sight line of the entrance, the counter, and the doors leading in from the greens—they sat down.

"Why don't you know how it went? Did you have fun?"

Tate blinked. It had never occurred to him that the purpose of a date might be to simply have fun. "I did. Jaime was great."

"Then it went well. Where did he take you? Did he kiss you? Did you have sex?"

"Whoa." Tate held up a hand to stop the torrent of questions. He told Kris about dinner and the movie, with Kris exclaiming delightedly when Tate mentioned the hand-holding and the sweet words Jaime had for him over dinner.

"And kissing?"

Tate's face went hot, and Kris clapped. "You kissed. Your skin gives you away."

Stupid face. He couldn't control his blushing, no matter how much he tried. The only times he could were when he kept careful control of his emotions, but when he was angry or flustered, his control deserted him. Jaime flustered the hell out of him, but not in a bad way, like when he was late for work or wasn't smart enough to figure out things like money.

"Yes, there was kissing." And it was good. Most guys he'd been with hadn't been too into kissing, and Tate had never pushed. He hadn't understood its appeal. Not until Jaime taught him differently.

"Mmm. Good for you."

"But he turned down a blow job." Tate didn't ever offer if he didn't want to give one, and he'd never been turned down. "Does that mean... I don't know what that means." Because Jaime had been hard—they both had—and he'd kissed Tate like he wanted to eat him up. When they'd pulled into the Area 52 parking lot instead of going to Jaime's apartment or a cheap motel or even a deserted field, Tate hadn't known what to think.

Kris squealed, then cut himself off abruptly. "Wait. Is there going to be a second date?"

Tate nodded. "Wednesday. He's picking me up here again."

"Oh, Tate, I'm so happy for you."

He was? "Why?"

"Because Jaime definitely wants more than just sex. I told you before, he liiiiiikes you. And not just for what's in your pants."

"How... I mean, I know he said something like that at dinner, but how can that be true if he doesn't want to have sex with me?"

"Haven't you ever read a romance novel?"

"You *have* read a romance novel?"

"Yeah, of course. They've got gay ones now, and I can read them on my phone so my parents don't know."

Gay romance novels. Who knew? "Okay, so, explain this to me."

Kris started a long-winded explanation, using as examples some rather improbable romantic scenarios he'd clearly picked up from fiction. Maybe it would work in book format—many of them had been incorporated into the romcom Tate had just watched with Jaime, and he'd liked the movie just fine. Of course, he hadn't been trying to apply any of the concepts to his own real life.

As he understood it, the general idea was for Jaime to prove that he was serious about getting to know Tate by denying them both orgasms. Tate hoped this denial wouldn't last too long, because he wanted in Jaime's pants. Jaime had been good about keeping Tate from feeling as though he owed Jaime for the money he'd spent, and everything Jaime had done and said showed Tate that he wasn't just searching for an interchangeable twink to fit on his dick.

Like Tate needed any more confirmation that Jaime was a good guy. That wasn't the issue. The issue was that Tate didn't deserve someone so good, and sooner or later, Jaime was going to figure that out. Mutual orgasms needed to happen before that so Tate had all kinds of happy memories to call on when he was alone again.

They talked, with few customer interruptions, until Area 52 closed for the night.

"Want me to drive you home?"

Tate chuckled. He was developing a regular stable of chauffeurs. "No, thanks. It's still a bit early for me to go home."

Thunderclouds gathered over Kris's rainbow world. "What do you mean by that?"

God. Tate had spent all evening sidestepping talking about his mother, and here he was, practically inviting Kris into his business. Friendship had better be worth this.

"My mom… drinks a lot. And it's just easier if I wait until she's passed out before I go home." Tate didn't need to add in anything about her boyfriends. Or the drugs.

"What do you do the whole time? I mean, it's gonna get cold out tonight."

"Eh. It's not that bad. I have a hoodie in my backpack."

"That doesn't answer my question—where are you going to go?"

Tate shrugged. "Walk around. Sit on a bench. Pretend to wait for a bus at a bus stop."

Kris looked horrified. "You can't do that. Come home with me."

"Yeah, right. If I remember right, you're not out to your parents, are you? You think they'd like you bringing home a gay high school dropout? Besides, don't worry about me. I've made an art of avoiding my house for years."

"God. You're going to give me gray hairs."

That made Tate laugh. From years of experience, he knew how to avoid the worst of the worst and could take care of himself. He only got into trouble when he lost his temper.

"Don't you worry about me. I'll see you Wednesday, if not tomorrow."

TATE PACED around the shelves of the Area 52 gift shop. He'd worried that he was going to be late, but he'd arrived just as Kris was opening. Which, given Kris's expression, was plenty early.

After an hour, Kris rolled his eyes. "Tate, calm down. My granny would say you're as nervous as a long-tailed cat in a room full of rocking chairs." Kris put a little lisp on it, making it sound like nothing anyone's granny would say ever.

"I can't. What if he doesn't show up?" Tate wanted to bite his lip. He hated sounding so needy and nervous. Relying on other people only led to heartache, and he was afraid Jaime would serve him up a double helping.

"You got through the hard part. The first date went well, and he wants a second date. You're golden."

He was fucking horny, not golden. And it was all Jaime's fault. No one had ever kissed Tate like that, turned him on like that, and then left him hanging. Left them both hanging, if the hard cock in Jaime's pants had been anything to go on. He'd barely slept for thinking about all the ways they could have made each other come, and managed to drive himself almost crazy. His skin was sensitive all over, he was so fucking horny. And that just never happened.

Maybe he should have worn one of his argyle sweaters. They were usually great about helping him get jobs... somewhat less great about helping him keep them. But maybe the argyle would help him with Jaime, give him more confidence, because this was an unfamiliar experience for him.

"I'll be back in a minute." Tate wandered outside for a bit, but that didn't help.

Then Jaime's car pulled into the parking lot. Tate dashed back inside and grabbed his backpack. "See you later, Kris."

He didn't even wait for a reply, but ran back out. Jaime parked under the shade of the UFO, but as far from the door as possible. Tate didn't know why he'd do that, since there were plenty of spots closer to the door, but it still suited him fine.

He opened the passenger door. "Hi, Jaime."

"Hi, Tate."

Simple words, but Tate heard the heat and yearning in Jaime's voice, the same as had been in his. He flung his backpack into the backseat and climbed in. After shutting the door, he clambered over to the driver's side so he was straddling Jaime's legs and facing him. Not the most comfortable position, but he didn't care.

"What are you doing?" But Jaime's voice had husked up—he knew damn well what Tate was doing.

Tate held himself just above Jaime's groin and took Jaime's face between his hands. "I appreciate your restraint. And I believe you that you aren't just interested in sex. But oh my God, Jaime. I haven't been able to think about anything but getting you naked since you dropped me off."

Jaime groaned, his eyes darkening. "Me neither."

Tate didn't know who moved first, but like magic, their lips and tongues tangled amid heated, heavy breathing. And hardness. Tate was so fucking hard; he let himself drop, grinding his cock against Jaime's full erection. Jaime clutched at him, hands delving under his shirt to get to skin.

The heat spiked in the car, and Tate thought they might burst into flames. Sucking at Jaime's tongue, which thrust into his mouth in a regular rhythm, Tate wiggled, imagining Jaime using the same measure to fuck him.

He was going to explode if they didn't slow down. Tate pulled his lips away, but Jaime looking dazed and horny was too fucking good. After kissing along Jaime's jaw, he moved on to attacking Jaime's ear. Desperate groans filled the car as Jaime bucked beneath him. The sounds Jaime made only made Tate want to suck and lick more of Jaime's body.

Fuck, fuck. That wasn't slowing them down at all. At this rate they were going to come before anyone was naked.

Tate lifted his head, but letting go of Jaime entirely was too much to ask. "Can we please go back to your place?"

Stunned, Jaime nodded. "As long as you allow me to buy you lunch afterward."

That little bit of silliness was what Tate needed to hear. Allow him? Jaime was fucking hilarious.

If only the law let him stay on Jaime's lap the whole way. But Tate reluctantly disentangled himself and sat back in the passenger seat. Jaime took a few deep breaths and scrubbed his hair with a hand. After adjusting himself—twice—Jaime got the car into gear and off they went.

Tate hated the fact that Jaime lived too far for Tate to get there by walking, and he certainly couldn't afford taxis. He hoped Jaime didn't mind driving—assuming they were going to do this again.

AT JAIME'S apartment—which was clean and airy and smelled so good—Jaime gave him a quick tour before they ended up in the bedroom.

Jaime fused their mouths together, but this time they were able to shed clothes, getting closer and closer to melding their bodies. They separated long enough to strip the last barriers away, and when Jaime wrapped his hand around both of their cocks, Tate threw his head back and moaned. Jaime stroked them a couple of times, precum beading on their slits and mixing between their flushed mushroom caps.

With his skin feeling too tight to contain his desire, Tate pushed Jaime toward the bed. Not hard, though, and since Jaime was bigger, if he hadn't wanted to move, Tate probably wouldn't have been able to do it.

Jaime lay back on the bed, expression welcoming, prick thrusting eagerly upward. Tate leaped on top of him, determined to taste every inch of Jaime's skin.

And Jaime let him. Not that Jaime wasn't involved. He touched and stroked and even bit when the opportunity arose, but mostly he let Tate follow his desires. Tate couldn't spend as much time as he'd like because he was already on the edge of coming. But he couldn't not taste that one part of Jaime that had dominated his dreams more than any other.

Tate licked Jaime's length, a much darker color than his own dick. The taste of man with a hint of clean sweat was like a drug, and he couldn't wait. He opened his mouth and sucked as much of that hot, hard cock as he could. Jaime shuddered and twitched, groaning like Tate was killing him.

"Fuck, Tate. You need to stop that."

Really? Tate lifted his head. "But you taste so good."

"Fuck, fuck." Jaime grabbed the base of his dick and squeezed, staring at the ceiling.

Tate's own cock twitched and another pearl of precum appeared in his slit. Jaime was going to slay him when he actually came. Tate had never found much pleasure in his partner's sexual satisfaction—maybe because they'd never much cared about his—but he wanted to make Jaime come. He was going to savor the shit out of that.

Jaime slowly opened his grip and stared at Tate, pupils blown wide. "There's condoms and lube in the nightstand."

Yeah, Tate didn't think he could prolong this any longer. He grabbed the supplies. Jaime took the condom and opened it up, preparing to roll it on Tate's dick. Tate reared back.

"What?" Jaime asked.

"You... I had thought you were going to uh... fuck me."

Jaime shrugged. "I don't mind. I'll do either; it just seemed like that's where this is going."

Tate reached out, grabbed Jaime's wrist. "You mean you'd be okay if I fucked you?"

"I *want* you to fuck me. But I also want to fuck you. I'm happy either way. Or we can do it one way now and go the opposite way next time."

"I... I've never done that before."

Those words hung there as Jaime looked at him, assessing. "Because you don't want to or because no one ever wanted you to?"

"The last one." Tate liked fucking just fine the few times he'd done it, but no one had ever given him the choice of *how* they were going to do it.

"Tate, I want to be with you. I'm having such a good time I've almost blown my load half-a-dozen times since you got in my car. Whatever you want is fine, just, please, please hurry, because you're so sexy I'm dying."

God damn it. Tate wrapped a hand around his own dick, choking back his orgasm. When he could breathe again without spilling his load, he grabbed the condom. "I'd like to fuck you."

Jaime smiled sweetly, like an angel who'd discovered the pleasures of sin. "Let me have the lube."

Instead of making Tate fumble with both condom and preparing Jaime—Tate didn't think they'd last that long—Jaime slicked himself up quickly and efficiently. Didn't stop it from being hot as fuck, and Tate had never been so glad to be wearing a condom before. He had a prayer of not coming the second he got inside Jaime.

Spreading his legs, cock lying hard and thick across his thigh, Jaime grinned and beckoned.

Tate didn't need to be asked twice. He slotted himself in the right spot and pushed. There was greater resistance than he imagined, but then Jaime just opened up and Tate sank home.

"Oh fuck." Tate's voice broke. He hadn't known. How could he? But the pressure and the heat were nothing short of perfect. Trembling with the effort, he stayed still, letting Jaime adjust.

Then Jaime bucked under him, and Tate let instinct take control of his hips. Out and in, he stroked, shifting and shifting until Jaime arched up with a shout. "There. Oh God. There."

Keeping to that angle, Tate sped up, bringing them into the home stretch. Sweat slicked them both, and just when Tate thought he couldn't last any longer, Jaime convulsed around him, cock shooting over both of them. The pulse and squeeze of Jaime's climax yanked Tate over the edge. He slammed home one more time, and his muscles locked up as he unloaded into the condom, lights sparking behind his eyelids.

He slumped over Jaime for a few moments, heedless of the jizz between them. Then he pulled out, careful not to move too quickly and lose the condom.

Once cleanup was taken care of, Jaime pulled him back into the bed and curled around him, his big body warm and comforting.

"That was awesome," Jaime whispered in between tiny, lazy kisses.

"It was," Tate agreed. "Next time I want you to fuck me, but I definitely want to do that again." He clamped his lips shut. Was he assuming too much? Usually guys lost interest in him after sex.

"Mmm. Whatever you want next time is fine with me. I'd like to suck your cock too. I didn't get a chance to do that."

Oh yeah. Jaime wanted a next time as much as Tate did.

Good.

CHAPTER EIGHT

JAIME'S MAMA'S house was already packed with family when he pulled into the driveway. Normally Jaime would have made Caleb drive him, especially since he'd worked a night shift the previous night, but it was Easter Sunday. The mamas in the Escobar clan weren't draconian about church attendance, but you had to have a damn good reason to miss church on major holidays. Fortunately for Jaime, the night shift on Saturday counted as a good excuse; Caleb and Raven wouldn't dare claim sexual exhaustion, so they'd been here hours ago.

The only shitty thing about that was he couldn't just throw money at Caleb for whatever food, drink, or hostess gift he'd brought. Jaime grabbed the enormous bouquet of white and yellow flowers and headed into the house.

Going directly to the kitchen, he found his mama first and handed her the flowers.

"Happy Easter, Mama."

"*Gracias, cariño*. I almost didn't recognize you, it's been so long since I've seen you."

Jaime almost bit out a sarcastic retort, but underneath the guilt trip, he saw genuine concern and hurt.

"I'm sorry, Mama. I've been busy." And feeling a bit like he wasn't important to his family, but he knew better. His mama loved him, she was just having difficulty overcoming some rather archaic notions about gay men. But aside from his understandable panic right before he came out as a teenager, he'd never truly worried that his family would disown him or kick him out. He certainly had a better mother than Tate had, and a more comfortable home life than either Tate or Kris. He needed to be better about showing his appreciation.

Jaime kissed her cheek. "I'll try to do better. How are the wedding plans coming along?" His brother wasn't getting married until next summer, but Jaime had been through enough weddings in this family to know the work started now and didn't let up.

"Don't you try to distract me."

"I would never, Mama. How are Maribel and the baby? Do we know what it's going to be yet?" He fluttered his eyelashes in an approximation of innocence.

"You're a bad boy." His mama laughed and patted his cheek. "Go get something to eat before your brothers and nephews eat it all up, the locusts."

Jaime laughed. The men in the family could pack it away, but the day one of his family events ran out of food, Jaime would know the world was ending. He wasn't worried about missing out on his mama's cooking or any of the other dishes his aunts brought to round out the meal for their virtual platoon of a family.

At the buffet table, Jaime piled his plate high. He'd have to remember to take home a bunch of leftovers. He hadn't had a chance to share any of his mother's cooking with Tate, but he was looking forward to seeing his reaction. Over the past month or so, he and Tate had seen each other as often as their schedules allowed—which wasn't nearly as often as either of them would like. Occasionally they went to a restaurant, Jaime taking a lot of joy in introducing Tate to various cuisines he'd never tried.

Sometimes he tried to treat Tate to more expensive dates, but so far Tate had denied him, always wary of Jaime spending too much money, even though he had more than enough to spare to make Tate smile. Most times they ordered in and watched a shit-ton of movies on his streaming service. He shared many of his favorites with Tate, none of which Tate had ever seen, and it was like seeing them again for the first time.

They talked about different books they'd read, Jaime buying a couple of Tate's favorites to read on his phone on the rare occasion he had time off work when he wasn't with Tate. Movies, books, food, sex— so much sex—sometimes he felt guilty about how simple their time together was, but if it made them both happy, it hardly mattered. After all, Jaime was looking for a long-term partner, and if his partner wasn't interested in the same everyday things Jaime liked, there would be a problem. He did want to take Tate out to a club some night, but it hadn't worked out. And he hadn't been ready to introduce Tate to his friends. Not yet.

Jaime took his plate outside, where Raven and Caleb were sitting in the sun with Nana, Raven all covered up in long sleeves like Tate usually was. If nothing else, maybe Raven and Tate could bond over their vampirically pale skin. Jaime had never discussed the specifics of

Caleb's sex life with Raven—aside from that one squicky, weirdly hot time he'd been making himself coffee in Raven's kitchen only to come out and find Raven ass up over the back of the couch, Caleb ready to fuck him. He hadn't wondered, until he met Tate, if Caleb found that pale skin hot as all fuck. Raven didn't blush quite as fiercely as Tate did, not that he'd seen anyway, but those crazy blushes only made Tate that much sexier, in Jaime's opinion.

"*¡Hola!* Happy Easter, Nana." He kissed her cheek and wedged a chair in beside her.

"*Hola, cariño.*" She patted his cheek, her skin soft and smelling like the rose-scented lotion that was so much a part of his childhood memories. "You look happy today."

He smiled at her. He was happy. Happier than he could remember being in a long time. There were only two things wrong: he didn't get to see Tate every day, and he was here at this warm, loving family holiday while Tate was… probably hiding from his mother at home. The library was closed today, and Tate didn't have to work. Jaime had thought long and hard about inviting him, but he had absolutely no idea how Tate would interact with his friends and family. He wasn't sure Tate knew either. The one time he'd brought it up, Tate had looked like a rabbit confronted with a dozen rabid wolves.

His family might take a little getting used to, but they were hardly rabid wolves.

"I am happy, Nana."

Caleb and Raven both leaned closer, speculative looks on their faces.

"Oh, my two best boys." Nana smiled at him and Caleb. "One with too much pressure to get married and have *bebés* and the other with no pressure at all. Your parents are blind."

Caleb and Raven both stared at Jaime. His nana was the sharpest knife in the drawer. She'd known all along how much it bothered him that his mother accepted he was gay but never tried to pressure him into building a family like she'd done with his siblings. He'd never said it aloud, so Caleb had never known—his cousin could be a little oblivious at times—but Raven suspected. He must have, considering how many times he tried to set Jaime up, even though it never took.

Nana gently placed her hand on his arm, and he put his plate on a nearby table so he could pay proper attention to her.

"When do we meet him?"

"Soon, Nana. Soon. He… I think we might scare him. There are a lot of us."

"*Sí, sí,* but our family are good people. Caleb's papa and Raven, here, fit in just fine."

Jaime nodded. He knew she'd specified those two people in particular because they also had little or no family to speak of.

Most people assumed the older generation was even more conservative, but Nana had never judged. Funny thing was, he hadn't realized why that was until he'd returned from his first tour overseas to discover Great Uncle Ricardo had passed away and left his estate to Jaime. Most of the family assumed it was because Jaime was the only one of his generation to have served in the military, and Ricardo had a number of medals and endless stories from serving in World War II.

It wasn't until Jaime signed the paperwork and noticed Ricardo had changed his will the same week Jaime had come out—in high school— that Jaime had realized the truth. Realized the real reason Ricardo had never married. And he suspected that Nana, Ricardo's sister, knew the truth too, especially since she was the one who'd witnessed the new will. If Caleb had come out when Jaime had, Ricardo might have split the estate between them, making the reason obvious to everyone, but as it was, that sweet old man had ensured Jaime had plenty of cushion to last him the rest of his life.

He was about to say something else when Caleb stood. "Nana, if you don't mind, I need to talk to Jaime about something."

She smiled. "Of course, *cariño.* Your sweet Raven can keep me company."

"Yes, Nana." Raven smiled, and it gave Jaime hope for Tate. Raven had been nervous about the family—he'd had a less-than-stellar introduction to them—but he and Nana had gotten along right from the start.

People were scattered all around the lawn, but Caleb dragged Jaime toward the shed, the area around which was deserted.

Instead of saying anything, Caleb merely crossed his arms and tried to look imposing and stern. Considering Jaime had once dared Caleb to put a marble up his nose and they'd both gotten in shit when Caleb had to go to the hospital to get it removed, Jaime wasn't exactly shaking in fear.

"Yes?" He had a plateful of *arroz con pollo* and sweet plantains getting cold, so they might as well move this along.

Caleb's expression became pained. "You met someone? Why didn't you tell me?"

In the face of Caleb's hurt, keeping secrets no longer seemed like such a good idea. "I don't know. No one sees me as anything but a player. A slut. No one seems to think I want a boyfriend." Of course, he should probably have the "boyfriend" discussion with Tate before anyone else, but nothing about his fledgling relationship was normal.

"Oh my God, Jaime. I'm so sorry. I'm sorry you couldn't tell me that. I might tease you, but I don't really think you're a slut."

Jaime lifted one shoulder. "It wasn't just you. Mama… she never harasses me to find someone and settle down."

Caleb huffed out a laugh and rolled his eyes. "Yeah, well, that can go a little too far, as you know."

Yeah, he did. Caleb hadn't come out until years after Jaime did, because of his own mother's pressure to give her grandchildren. "Anyway, the way I met him was a little… odd. And he's… different. In a good way. At least, good for me. But it's still new. I don't want to jinx anything. We've only been seeing each other a month."

"A month?" Caleb practically yelled. "You've never dated someone that long. They're usually lucky if they get a week out of you."

Okay, maybe part of this was on Jaime. His behavior wouldn't have told people he was actually looking for something serious. "None of those guys lasted because they wouldn't have lasted. No point in wasting anyone's time, right?"

Caleb squinted at him. "How could you know after a week?"

"Really? You're asking me this when you lost your fucking mind after finding Raven in a hotel room? He fucked with your mind in mere minutes, *mi amigo*."

At least his cousin had the grace to look ashamed. "So tell me about your new guy. I want to know how you met and why he's different. I want to meet him."

"Fine. But not here. I'll tell Mama about him, but not today. Let's go to a bar or something after we're done here. It'll save time if I tell you and Raven at the same time." He'd have to make a point of stopping by the house sometime when it wasn't packed to the rafters with family, but until he was ready to introduce Tate, he didn't see the point. Starting with

Caleb and Raven was the baby step Tate needed before ramping up to the entire crazy Escobar clan.

"True. He'll want to know all the details too." Caleb paused for a moment, mouth open. "Shit. I just realized he's been telling me for months that you weren't a player. I just thought he wanted to set up everyone he knew. Damn. He'll be crowing about this for a long fucking time."

"We good now? Because I'm starving."

"Yeah, yeah, let's get you fed. Hey, wait a minute. What's this guy's name?"

"Tate."

"Tate. You look so happy when you say that. I'm happy for you, *papi*. You deserve the best."

Jaime grabbed Caleb in a one-armed hug before zeroing in on his loaded plate.

TATE PULLED his legs up on the bench and rested his forehead on his knees. His pants were torn, his knees were skinned, and he was covered in drying mud, but that all smelled better than the piss-vomit-shit bouquet of his holding cell. His muscles were tight, both from the fight and from a night spent in jail. At least he'd been alone in the cell and wasn't forced to worry about his virtue or whatever, but that didn't mean he slept well.

They'd asked if he wanted to make a phone call. What a joke. Who would he call? His mother? Jaime? Even if he wanted to let Jaime know he was a colossal fuckup, he didn't actually know Jaime's phone number. His mother wouldn't have money to bail him out, even if she'd been inclined to help. And that was assuming he'd even remember the number. He'd be just as likely to accidentally put a call through to Manila or Athens or Moscow as he'd be to call home.

Better just wait and they'd either let him go or send him to prison. Jaime would find out, eventually, that Tate had fucked up again, and he'd realize Tate was a waste of space.

He sniffed and let a few tears leak onto his pants. Things had been going so well too.

Spending time with Jaime at his apartment had been like heaven. He'd never had so much fun, he'd never eaten so well, and he'd never known sex could be incredible. But it was more than that. It wasn't the stuff, it was Jaime. Jaime was the nicest person Tate had ever met, and for some reason Jaime seemed to like him. And Tate liked him back. Maybe even loved him, although he was still considering that. He needed to read a few more romances to be sure.

A few days after Kris had told him about gay romances, he'd screwed up his courage to check the romance section in the library, and to his surprise, he found some. Mrs. Birenbaum had laughed kindly when he'd added a couple to his stack behind the desk, and said she'd wondered how long before he found them. His face had been red for hours afterward.

He'd also learned pretty quickly to limit his selections to the less racy ones, because getting turned on in the library was just embarrassing. He thought maybe, at some point, he might be able to ask Jaime if he could download some and they could maybe have some fun with them together. But he had more research to do, trying to figure out if these intense yet comforting feelings he had for Jaime were love.

If only he hadn't screwed it all up.

Easter Sunday, the library was closed. Kris was off doing family stuff, and Tate didn't think Mr. Singh would let him hang out at Area 52 if Kris wasn't there. Worst of all, Jaime was also spending time with his family. He'd been weird about it too, like he hadn't wanted to tell Tate about it. Obviously he wasn't going to invite Tate. Tate should have been fine with that. He was terrified of meeting Jaime's friends and family. Simply terrified they'd take one look at him, deduce he was white trash who shouldn't be anywhere near Jaime, and Jaime would realize it for the truth. So he'd been shocked to realize that *not* getting invited to meet Jaime's family hurt like knives in his gut.

Jaime never minded if strangers in restaurants and movie theaters knew they were dating, but the fact he didn't want his family to know about Tate made him want to curl up in a ball and cry. It hurt worse than all the black eyes and bruised ribs and broken noses he'd ever had.

He should have seen the warning signs, his mood simmering on a half boil, with nothing to do and nowhere to go. Instead, he walked and walked, farther than normal. He'd hoped wearing himself out would settle his mind, but with only himself for company, he kept imagining Jaime having fun without him, and it had killed him.

When dusk had fallen and he'd walked he didn't know how many miles—and knowing he was going to regret his marathon during his next shift at work—he sat down on a bus stop bench, then made the mistake of falling asleep.

A patrol officer rousted him and chased him off rather than dragging him in for a misdemeanor like loitering, which was hard as shit to prove—he'd beaten those charges more than once when he was a kid. But being startled awake and groggy, he'd only thought about getting out of sight of the cop in case he changed his mind.

More proof he was stupid. Getting picked up for loitering would be a hell of a lot better than his current situation.

After he'd put enough distance between himself and the bus stop, Tate tried to figure out where he was, and realized he was fucked. Lost. He'd intended to just stay on Irlo Bronson the whole way, but his "escape" included a bunch of turns he'd failed to take note of. There were no street names he recognized and no bus stops he could use to orient himself.

On his own, he tried to stay within certain prescribed borders, because he got lost as easily as he fucked up phone numbers. Trying to find the new library when it had been built had been horrifying—getting lost in richer neighborhoods only increased the likelihood of someone calling the cops on him.

He didn't know how long he'd been asleep, but it was full dark, and there was minimal activity in this neighborhood. It could be well after normal people went to bed, or they could all be at family gatherings, having fun. Either way, his choices were limited. Keep walking despite his exhaustion and aching feet, or find another, more secluded bench to sleep the rest of the night. The idea of spending the night on a bench in an unfamiliar area, where he could encroach on the wrong person's territory, sent panic zinging through his veins, piling on top of his hurt.

He ended up aiming for the sounds of heavy traffic, hoping to at least find Irlo Bronson again and maybe a gas station to ask for directions. Once he was back on Irlo Bronson, he wouldn't have to worry about mixing up his left and right; he'd just need to be going one way or the other, and he'd ask for someone to actually point.

When he finally broke out of the run-down residential area with a number of overgrown, abandoned, boarded-up homes, he found an equally run-down motel with an attached bar. Farther down the street, barely visible, was a gas station that looked like it still might be lit.

Holidays could make it hard to find anywhere that was open. If he didn't have any luck at the gas station, he'd come back to the bar, which appeared to be busy enough. Tate had learned a long time ago that bar patrons were rarely helpful when it came to giving directions. Those who weren't too drunk to remember where things were often found it funny to give wrong directions. Bartenders were more reliable, but they usually required him to buy a drink—a real one, not just soda—in return for the information. Rent had cleaned out his pockets, and there'd be no more money until tips after his Tuesday shift.

Between the bar and the gas station, in front of a darkened motel that more rightly belonged in a horror movie than a touristy Florida city, Tate heard a scuffle behind a giant black pickup truck. The pickup had been raised to an obnoxious degree, so Tate couldn't see over it. Tate didn't *want* to see over it, but then he heard the vicious names. Faggot. Goddamn homo. Cocksucker. Fudge-packer. And the savage joy in the man's voice as he outlined the punishment he was going to dole out for being gay. Not too loud, though. If Tate hadn't been walking past at that very moment, he might never have heard it. If someone was asleep in the nearest motel room, the door might be enough to muffle that foul voice.

Anger ignited the flammable roil of emotions already seething. Damned if he'd walk past someone getting gay bashed. Fuck that shit.

IN HIS cell, as miserable as he was, just remembering it made his anger smolder and rise. He'd learned a long time ago that quiet fights usually meant someone died. When he'd fought off Kris's attackers, he hadn't been too worried about noise, knowing Kris was going to call the cops as soon as he got to a phone.

When Tate rounded the truck, a solitary man lay on the ground, his assailant standing over him, boot poised to kick. He wasn't as big as the guy who'd pulled a knife on Tate at Area 52, and didn't appear to have a weapon, although in the grips of his anger, seeing a weapon likely wouldn't have stopped Tate. Without another thought, Tate waded right in, making as much noise as he could, trying to create a disturbance worthy of calling the police.

For good or bad, the fight had come to the attention of the authorities. The police who arrested Tate hadn't cared about explanations, and the guy on the ground had been too injured to offer a statement before he was whisked away to the hospital by EMTs who weren't Jaime.

Wherever the other guy had been taken—maybe he'd called someone to bail him out—at least he hadn't been put in the same cell as Tate.

More than one police officer had asked Tate if he had someone he wanted to call. But he didn't. Or at least, the one man he wanted to call wouldn't want either his family time or sleep—depending on how late it was—interrupted by a giant fuckup by the guy he was dating, demonstrating just how fucked-up and stupid he was.

Every cop who asked, though, thought Tate was just being difficult, and the last one seemed to think a night in the cells would be just the thing to teach him a lesson about cooperating with the authorities.

If this went before a judge, Tate would be going to prison, of that he was certain. He'd had too many near scrapes for a judge to do anything else. Tate better start getting used to the smells and the confinement now, as well as the loss of the best thing to happen to him. No matter what Jaime had said about no judgment and accepting him as he was, there was no way Jaime would wait for him. Last time Tate had hung out with Kris at Area 52, Kris had referred to Jaime as Tate's boyfriend, but he'd never heard Jaime call himself that. No surprise, really, and it was even less likely to happen now. Who'd want an ex-con boyfriend who was too stupid to avoid getting arrested all the time?

Tate was going to miss their date tomorrow, and maybe Jaime would be mad that he'd been stood up. Maybe he'd even go and ask Kris about Tate. But Kris wouldn't know anything either. At that point, maybe Jaime would start looking for him. Once he got around to calling the police and found out Tate was in jail? He'd probably give up on Tate right then.

More hot tears trickled onto Tate's knees, soaking through the abused fabric. Why couldn't he be smart like Jaime?

CHAPTER NINE

A SHRILL and insistent ringing pulled Jaime out of sleep. Years of experience had him shaking off his stupor, and he grabbed up his phone. It might be nothing more than someone asking him to cover a shift—although he'd eased up on the extra shifts since meeting Tate—but it might also be an emergency.

"Yes, hello?" He was too sleep-fuddled to think of looking at the caller ID, though. It could be anyone calling.

"Did I wake you up, princess?" Diego's teasing tone and words confirmed there was no emergency, and neither would Diego be calling about covering shifts.

Princess. "Fuck you. Yes, I was sleeping. Still working the late shift." Jaime squinted at his bedside clock. "It's not even eight o'clock, Diego, what the fuck?"

"I'm back on days now."

"And what, you just called to rub it in?"

Diego made a lewd purring sound, and Jaime laughed. "Seriously, what's up?"

"We haven't talked in a while, but last time we talked about Tate Buchanan."

Adrenaline spiked, and Jaime flipped the covers off and started pacing, heedless of his nudity. Calling this early about Tate? He had a bad feeling. "What's wrong?"

"Did you end up tracking him down? Talking to him?"

"Yes." Jaime snatched a pair of jeans from the laundry basket filled with clean clothes. "We've been dating for almost a month now."

"Dating? Like... for real?"

"Yes. Why? What happened?"

A small part of him realized he'd be facing this disbelief from just about everyone he introduced Tate to, but that was a problem for another time. He pulled on the jeans, commando, and grabbed a plain white T-shirt. Being naked when getting bad news made him feel almost as vulnerable as if he'd gone out in the desert without body armor.

Diego sighed. "I'd have called you earlier if I'd known, but I just got to the station."

Dread sent bile into his throat. Surely this wasn't... surely Tate wasn't hurt. Or worse. Jaime swallowed heavily.

"One of the newbies picked him up for causing a disturbance. He didn't know Tate, just saw how many times he'd been arrested and pulled him in. Left him in the cells overnight as some sort of scared straight shit. I'm getting him released now, but he could probably use a lift."

"I'm leaving in two minutes. Can you tell me anything else? What kind of disturbance?"

Another sigh drifted over the phone line. "What else? Fighting. From all appearances, he stopped a gay bashing, with his fists rather than calling the cops. The victim is undergoing surgery right now, and the prognosis is good. As soon as he corroborates Tate's version of events, that'll be the end of this. If he'd called anyone last night, he'd have been sprung already, but he stubbornly refused to make a phone call."

Jaime wanted to throw up. Tate probably didn't know who to call. He didn't even have Jaime's phone number, because he said he never had access to a phone. Jaime would have pressed the matter if he'd had any idea something like this could happen.

Shit. He'd probably been at a bar with Caleb and Raven, telling them about Tate, at the same time Tate had been getting in another damned fight. If only Jaime had insisted Tate come home with him to meet the family. He'd have coaxed Tate into staying the night—they hadn't gotten to that point yet, but Jaime wanted to be there soon.

"Thanks for calling, Diego. I'll be there as soon as I can." Jaime flung down the phone, yanked on his shirt, and ran for the door, grabbing keys and wallet as he passed the hallway table.

APPARENTLY, LIKE many things in life, waiting for someone to get released from lockup was hurry up and wait. Jaime had barreled down the highway at full speed, despite the lingering early morning fog in the low-lying areas, but he probably could have showered and had brunch before making his leisurely way down to Kissimmee. Not that he could have eaten a fucking thing.

Thank God for Tate's hair, almost garish in the fluorescent lighting. Otherwise Jaime might have missed him when he finally came out into the lobby.

Tate was shorter and thinner than Jaime, but he'd never looked small before. Dejected. His clothes were filthy and wrecked, and he looked transparently pale. He held his arms close to his body, and he moved stiffly, but Jaime couldn't discern any obvious injuries.

Seeing Tate standing in the lobby, looking lost, alone, and younger than his age, drove home the realization that Jaime wanted to slay all his dragons, and he knew it was time to introduce him to the family. Because Jaime was pretty sure he'd fallen for this man.

"Tate."

Tate swung toward him, and Jaime was pleased to see there weren't any black eyes or broken noses this time, but the shadows under his eyes and the emptiness in his expression tore at his heart.

"Jaime. What are you doing here?"

He smiled. "Picking you up."

Tate held himself stiffly, arms wrapped around his torso, otherwise Jaime would have pulled him into a hug. Tate had sort of gotten the hang of cuddling during their time together, but his comfort level with hugging wasn't there yet. That was an even better reason to introduce him to the family. They'd taught Raven to love hugging, and they'd teach Tate too, although Jaime suspected Tate would be more of a challenge.

"Why?"

God. Tate shouldn't have to ask that.

"Because you're my boyfriend and a little birdie told me you had a rough night."

It was a measure of just how bad his night had been that Tate didn't protest. Tate was so used to being independent—through necessity rather than choice—that he had a hard time accepting Jaime doing nice things for him. But Jaime wanted to do all the nice things for him because Tate's smiles were a treasure.

"What birdie?"

"Diego."

A flash of something sparked in Tate's eyes, but it didn't last long enough for Jaime to decipher it, although he could guess. Tate had an ingrained mistrust of authorities in general, and police specifically. Which was kind of funny, since most of the cops who knew Tate looked the other way more often than not. But Jaime hadn't quite been able to figure out yet if Tate disliked Diego on general principle because he was a cop or because Jaime had told him not long ago that he and Diego had dated for a while.

They walked in silence to the car, the morning sun just starting to heat up the humid air.

Then Tate stopped and stared at him. "You're my boyfriend."

Jaime couldn't decide if Tate was telling him or asking him; he'd almost forgotten he hadn't talked to Tate about it. "Yeah, I am. I don't want to see anyone else, and I'd like it if you didn't either. If you're okay with that."

"I'm okay with that," Tate whispered. He started to smile, but then his face grew blotchy and the lower lip he so loved to suck on started to tremble.

To hell with Tate's unfamiliarity with hugging. Jaime wrapped his arms around Tate and pulled him close. For a moment it was like cuddling a high-tension wire, but then Tate sagged against him.

Relaxing the muscles opened the dam, and Tate cried silently into his neck, his whole body shaking.

"It's okay. It'll be okay." Jaime rubbed gentle circles on his back and kissed the top of his head.

After several minutes, the storm passed and Tate pulled back.

Oh, his poor boyfriend. Tears had ravaged Tate's face, leaving him blotchy and swollen. Tate sniffed, and Jaime opened his car door to rummage in the glove box for a fast-food napkin. His mother would be able to magic up a tissue from her purse or wherever, but Jaime only ever bought tissues when he was sick, and he certainly didn't carry them in the car.

Perhaps not the most romantic "exclusivity" conversation he could have imagined, but at least it still ended up the way he'd hoped.

Tate blew his nose, and he refused to look Jaime in the eye. "I'm sorry."

"For what?"

"For getting arrested. Making you come down here. Crying."

"Oh, *mi fuego*, don't apologize for any of this. You saved that man. Diego said he might have died if you hadn't intervened. And even if you'd just made a terrible mistake, I'd still be here for you."

It was too soon for the words he wanted to use, but they welled up in his throat.

"I don't know why, but thank you."

"Are you hurt? Did they get you medical attention? Maybe we should go to the hospital." Judging by the rips in Tate's clothing, it truly had been a brawl, and there was a hint of a bruise forming on his jaw that Jaime hadn't noticed until they were out in the bright daylight.

"No hospital. I'm fine." Tate's jaw firmed up again, and Jaime wondered if he had something against the place above and beyond the cost. Jaime had his medical kit in the car if any patch-up jobs were needed, and although Tate seemed to move a little stiffly, nothing screamed fractured or broken bones.

"C'mon. Let's get you back to my place. You can shower and I'll feed you."

"I messed up our date."

Jaime had finally convinced Tate they should go out and do something super touristy for their date today. They'd narrowed down the options and were going to make a final decision when Jaime picked him up. But he didn't think Tate would enjoy any of them today. He did think today of all days, it wouldn't be wise to hole up in the apartment. Tate would only brood about his arrest. Jaime had an idea for something in between, but he'd wait until he was sure Tate wasn't lying about being hurt.

Poor Tate fell asleep on the drive back to Jaime's; Jaime felt bad waking him up, but if he wanted to sleep, the bed would be better.

They got into the apartment. "Can I borrow some clothes?"

"Of course." In the bottom of his dresser, Jaime had a couple of things that wouldn't make Tate look like a kid playing dress-up. "Can I look you over before you shower, make sure you don't need a doctor?"

Tate frowned at him. "I'm fine. Only bruised. I'd rather you just be my boyfriend, not my keeper."

Jaime didn't want to fight, and he understood that, for whatever reason, this pushed Tate's boundaries. He wondered if Tate's mom used to hit him as a kid. Abused kids got good at hiding things.

He muttered "*mi fuego*" under his breath. Tate's inner fire was what drew Jaime in, but he also suspected that the more comfortable Tate got in their relationship, the more he was going to let Jaime see of it, especially the stubbornness. But he'd be happy to see it. As skittish as

Tate still was after these weeks together, Jaime wanted Tate to feel free to share everything with him, good or bad.

"What was that?" Tate narrowed his eyes.

Jaime just smiled. He had a feeling the endearment he'd been thinking for days now would make more frequent verbal appearances—and he'd rather explain it when Tate wasn't spoiling for an argument.

"I don't want to be your keeper, Tate. But you have to take pity on me—helping injured people is kind of my thing, you know? And it would kill me if I didn't help you if you needed it. It's even more important to me because that's part of being a boyfriend."

The defiance in Tate's eyes softened and faded away. "If I'm hurt badly, I'll let you help me. But I'd like you to trust me that I'm not badly hurt. I just need a shower and some clean clothes."

Jaime stepped close and cupped Tate's cheeks in his hands. Even wrecked by tears, sleeplessness, and a fight, this man was rapidly becoming the most important thing in his life. "I think I can live with that compromise." He pressed his lips against Tate's, thrilled to feel Tate kissing him back.

After a moment Tate pulled away. "But I don't think I'm up for sex."

"I wasn't expecting you to." Out of everything that had happened, Jaime didn't think he'd ever been so happy to know sex was off the table. In their early few dates, Jaime had worried Tate had initiated sex to repay him for what he'd spent; the fact that Tate would come out and say no sex meant a lot to Jaime. And he was going to have to trust his boyfriend that it had nothing to do with being more hurt than he claimed.

TATE WALKED slowly into the bathroom and closed the door firmly behind him. He ran a finger over the lock, considering. He knew how much Jaime needed to help people—maybe it was the only reason Tate had even attracted his notice. But if they were truly boyfriends—real ones like the ones he'd started reading about in romances—then he needed to trust Jaime.

He slipped out of his runners—looser, filthier, and more damaged than they'd been yesterday.

The ache in his feet and ribs paled in comparison to how happy he was. Tate closed his eyes and just enjoyed the moment. Jaime had come to pick him up from jail. Jaime didn't hate him but instead wanted to be boyfriends. This might be the happiest moment of his life, and he really, really wished he could have taken Jaime into the bedroom and showed him just how happy he was. But the fact that Jaime hadn't even for a moment looked angry when Tate said he wasn't up for sex? Made this day even more special.

He started the shower to heat it up—Jaime's water got nice and hot, with pressure enough to scour the stink of jail off his skin. After undoing his pants, he let them fall to the ground. A flick of his fingers sent his briefs to the floor as well. Stripping out of his shirt wasn't easy, but after putting his foot down, he wasn't about to ask Jaime to help him. Grimacing at his reflection, he leaned a little closer to the mirror. God, the bruising around his ribs was going to be bad. Jaime would be furious the next time they had sex.

But his ribs weren't broken—he knew what that felt like—and the guy he'd fought had confined the majority of his blows to Tate's body rather than his face.

Mostly naked, he sat on the closed toilet and contemplated his socks. He hadn't exactly expected dried blood to decorate them, but his feet hurt almost as much as his ribs, enough so he'd been afraid to take his shoes off for fear he wouldn't be able to put them on again.

Now he wasn't sure if he could take his socks off, because they were firmly stuck to blisters that had broken and bled on his far-too-long walk. Leaning over to try to tug on them made him groan.

Fuck it. He'd just get in the shower like this; the water should make it easier to peel them off.

Steam curled through the bathroom, beginning to fog up the mirror. Just as well. Tate was sick of looking at himself. Bruises always looked so damn obvious and ugly on his skin.

He stepped into the shower and let the hot water flow over him, soothing tight muscles. Jaime's shower was so bright and clean, without any black mold climbing between the tiles. Mold would probably be afraid to set foot in Jaime's apartment. For a single man, he kept his place super clean. Tate had wondered when he found the time and found out Jaime hired someone to come in and clean. That had been a real shock, knowing Jaime could afford such a thing. He also knew Jaime's mother kind of hated that he did, because she felt Jaime ought to do it himself, but when Tate realized how much time Jaime spent at work, it seemed a sensible solution.

Then the water fully soaked through his socks, and he let out an undignified yelp as every broken blister stung like he was standing in lemon juice. Holy fuckarama, that hurt.

Gritting his teeth, he breathed through the pain and waited until it faded to a dull throb. As he washed his hair and soaped up his body, he realized trying to take his socks off in the shower was a concussion and possible drowning waiting to happen, so he cleaned everything he could reach without too much pain.

After drying himself as best he could, he slopped back to the toilet and sat down again to pull off his socks. They landed with a wet plop, and Tate inspected the damage. Worse than he'd thought, to be sure, and reddened from the hot water. But at least they weren't bleeding again, and Jaime had all the first aid supplies anyone could wish for. Wincing, he stood and hobbled to the drawer where Jaime kept such stuff and found a bunch of bandages and ointment.

When his feet were almost covered with plastic strips, he eased on the clean socks Jaime had given him. Then he got dressed and felt mostly human again. He gathered up his dirty clothes, which probably needed to be burned. But he didn't have the money to replace them, so he was going to have to get out his sewing kit when he got home and repair the pants at least.

It had been embarrassing as all fuck that one of his last high school classes had been Home Economics. He'd done surprisingly well with the sewing, never realizing how useful the skill would become, but getting laughed at for being unable to follow a recipe, and in danger of failing that class too, had been one of his last breaking points, convincing him to drop out.

He bundled the socks in the middle of his other clothes so Jaime wouldn't see the blood, then left the bathroom in a whoosh of steam and put his clothes in the washing machine. He hadn't gotten to the point of asking Jaime if he could do his laundry here to save some money, but with all the sheets they'd gone through humping like bunnies on coke, Tate was almost as familiar with this washer as the ones at the laundromat.

Jaime met him as he started the cycle. "C'mon. I heated up some leftovers from yesterday. Maybe not the best breakfast food, but it's quick, filling, and good."

A yawn cracked Tate's jaw, exhaustion warring with the emptiness in his belly. He hadn't eaten anything in almost two days, when he and Jaime'd had lunch on Saturday before work. From his shift, Tate still had a few slices of leftover pizza he'd swiped from stuff destined for the garbage—but his mind had been so messed up, he hadn't been interested in food. He should probably throw that out now too.

Tate followed Jaime to the kitchen, where two huge plates of food sat alongside a properly set table.

"What's going on?" They usually ate most of their meals together in the living room, in front of the TV.

Jaime laughed, although he looked a little uncomfortable. "Nothing really. Just thought we could make our first meal as boyfriends a little special. Also, I have a hell of a time eating rice and not getting it everywhere. Eating at the table will be a little less messy."

Huh. Yeah, Jaime didn't avoid rice when they went out to restaurants, but maybe they hadn't gotten takeout of anything that had rice. He imagined Jaime on the couch, rice scattered liberally around him, and laughed.

"Yeah, yeah, but you've never gotten yelled at by Amalia for getting rice stuck in the carpet."

That didn't stop Tate's laughter. The carpet in the living room was very thick and fuzzy—lots of rice could get lost in there.

But Tate didn't want to waste any more time teasing Jaime—he was too hungry, and the food smelled amazing.

"So what's all this?"

Like he'd done so many times now, Jaime explained everything, and Tate tried everything. In this case, there wasn't anything he didn't enjoy. If Jaime's mom had cooked like this while he was growing up, it was amazing he wasn't fat. Tate's mom's idea of home cooking had been cereal, sandwiches, or pasta with canned sauce, but even those delicacies had tapered off as he'd gotten older.

Thirty minutes later Tate had filled up every available crevice in his stomach, and staying awake was almost painful.

Jaime smiled at him. "Go have a nap."

"I want to spend time with you." Because of shifts Jaime had promised to cover, they wouldn't be seeing each other again for almost a week. He didn't want to sleep through the day of the boyfriend discussion. Some celebratory date that would be.

"Hey, Diego's call woke me up way too early this morning. I'll be in soon, but I won't let us sleep too long. Then we can have our date. Something calm and easy."

Jaime pressed his lips together like he did when he was figuring out what to say. Tate wanted to follow instructions to go have a nap, but he waited for Jaime to sort the words out in his head.

"Will you stay the night? Please?"

Jaime had been obvious about wanting him to stay, but he'd also been great about driving Tate back to Area 52 and dropping him off each night without complaint. Sleeping at Jaime's had seemed like one more thing he'd be sponging off the guy, but maybe now Tate could stay over without feeling guilty. It was a boyfriend thing to do, and from the first time Jaime had offered, Tate had wanted to stay with every fiber in his being. But protecting himself had been more important. Now he trusted Jaime to not fuck him over, and he wanted this. Wanted to know what it was like to sleep next to Jaime, who gave off heat like a furnace. Wanted to know what it felt like to wake up in someone's arms, then make breakfast together.

With his injuries it would probably hurt like hell, but it was a price he was willing to pay.

"Will you drop me off at the library tomorrow?"

"Of course."

Settled. He was having his first overnight at his boyfriend's apartment, and amazingly, there would be no sex. Would his mother even notice if he didn't come home?

JAIME HUMMED to the song on the radio, letting himself enjoy the drive as he never did when he was working. Traffic was light, his boyfriend was asleep in the passenger seat, and he was taking Tate to one of his favorite—and free—places in or around Orlando.

When he'd woken them up from their nap, Tate had been full of questions about where they were going, but Jaime wanted it to be a surprise, and it hadn't taken too long before Tate had nodded off again. At least Jaime'd had the foresight to bring a small pillow in the car, because he didn't want Tate to stiffen up any more than he had after their nap.

Jaime was content to brave the thorns for the hidden rose. He snorted, imagining Tate's reaction if Jaime ever called him a rose. Maybe a fire lily? But those didn't have thorns. Whatever. He wasn't a literature professor or a poet. His mangled metaphors, however ridiculous, could stay in his head.

Tate woke up just as they started over the causeway west of Tampa.

"What? Where are we?" Tate peered out of the window, face almost mashed up against the glass.

Jaime smiled. This particular part of the drive was definitely the most scenic. "On the other side of Tampa, crossing over the bay."

"Tampa? How long have we been driving?"

"Just over an hour. We'll be there in about forty-five minutes more."

Tate pulled his attention from the window. "We're driving two hours. For what?"

Jaime smiled. "You'll see." He just hoped Tate would find it as special as he did.

They passed the rest of the drive learning about what sort of music they both liked. Perhaps unsurprisingly, Tate liked mainstream pop, the kind that was frequently played as background music in public venues. Fortunately Jaime liked a lot of the same stuff, since Top 40s were what he usually heard in the clubs unless he ended up going to eighties night or indie rock night.

When Jaime finally pulled into the parking lot at their destination, Tate lifted an eyebrow. "The Florida Botanical Gardens?"

"Yeah. Have you been here before?"

"Uh, no. Orlando, Kissimmee. Jacksonville once. That's it. The sum total of where I've been."

Jaime hadn't traveled a lot for pleasure, although he'd been a number of places as part of his enlistment. He didn't know if he'd have traveled away from his family very often if he hadn't joined the Army, and he had pretty much zero desire to get on a plane again after he'd returned to civilian life, but he was already mentally preparing some vacations he and Tate could go on. It might be fun for Tate to get on a plane, or maybe they could go on a short cruise together. Jaime had never gone on a cruise before either. It would be new for both of them.

He could see it already: him and Tate in skimpy swimsuits, playing in the sand—under a beach umbrella so Tate didn't lobster up—with deep teal ocean as far as the eye could see. Beach sand he could handle—it was nothing like the desert.

"Uh, Jaime?"

He blinked, shaking off visions of him and Tate in the Caribbean, and realized he'd missed what else Tate had said.

"Sorry. Zoned out for a minute. What did you say?"

"Just wondering if there's a bathroom. I gotta take a leak."

"Of course. Then we'll wander around for a bit."

Jaime helped Tate get out of the car—he had stiffened up even more.

"I'm looking forward to seeing one of your favorite places. I have to admit, when you said it was free and not the sort of place you'd expect, I had figured you were talking about Old Town or something." There was no mistaking the sneer on Tate's face.

"You don't like Old Town? I mean, it has its place... but wait. Those rides and all aren't free, are they?" It had been a long time since he'd bothered with Old Town, which was pretty much the definition of tourist trap.

Tate shrugged. "Oh, yeah, I've never been on the rides. You have to pay for those. But the stores and stuff you can wander around for free."

"And if I offered to take you there?"

Another negligent shrug. "I guess I'd go, but I don't go there anymore."

"Bad experience?"

Tate's face flamed the red of shame. "Kind of. One of my first arrests."

Jaime waited, breathless. He'd only heard about a couple of Tate's brushes with the law. He could probably get Diego to give him some more details, but he'd been hoping Tate would start opening up more. Hearing it from Tate, knowing Tate trusted him with the information, made it special.

TEN MINUTES later they'd chosen a path and wandered along it. Tate was closer to hobbling, but he brushed off Jaime's concerned questions. Instead, Jaime merely dropped their pace—it wasn't like they had to see the whole thing today. There was even a historical heritage village thing on-site as well, but he wasn't about to drag Tate through that today.

Jaime had really wanted to show him the nature paths, not the village. Along one of the boardwalks, they stopped at a well-shaded bench. Tate dropped awkwardly onto it, wincing as he jarred himself. Jaime was proud of himself for not asking if he was okay. Gold star for him!

They weren't the only people visiting the gardens, but between the winding paths and the extensive foliage, it was easy to imagine they were the only people in the world.

Jaime relaxed against the back of the bench, listening to the birds, the hum of insects, a breeze ruffling the leaves overhead. Beside him, he could almost sense the lingering tension and worry leech out of Tate. He shifted his hand to hook their fingers together. Tate squeezed briefly, and they sat there in silence for a while.

A family of five, from the UK judging by the accents, interrupted their solitude, and they both sat up a little straighter. The family smiled and continued on, chatting and pointing out various plants and flowers.

"I can see why you like this place. I didn't know... I didn't know places like this even existed."

"Honestly, I didn't either, for a long time." Jaime let out a breath and shifted to face Tate. Tate mirrored his movements, if slower and less gracefully. "I saw a lot of stuff in the Army. Bad stuff. I lost friends, including a very close friend. I watched him die." He didn't need to go into the details, that all his skills hadn't been enough to save Mario. His pulse picked up, and a small amount of adrenaline leaked into his system. This was only the second time he'd said those words to anyone.

Tate gripped his hand tighter. "I'm so sorry, Jaime."

There was no pity in those amber eyes, though. Just the bone-deep understanding he'd been expecting. Both of them had seen and experienced some of the worst things life had to offer, and that more than anything made them comrades-in-arms. This was part of the reason Jaime had never been able to click with any of the guys he met in clubs. He needed someone who understood he'd seen some truly awful things and had come away just a little bit broken. Tate hadn't had to travel to Afghanistan for his bad shit, but Jaime had seen just a tip of his iceberg.

"Anyway, when I got back, I was pretty fucked-up. My therapist did wonders, but this was one of the things he suggested to help keep me calm. The fact that it doesn't look like a fucking desert? Helps a lot."

"It works. I feel almost like a different person." Tate's words hadn't acknowledged their similarities, but he didn't have to. His expression and the way his thumb stroked against Jaime's hand said everything.

"Anyway, I don't have to come out here as often as I used to, but it recharges me, and I'm happy to bring you out here whenever you want."

"Thank you. I think we can assume I'll want to come out here every time I get arrested."

Jaime stared at him for a full half second before he burst into laughter, and Tate laughed with him. He'd have thought it too soon for Tate to want to joke about it, but borderline morbid humor was another way to deal with the bad shit, and it was yet another thing he and Tate had in common, even if Tate had been a little slower to open up that side of himself.

A sudden thought struck Jaime, and this time his laugh was bitter. "Uh, by the way, I'm still a little fucked-up, even after all these years." He paused for Tate to ask how many, but he simply waited for Jaime to continue. "I already told you I don't like movies with explosions. Or military ones either. But I also get nightmares. I can't really predict when I'm going to have them. They're much less frequent than they used to be, but… um… if you're going to be spending the night sometimes, you should know."

"Is there anything you need me to do?"

Jaime frowned. He didn't actually know. He'd only had a couple of guys ever spend the night, and those had been mostly by accident, when he'd fallen asleep before kicking them out. "Just… do what you can to wake me up, and if I'm thrashing, try to keep out of the way."

"I can do that."

Jaime dared to give him a kiss but was careful not to let his lips linger. "Want to walk a little more? We can take it slow, and lots of breaks."

"How long can we stay?"

"They close at sunset, which will be close to eight, but I think we'll get hungry long before that. We'll give it a couple of hours, then go find a place to eat. This close to the coast, there are a ton of great seafood places. Casual ones," Jaime said before Tate could object. Jaime's clothes looked okay on him, but Tate's runners were filthy, and there was no way Tate could borrow Jaime's shoes.

Tate smiled, and this time it was him pressing a kiss on Jaime.

Jaime helped him to his feet and began guiding him along the path.

CHAPTER TEN

JAIME HAD promised weeks ago to fill in for this Tuesday shift, which would end up being a double for him, and even though he'd wanted to stay home cuddling with Tate, he'd grudgingly woken up early and dropped Tate off at the library, where he was planning to spend the day before going in for his own shift.

Two hours after Jaime dropped Tate off, he and his partner—Angelica again—were racing back to the library, responding to a call that someone had collapsed. Dispatch said an eighty-two-year-old.

Heart attack or stroke, probably, although the old dear might have also broken a hip depending on how hard they went down. At least the library was near the hospital.

Sirens wailing, they parked close to the doors and in efficient, practiced moves had a stretcher and medical case out of the back and into the library in no time at all.

They didn't need to ask anyone where the patient was—a small gaggle of professionally dressed women and one man hovered around a figure on the floor.

"Clear away, please, we need to get in there to work." Jaime rarely used that stern voice in real life, but most people experiencing a crisis responded exactly the way he needed them to.

Everyone was pale and drawn-looking, one of the women crying. She was heavyset and short, and it took her longer to move away because she'd been on her knees, holding the patient's hand. Another, much younger woman helped her to her feet.

"Can anyone tell us what happened?" Angelica asked.

Jaime was waiting for his chance to get at the patient. If they were conscious, even if they couldn't speak, he was usually good at soothing and interpreting.

The older woman finally moved away, and Jaime fell to his knees with a pained gasp, blood rushing through his veins so hard for a moment all he could hear was his pulse thundering in his ears.

"Jesus. Tate. What happened?"

Tate's eyes were glazed, unfocused, and he cradled his middle section with his left arm. "Jaime? What are you doing here?"

Angelica knelt on the other side of Tate and started taking vitals. "You know him?"

Jaime thought he might throw up. "He's my boyfriend."

"Shit," she muttered under her breath. "He'll be fine," she said a little louder.

"What happened?" Jaime stared at the woman who had been holding Tate's hand. "Do you know?"

She dabbed at her eyes with a tissue, but her tone was precise and brisk, exactly the sort of person Jaime liked best to deal with at a call. "He came up to my desk, and he didn't look good at all. Paler than normal, and he seemed unsteady, like he was dizzy. He said his stomach hurt, and then he just fell."

"Was he unconscious at any time? Do you think he hit his head?"

"No. Not unconscious, just confused and dizzy. I don't think he hit his head, but it happened so fast."

Tate had borrowed one of his button-down shirts that morning, and Jaime didn't waste any time getting it open. He suppressed a gag at the sight of Tate's chest, mottled black and purple and red. Several of the onlookers gasped. God. He had an iron stomach, but seeing evidence of Tate's beating had him wanting to heave up his breakfast. The breakfast Tate had helped him make. Why hadn't Tate told him it was this bad?

Angelica gripped his forearm. "Jaime, do I need to call another team?"

He shook off his shock as best he could. Damned if someone else would work on his boyfriend. "I'm fine. Fine."

"From this bruising, I'm guessing ruptured spleen." Angelica tested her theory, making Tate gasp. "Yup. Let's go. He could have other internal bleeding too."

They worked as quickly as possible and got him into the ambulance. Angelica drove while Jaime monitored Tate in the back, hooking up an IV and telling him it would be okay. But Tate's fingers were freezing, his freckles were stark against abnormally pale skin, and he wasn't exactly with it.

"Fuck, Jaime, I was sure Dispatch told us an eighty-two-year-old."

Jaime didn't bother responding. Someone must have gotten their wires crossed somewhere. No point in worrying about it now, not when he had so many other things to worry about.

He did everything by rote, somehow playing the part of a competent EMT. After they reached the hospital and the emergency medical staff took over, Jaime watched as they wheeled Tate away, colorless except for his hair.

Angelica steered him into an empty room. "What the hell, Jaime?"

Jaime stared at her, fingers trembling, not sure what she was asking. "What?"

She scowled at him. "You think I don't recognize the signs of a beating? You said he was your boyfriend. Give me one good reason that I don't call the cops." She was practically hissing she was so furious.

Her anger worked almost like a slap across the face. "*Dios*, Angelica, I didn't do it. He stopped a gay bashing Sunday night and ended up spending the night in jail. He told me he was fine, but I haven't seen him naked since it happened." Tears slipped down his face. "He wasn't moving well, but he said he didn't have any broken ribs. And there was only a faint bruise on his jaw. He didn't... he didn't want me to be his keeper, he said."

His last words came out broken, battling past the lump in his throat.

Angelica leaped at him, wrapping him in a giant hug. Jaime hugged her back, and they stood there until Jaime had himself under control.

"I don't... I don't know what to do now."

"I do." Angelica dragged him to the waiting area. "Sit. And wait. I'm going to get you a cup of coffee and call the bosses. You're off as of this minute, and for tomorrow too, at the very least."

Jaime did as he was bid, hollow inside, staring at the television but not comprehending anything.

At some point Angelica returned, bearing excessively sweetened black coffee. "Drink it."

Without any reason not to, aside from the nauseating twist of worry in his stomach, he obeyed.

"Can I call anyone to come and sit with you? He's in surgery now, probably won't be ready for visitors for a couple of hours."

God. He wanted to wait. Odds were good Tate would be fine, but life and death didn't always play to the odds. Sitting here would accomplish nothing, and he'd spend the whole time imagining the worst. What he needed to do was find something to keep his mind occupied until Tate was out of surgery.

"Thank you. I'll call my cousin in a few minutes."

"Do you want me to wait with you?"

Jaime shook his head. "I'll be okay. Thanks again." He wanted family, but he wasn't sure he wanted to give the explanations needed. Once Angelica left, he'd figure out whether he was going to call Caleb. He wanted his best friend there with him, but he hated exposing his cousin to the pain in his life. Maybe he needed to stop protecting Caleb, though. Maybe it was hurting Jaime more than it was keeping Caleb safe and ignorant.

He drank more of his coffee, unsure if it was terrible because hospital cafeterias were hit-or-miss on coffee quality or if everything would taste like shit right now.

Angelica hugged him again. "Let me know how things go, okay?"

A few minutes later, she returned. "Here. It's Tate's wallet. Must have fallen out of his pocket in the ambulance."

Jaime curled his fingers around the slim, ragged nylon. "Thanks."

"Did you call your cousin?"

"I will. I promise."

Angelica nodded but didn't look like she believed him. Smart woman. Jaime wouldn't have believed him either.

Regardless, she still left, leaving him with a few other people who were in similar states of zombie-tude. Jaime set his half-finished coffee on a nearby table and turned Tate's wallet over in his hands.

What he should do first was tell Tate's mom. Tate had mentioned recently that he thought their phone line had been disconnected, so even if Jaime had known the number, he couldn't call.

Gingerly, Jaime pulled open the Velcro closing, the sound loud and harsh in a waiting room, where no one spoke louder than a whisper. He tried desperately not to remember sorting through Mario's personal effects for ones still in good enough condition to ship home to his family. *Please not again.*

Unlike his own bulging wallet, Tate's had almost nothing in it. A ten-dollar bill, a smattering of buy-one-get-one-free coupons for various fast-food places, a birth certificate, a social security card, a library card, and a Florida ID card. Jaime smoothed a finger over the picture. Tate really hadn't been kidding when he said he didn't drive. Coming across non–driver's license ID cards was rare. Most importantly, it had an address on it.

Visiting Tate's mom had to happen sooner or later, but Jaime needed either his car or a ride. He'd rather wait, at least until Tate was out of surgery and in the recovery room, but that wasn't fair to Tate's mom. She should at least have the option of coming to get information sooner rather than later.

He went outside and walked a bit away from the emergency entrance—he was still in uniform, and he didn't want to get roped into another emergency with someone who thought he was still on duty.

After pulling out his phone, he stared at it for a moment. Was it only two days ago he'd told Caleb and Raven all about Tate and how well things were going? It seemed like years ago.

He pulled up Caleb's contact information and initiated the call.

"Jaime? What's wrong?"

Maybe he'd underestimated Caleb. After all, he figured out there was something wrong just because Jaime called instead of texting in the middle of a workday.

"Hey, *papi*. Can you pick me up at the hospital?"

It took a few minutes to explain that he wasn't hurt, but Caleb said he'd finish up the job he was in the middle of and would be right down. No more than thirty minutes.

Jaime sighed and sat on a nearby bench. All of the bliss and contentment from the previous day's trip to the botanical gardens had vanished. There was too much ambient noise and traffic for this bench to provide any solace, not that he was expecting to find any peace. Not until Tate was out of surgery and on the mend.

JAIME LET his head fall back against the wall and closed his eyes against the sun. It was bright enough that he could still see the light through his eyelids. A faint breeze ruffled his hair, keeping the midday heat from being too oppressive. His phone buzzed, and he opened his eyes to read the text.

I'm here.

Jaime stood and walked toward the entrance, quickly spotting Caleb's work truck in the short-term parking. He walked toward it as Caleb got out and moved to meet him.

Before he did anything else, Caleb wrapped him in a big hug. The hug was warm and secure and provided far more comfort than Jaime had expected.

Perhaps he'd been wrong not to tell Caleb about his experiences overseas. But rectifying that mistake was a job for another time.

"I'm so sorry, Jaime. I can't even imagine how awful it would be to find Tate like that."

Caleb pulled away, and Jaime nodded, not really wanting to talk about that. At least there hadn't been any blood. That might have triggered a full-blown flashback simply because of his feelings for Tate.

"Okay, so you said he's in surgery now? What did you want me to do? I can wait with you. I cleared the rest of my day."

Jaime sighed. "I really just need a lift to pick up my car." He waved Tate's wallet. "I need to go and tell Tate's mother what happened."

"No. No way. You're not driving anywhere right now. I'll take you. There's enough room that I can bring both you and Tate's mom back to the hospital, or whatever. Then you can let me and Raven worry about getting your car to you."

"Are you sure?"

Caleb gave him a look that suggested Jaime was talking crazy. "Of course I'm sure. Get in the truck."

Jaime punched the address into the GPS while Caleb maneuvered out of the parking lot. Tate's place was definitely a long fucking walk from the library, but surprisingly close to Area 52. It made sense that most of Tate's jobs were in that area.

"Everything's going to be all right." Caleb reached over and squeezed his forearm.

Just a platitude—Jaime knew better than most all the things that could go wrong—but somehow Caleb's faith helped calm some of his jitters. Having something to do, a plan, helped too. Or maybe it was nothing more than not having to face all this alone. Because he wasn't alone in this life, and he needed to do a better job of recognizing that.

It was in the hands of the surgeon now, and Tate's will to live. If there was anything Jaime could take as a given in this world, though, it was that his boyfriend was a fighter.

Several minutes later Caleb pulled up to a curb and parked. "Is this it?" His voice was carefully neutral.

Jaime checked the address on Tate's ID. "I think so."

They both stared. The tiny dilapidated house sat on a good chunk of property and was well shaded by mature trees, but those were the only good things he could say about it. The roof sagged and was covered with detritus from the trees. Part of the eaves had broken away, and another section hung at a jaunty angle, neither of which would do anything to funnel water away from the house. Paint was a long-lost memory, and the yard was weedy where it wasn't covered with rusting-out car hulks and broken fencing. It looked almost as though someone had considered starting a junkyard but then got bored somewhere around 1987. Plywood covered one of the front windows, the chipped wood gray and water damaged, showing the evidence of months or, more likely, years of use.

"It looks abandoned."

Jaime agreed. "I have to find out for sure." This house would definitely explain some of Tate's behavior, though, like why he never told Jaime where he lived and wouldn't allow Jaime to pick him up or drop him off at home.

"I'll wait here. Let me know if you need me for anything."

Fuck. He didn't want to do this. Jaime climbed out of the truck and strode up the dusty path to the front door. The doorbell was cracked and broken. If it still worked, he'd be asking to be electrocuted, so he knocked firmly.

After a minute he knocked again. This time he could hear movement from within, but for all he knew, a family of possums or armadillos had taken up residence inside.

The door opened and a bleached-blonde woman hung seductively on the frame. Or at least, a drunken, drugged-up version of seductive. She wore a red satin teddy, and she could be anywhere from his age to twenty years older. Heavy drinking and drug use could radically affect someone's appearance, but much of her beauty remained despite that.

"Well, hello, there. What can I do for you?"

Jaime winced at the unsubtle invitation. "Do you know Tate Buchanan?"

Her expression changed from seductive to disdainful in an instant. "What the fuck has that idiot done now?" She squinted at him. "Are you with the police?"

"Um. No. Are you his mother?"

"Unfortunately. That deadbeat is late on his rent. Again."

Jaime plowed on. "There was an accident. He's in the hospital. He's in surgery now, but the prognosis is good."

"Oh for fuck's sake. I'm sure there was no accident. That stupid fuck can't figure out not to start a fight with men bigger than him."

"Did you want to go to the hospital?"

Tate's mother—he didn't think she was Mrs. Buchanan, from the things Tate had said—rolled her eyes. "Hell no. Last time I showed up, they tried to make *me* pay for it. Fucker can pay for that shit himself. And make sure he gets me rent if he wants to come back here after."

Jaime clenched his jaw, trying to quash his own sudden desire for violence. How could Tate's mother hate him so much? He now understood Tate's desperation for a job—any job—and his desire to live on his own, but that might never happen if he didn't find something that paid more than minimum wage.

"Can I at least come in and get him a change of clothes?"

"Fine. But if he don't have money or he don't take Bertie up on his job offer, he can forget about getting in the door."

"And what job offer would that be?" Jaime did his best to be polite, but he didn't imagine Bertie was up to any good.

She smirked and tapped a long red fingernail at her temple. "Pays a lot better than slinging burgers, but just proves my boy isn't all there." She stepped back from the door and grabbed a pack of smokes from a table. She lit one and inhaled.

"Put his stupid mouth to better use than riling people up, if you get my drift." Cigarette smoke curled about her hair, and she laughed, the harsh, grating sound of a well-seasoned smoker. For the second time that day, Jaime wanted to throw up. Was she seriously expecting her son to whore himself out in order to have a roof over his head after surgery?

"I'll just grab some clothes. Which one is his room?"

"Door at the end of the hall, honey. But you don't need to be in a hurry to leave."

Oh, yes, he did. He detoured into the kitchen. "Mind if I get a glass of water?"

"Not at all." Tate's mom sank down on the couch, cigarette dangling from her fingers, and stared glassily at the television.

Not that Jaime had wanted to take a drink, but now that his eyes had adjusted to the dim interior, he had some grave reservations about whether Tate could recuperate here, money notwithstanding.

He flicked on the faucet to let the water run.

Everything was yellowed with years—decades—of nicotine in the air. Dust lay heavy, tiles were cracked, grout was falling away. Jaime had been expecting filthy dishes piled up in the sink, covered in roaches or ants, but there wasn't anything. Under the sink, though, was a vast field of empty booze bottles.

He opened a few cupboards and found plates and glasses and a few sad cans of pasta and some packets of "just add boiling water" soup that were more salt than food.

The fridge was next. Inside, vodka. And nothing else. What the fuck? No wonder Tate didn't know anything about food or cooking.

He shut off the tap and headed into Tate's room. There were a few faded posters that looked like they'd been swiped from bus shelters tacked up on the walls. A single mattress lay on a frame that had more in common with a cot than a bed. A few clothes hung in a closet with no door; spare sheets and some towels lay on top of the shelf. A couple of stacking plastic tubs in the corner held more clothes. Another plastic bin doubled as a bedside table, bearing half a roll of quarters and a rickety lamp with a torn shade. This bin only held a couple of plastic garbage bags.

Turning around, he looked for anything else. Anything Tate could call his own. That was when he noticed the mold. Black mold covered the baseboard in the corner and streaked up the wall to the ceiling. After a few mental calculations, he figured out this part of Tate's room must be right below the missing eaves.

"Hell no," he muttered. There was no way—no fucking way—Tate was staying here another day, especially not after surgery. There was only one solution: Tate was coming back to his place.

Grabbing one of the plastic bags, he turned his attention to the clothing bins. Everything easily fit inside the single bag. Next, he went to the closet and inspected the towels and sheets. Both were threadbare, the sheets nearly transparent with age, but as much as he wanted to throw them out and replace them, he had a feeling Tate would have angry words about that.

Into the bag they went, leaving only the clothes hanging up. Two button-down shirts hung side by side with two argyle sweaters and two argyle sweater-vests. Jaime wouldn't have ever taken Tate for an argyle fan, but he wasn't about to leave them here, not when they'd been so well taken care of. He folded them carefully and put them in the bag.

Finally he swiped the roll of quarters and tossed it in on top of everything else. He wasn't even going to brave the bathroom. Tate could share his toiletries, and he was just going to have to live with the burden of having Jaime buy him a new toothbrush.

He almost swept out of the place without another word, but his sense of responsibility made him pause. After setting down the garbage bag full of Tate's clothes, he pulled a small notebook from his pocket, scrawled his cell number, and walked over to Tate's mom.

"Here. If you want to get in touch with Tate, you can call him here."

Already smoking a fresh cigarette, she made absolutely no move to take the paper from him. "Yeah. Okay."

Duty done, he left his number beside her lighter. Then he grabbed the garbage bag and left, desperate for another shower, even though he'd had one that morning.

Practically running, he returned to the truck and slung the bag in the back.

"What's up?" Caleb asked. Jaime buckled in and Caleb started driving. "Where to now?"

"We need to make a stop at Walgreens. Maybe IKEA too."

Caleb stared at him. "IKEA? What on earth for?"

"I need to get a small dresser for Tate's clothes. I don't have enough spare room in mine."

"Have you lost your mind, *papi*? You're going to move Tate into your place? You barely know him."

"Aside from the fact that I know him better than you think, Caleb, it was horrifying." He related everything, including that woman's—he refused to think of her as Tate's mom any longer—suggestion that Tate might want to take up selling himself for rent money.

"Okay, okay. I get it. He definitely can't stay there, but is your place the right alternative? I mean, none of us have even met him yet."

"So? Do you think he's going to rob me?"

Caleb huffed in frustration. "I don't know. Maybe. How can we know? Again, we haven't *met* him."

"After what I just saw in there? If I came home one day and found my apartment cleaned out, it would be okay."

Caleb's mouth dropped open. "It would be okay?"

Jaime thought about that for a second. "Not okay. I mean, it would also mean Tate had gone, and that would suck, but I wouldn't begrudge him the stuff. Because I'd understand why he'd be tempted by things he's never had, and if he thought my stuff might lead to a better life for him, I'd accept that. But I think when you meet him, you'll realize he's not like that." There was no doubt in Jaime's mind. "I'll have a harder time convincing him to stay than you'd think."

"Are you sure?"

"I'm sure. Besides, this is what I'd want soon anyway. I'd rather not worry about him being somewhere else, somewhere more dangerous." And there was the little matter that he'd probably get some awful infection from that hellhole of a house and die. Assuming his mother didn't kill him first through neglect.

"Fine." Caleb might sound begrudging now, but he'd come around.

"Oh, before we do that, can we stop by the Flying Pizza Pie? I need to let them know Tate won't be able to work for a while." Those errands should keep Jaime well occupied until the evening visiting hours, which would probably be the earliest he'd be allowed to see Tate, since they weren't family.

"Cool. We can get some lunch while we're there. I'm starving."

Jaime's stomach lurched, this time from hunger rather than sickness. "Yeah. I could eat."

"I'VE NEVER been here. Is it any good?" Caleb stared at the giant pizza hovering over the doorway. It reminded Jaime of the UFO at Area 52, and he wondered if the pizza place had been hoping to capitalize on the proximity and similarities. Stranger things had happened—this was Florida, after all.

"No idea. I'd never heard of it until Tate. But he never suggests eating here. I don't know if that's because they feed the employees on shift and he's had enough pizza, or if it sucks. Guess we'll find out."

Inside, they placed their order at a counter, and the cashier handed them a number to take to their table so the server could find them when their food was ready.

"Hey, is there a manager I can speak to?" Jaime asked.

"Is something wrong?" The cashier looked horrified, as though she'd mortally offended them or something and they were going to try to get her fired.

Jaime smiled. "No, no, I just want to ask him or her something."

"Oh. It's a him. Gary. If you want, I'll send him over to the table."

"Thank you."

They got soft drinks from the self-serve dispenser and had been sitting for only a few minutes when a mousy-looking man, probably just a few years younger than Jaime and Caleb, approached the table.

"Hello. One of you was looking for a manager? What can I help you with?"

Jaime stood and saw the man take in the uniform he was still wearing. That was another thing to add to the errand list for the day—get into some civilian clothes.

"Yes. It's about one of your employees." Jaime glanced around. It was a little later than normal lunchtime, but the tables were still crowded. "Is there someplace private we could talk?"

Gary exuded an air of concern, although Jaime suspected it was mostly feigned. "Of course. My office is in the back."

Gary led Jaime through an Employees Only entrance and into a small, windowless, cheerless room. Gary sat behind the desk, and Jaime sat across from him. If Jaime worked for him, this would be an unsettling room. Probably Gary only brought employees in here to yell at them.

"One of your employees suffered an accident earlier today. He's in surgery now, but he was supposed to work tonight. Obviously he won't make it, and he'll be unable to work for a while. A couple weeks at least."

"That's terrible. I hope he feels better soon. Who did you say it was again?"

"Tate Buchanan."

Gary's lip curled up in a sneer. "That guy? God. I was ready to fire him anyway. I'll consider this his resignation. He can pick up his last check on Monday."

Jaime couldn't quite catch his breath. What the hell had just happened? "Why are you doing this? I know he'll be anxious to come back to work after he's well again."

"Like I care. He comes in late more often than not, and I can't even put him on as a cashier because he keeps fucking it up. Tells people wrong totals, can't figure out change even when the cash register tells you what to give them. Impossible to teach. I've worked with some stupid people in my career, but Tate's a special case. Good riddance."

Again, Jaime was starting to see the appeal violence had, because he wanted to punch this fucker in the mouth. How dare he speak about Tate like that? This was the second person today who'd called Tate stupid, which Jaime didn't understand at all. He also couldn't understand why Tate was late to his shifts; he never gave Jaime the impression that he hated his job or that he'd procrastinate so he wouldn't have to go to work. With the possibility of his mother pimping him out as an alternative, Tate probably had a better work ethic than most people Jaime knew.

"I see." He didn't, but Tate could find a new job with a manager who wasn't a giant douche-mobile. "Then someone will be in on Monday to collect his check."

Jaime slammed the door behind him and strode to the table. Their lunch had just arrived. "Let's go."

"What?" Caleb pointed at the food. "In case you've forgotten, we haven't eaten yet. And there's food right here, begging to be devoured."

Like he would eat here now. Jaime sniffed. "It's swimming in grease and smells like week-old socks."

"You're the one who asked for gorgonzola on yours."

"I'll treat you to something else. Anything else. Let's go."

Out in the truck, Caleb aimed them for the nearest drive-through. On this stretch of 192, they were littered like leaves on the ground. It took mere minutes to get a couple of burgers and fries.

"What the fuck just happened back there?"

"Apparently ending up in the hospital was the equivalent of quitting."

"What? They can't do that, can they?"

Jaime sighed. "Yeah, they can. People can be fired for just about any reason, and *Gary* said he'd either fire Tate or consider it a resignation."

Caleb huffed. "I haven't even met the guy and I already feel sorry for him. No wonder he fights all the time."

Jaime had a theory about that too, but he needed more information before he was willing to air it. He just couldn't figure out why everyone called his boyfriend stupid. Sure, there were some things he didn't know and technology had mostly passed him by, but…. "Wait. I also need to go to Best Buy."

"Jesus, Jaime."

"What? You said you'd drive. And that you cleared your day. What else were you going to do? Or am I keeping you from hide-the-sausage-under-a-kilt with Raven?"

"Shut up." Caleb tried to sound offended, but he was laughing too hard. "You'd never even say that if you weren't a perverted voyeur."

"Uh-huh. I was making *coffee* and you knew that, but the second I was out of the room, you still had Raven ass up over the couch. You just have no self-control."

"Yeah? How's that self-control working out with Tate, hmm?"

"Fine. Fine. I get it. Now. Best Buy, Caleb. IKEA. Walgreens."

Caleb shoved some fries in his mouth and glared at Jaime. But he headed in the right direction.

CHAPTER ELEVEN

AFTER AN afternoon of getting ready to move Tate into his apartment, Jaime felt more grounded and pleased he had a solid plan. Caleb had dropped him back at the hospital with a promise that he and Raven would rescue his car from work and leave it in short-term parking.

Before anything else, Jaime let Bethany, one of the emergency nurses, know Tate would be going home with him so she could make a note in his file. If things worked out the way Jaime hoped, Tate could change his home address permanently once he was feeling better. Bethany had smirked at him, but it had only taken a tiny description of Tate's house and how his mother had unceremoniously turfed him out, and Bethany let out a little gasp, her expression softening.

Most of the nurses had already heard the circumstances under which Tate had gotten injured and thought Tate was a hero and cute as a button. Jaime didn't exactly growl at hearing that, but at least Tate wouldn't have his head turned by the female nurses. Hopefully not by the male ones either.

He found Tate's room with ease. Three other beds in the room were occupied, and Tate's bed was curtained off. Jaime pulled a chair next to the bed. The scrape of metal against the floor made Tate blink sleepily at him.

"Hey, there." Jaime pulled the blanket higher and took Tate's hand in his. "What's the verdict?"

"Hi." Tate's voice was thick with disuse. "My spleen ruptured and they took it out."

Jaime nodded. Exactly as he and Angelica had surmised.

Tate blinked. "What are you doing here?"

"Visiting my boyfriend after he had his spleen removed." Jaime smiled gently.

Tate's expression was part smile, part grimace. "I can't believe I just fell down. I guess I should have let you take a look at me."

Amazing. Jaime had been expecting a demand to get him out of here. Maybe the nurses in the recovery room had managed to convince him that a ruptured spleen was actually serious.

"Yes and no. I mean, I might have been able to tell your spleen was swollen, but it might not have gotten swollen right away. But if I'd known how bad you'd been hit, I would have been able to at least warn you what to look out for."

Tate glanced away. "I'm sorry."

"Hey." Jaime squeezed his hand tighter. "I'm not scolding you. I'm just telling you how things could have been different, and I'm hoping you'll keep that in mind for next time."

"I don't want there to be a next time. But sometimes… the anger just takes over and I can't stop it."

Jaime wasn't a therapist, but he had some ideas and would spend some time doing more research. "I don't want there to be a next time either, but maybe together we can figure something out."

The pain and fury and fear of the day caught up with him, and he clutched Tate's hand tighter so he wouldn't notice Jaime trembling. Unable to bear being even this far from Tate when he'd been afraid someone was going to tell him Tate hadn't made it, he leaned over the bed, avoiding Tate's midsection, and buried his face in Tate's neck. Underneath the antiseptic smells of the hospital he was able to pick up musky traces of Tate's normal scent. His eyes burned and his shoulders shook as he suppressed a sob.

"I was so fucking scared when I saw you lying on the ground. For a second I thought you were dead."

Tate lifted a hand and stroked his hair. "I'm sorry for that."

They stayed like that, just being with each other, until Jaime's spine couldn't take the pretzel shape he'd twisted it into. After sitting back in the chair, he took Tate's hand again.

"I have to call work and let them know I won't be in. Will I be able to go home tonight?"

"No, I'm afraid not. And probably not for a couple more days. Your work is taken care of, so don't worry about that." The truth, although not as Tate understood it. Jaime would feel guilty for deceiving Tate, but he didn't want to stress him out. Not yet.

"Thank you."

Jaime flipped up the lower part of the blanket and carefully kept his expression neutral when he saw the bandages. Bethany had told him Tate was going to need new shoes, but not why. From her expression, though, he'd deduced it wasn't simply dirt or blood that made Tate's old shoes unwearable.

"What happened to your feet?"

Tate shrugged, then winced. "Blisters. I guess I walked too far."

Jaime held in a snort. Walked his shoes into tatters, more like. Well, Tate was also going to have to deal with the additional burden of brand-new shoes courtesy of Jaime. He'd stop somewhere in the morning and pick up something before Tate was released, along with some nice cushy socks.

Tate's fire had been muted to embers by the narcotics he was on for the pain, but Jaime could see the spark underneath. He suspected Tate would be an irate, testy patient, and Jaime still looked forward to being able to take care of him.

They spoke of nothing much for a few minutes before Tate's eyelids started drooping.

"You go to sleep, *mi fuego*. I'll stay until they kick me out." It was hard to tell how people would react to the drugs. Tate might sleep for a few minutes, an hour, or all night. But Jaime would stay until visiting hours were over.

Tate's lips moved, but he was asleep before any words escaped. Jaime pulled out his phone and launched the e-book he'd been reading— the sci-fi trilogy Tate had raved about. Within moments, he'd been sucked back into the story.

"Excuse me?"

Jaime looked up. The woman standing by the end of Tate's bed wasn't a nurse, but she was familiar. "Oh. You were at the library this morning." So much had happened   had it really only been that morning?

"Yes. I'm Mrs. Birenbaum."

"Of course. Tate's said great things about you."

She smiled faintly.

"Let me get you a chair. Thank you for coming by."

Jaime grabbed an unused chair from the hall and brought it in.

"Thank you. You are the EMT who responded, aren't you?"

"Yes, I'm Jaime. Jaime Escobar."

"And did I hear you say you're his boyfriend?"

How should he respond? He didn't know if Mrs. Birenbaum cared if they were gay or not, but then again, he'd already admitted it. "Yes, I am."

"You poor dear."

Because he was gay?

"That must have been awful, finding your boyfriend like that. It was a shock to us too, but well, it's a different relationship, obviously."

"Thank you, yeah." Jaime let out a little bleat of laughter. "Dispatch had told us it was an eighty-two-year-old, so it was extra surprising."

Mrs. Birenbaum's lips twitched. "Oh dear."

Finding the humor in it now that Tate was on the mend was okay by Jaime.

"Do you… can you tell me what happened?" Mrs. Birenbaum asked.

Jaime glanced at the sleeping Tate. Jaime hadn't had much chance to see Tate in the soft repose of slumber, but he hoped to see much more of it. He wasn't entirely sure how much Tate would want him to tell people, but too bad. He was going to spread this story far and wide— the last thing he needed was anyone else thinking he'd beaten up his boyfriend like Angelica had first thought.

"He stopped a gay bashing on Sunday night and got banged up good in the process. Damaged his spleen, and it ruptured this morning."

This time there was no humor in Mrs. Birenbaum's eyes. "How awful. But how like Tate. He's very sweet."

Someone else thought Tate was sweet? And wasn't calling him names? Jaime smiled widely at her. Obviously she was good people, and insightful too.

"Yeah, he is." Jaime knew he sounded dopey, but he couldn't help it.

"I called the hospital before I left work, found out he'd been admitted, but that was it." She pulled up an enormous bag, one that looked like the knitting bag Nana used to carry around before the arthritis got too bad.

"I have a few things for him." Out of the bag, like magic, came Tate's backpack. He didn't carry much in it, and the nylon was cheap and thin, but Jaime would never have expected it to fit in Mrs. Birenbaum's purse.

"Where did you get that?" He hadn't even thought about the backpack that Tate almost never went without.

"I guess he'd left it by one of the carrels. He really was quite disoriented when he came up to my desk, so I'm guessing he just forgot about it."

"Thank you so much. I know he'll be glad it's not gone."

More things emerged from the bag. "Here's a little get-well gift from me and the other librarians. We haven't been able to get this through the system for him—it's quite popular—so we thought he might want his own copies."

Jaime peeked in the bag. It was the second trilogy to the sci-fi one he was reading now. He was both amazed and touched. He'd never realized Tate had spent enough time in the library to warrant a gift of any sort, never mind one that suited Tate so very well. Why couldn't this woman be Tate's mom… or maybe grandma?

"I know he's going to love it. Can you stay until he's awake again?"

"I wish I could. Mr. Birenbaum will have dinner on the table soon, and he'll be cross if I'm late."

What? He knew his sister and female cousins his age weren't all into the standard gender roles their parents seemed to go for, but Mrs. Birenbaum seemed around his mother's age, maybe even a bit older.

She snickered, surprising Jaime yet again. "Mr. Birenbaum was able to retire early, so it only seemed fair that he take over more of the household tasks. Fortunately he agreed with me."

Jaime nodded. "Good for you." He should know better than to make assumptions.

He expected her to get up and leave, but there was more magic in her bag of tricks. Several sheets of paper, folded like homemade cards, came out, and she handed the small stack over to Jaime.

All of them had been addressed to Tate, in various colors, in the unsteady penmanship of small children just learning how to write. He opened up a couple of them. The messages were all simple, like *Get well* or *We miss you*, and signed with a different name. There were a lot of drawings all over them as well.

"I don't understand."

Mrs. Birenbaum sighed. "How long have you and Tate been dating?"

"Almost a month."

"Oh my. So new. Well, there will be many more mysteries to be revealed over time. I should know. Mr. Birenbaum and I have been married for thirty-three years now, and he can still surprise me."

Jaime loved that she had faith a gay couple could make it long-term when his own mother wasn't so sure. "I know there's no way to know everything about each other this soon, but I still don't get it."

"When it doesn't conflict with his shift, Tate does story circle on Tuesdays and Thursdays. I'm just…." Her hand fluttered. "I'm just glad the children hadn't arrived yet. It would have been awful for them to see him like that."

"Children?"

"Yes. We've got a few programs for the younger kids. Sometimes the moms will stay with their kids during story circle, but more often they take that hour to browse the library for themselves. One day about a year or so ago, we were short-staffed and had another medical emergency. Tate was literally the only adult within range. I made a snap decision, asked if he could watch the kids for a few minutes. When I got back, it was like those children hadn't noticed I'd even gone. Tate was reading to them from the book I'd started, and they were enthralled. He's been doing story circle ever since, when he's available."

That Jaime had to see someday, even if that much cute might make him cry. Just hearing about it had him tearing up. He sniffed and tried to pretend his eyes weren't watery.

"I know, I know. I had no idea he'd take to it so well."

"I am surprised, though, that you'd leave a strange guy in charge of kids." Even more shocking in days like this, when it seemed every other day there was a news story about child molestation or pedophiles.

"Oh, Tate's not a *strange man*. Tate's been coming in to my library since he was just a boy. He was a little volatile when he was younger, but he's calmed down a lot, no thanks to that mother of his."

Mrs. Birenbaum's mouth pinched up, and Jaime almost high-fived her. He had a feeling he was going to love Mrs. Birenbaum as much as Tate obviously did.

"What about background checks?" Jaime didn't want to bring up Tate's brushes with the law if Mrs. Birenbaum didn't know.

"Of course we did one, once Tate expressed an interest in continuing to volunteer. But his arrests were all as a juvenile, there were no convictions, and there are always at least two volunteers with the children's groups anyway, which alleviated many concerns. Also, my personal recommendation weighed heavily."

Of that Jaime had no doubt. Mrs. Birenbaum was a force of nature. But he also understood that she'd taken a leap of faith with Tate, and he appreciated that someone else saw the good in him.

She checked her watch. "Oh dear. I really must go. Please let him know we're all thinking about him, and we're looking forward to seeing him again when he's better. I know the children will too."

"I will. I'll make sure he gets back to the library as soon as he's well enough. Thank you." Jaime stood up as she did, and waited until she'd left before sitting down again. He propped a couple of the cards up by the water carafe, but he was going to take the rest of Tate's things home with him so they didn't get misplaced.

A few strands of Tate's bright hair were tousled, and Jaime smoothed them away from his face. "Story time for young kids. I think Mrs. Birenbaum was right. You'll be surprising me for years yet to come."

Then he pulled out his phone. Before getting back into his book, he texted Kris, who'd probably want to know Tate had been hurt.

AFTER VISITING hours, Jaime walked slowly out of the hospital. Fortunately the short-term parking lot was fairly small, and thumbing his key fob located his car without any difficulty. Tate hadn't fully woken up again the whole time Jaime was there, but he needed the rest to mend. Jaime hadn't even managed to get back to his book. Area 52 apparently wasn't busy, and Kris's texts kept him occupied. Jaime understood why Tate liked the kid. Considering Kris was an eighteen-year-old who practically molted glitter at the least provocation, many people might miss that he was also smart, funny, and caring. Jaime was glad Tate had a friend like that, although he did wonder how his friends would react to Kris, and he to them. Assuming a meeting like that happened before Kris went away for college, anyway.

As he started driving away, he activated his hands-free and called his mama.

"Jaime? Is everything okay?"

For a moment he wondered if Caleb had spilled it all, but there was no reason to think that. Unless Caleb had spilled it all to *his* mother, and Tía Maria had called her sister-in-law.

"I'm fine." Because everything wasn't exactly okay. But it had been a long day—too long. He needed to tell his family about Tate, but he didn't have the energy for an interrogation today. "I'm just calling to see how you are."

"*Cariño*, I'm just fine. But I worry about you."

"I know, Mama, and I'm glad you do. I love you."

His mama started sniffing. "I love you too, *querido*. Are you sure nothing's wrong? Come over. I have food."

He'd definitely been too harsh in his judgment of her. She had her flaws, but that was only human. Tate's mother had been almost inhuman in her callousness.

Food. Some of his mama's cooking would hit the spot, and he hadn't realized until just then how hungry he was. But…. "I can't. Not tonight. Soon, though. I'll come over for a visit."

Sometime when he could be sure there weren't too many siblings and kids hanging about, when he could be sure Tate didn't need him. Tonight there were still some things he needed to get ready for tomorrow.

"Promise?" The word was as much an order as it was a plea.

"Promise."

THE DRUGS were fabulous. They suppressed the worry about how he was going to pay for all his medical bills. They let him accept that Jaime had sat with him, holding his hand, until he fell asleep last night. Under their influence, he got into Jaime's car after being released, letting Jaime drive him home without offering to walk. Sure, last night he'd dreamed about lemon-scented monkeys who wanted to knit his hair into socks, but that was a small price to pay.

Woozy as he was, it took him a while to realize Jaime wasn't headed toward his home but to Jaime's apartment.

"Don't get me wrong, I like your apartment more than my mom's place, but shouldn't you be taking me there?" Oops. The drugs made the thoughts in his head fall out of his mouth. Normally he didn't talk so bluntly about his home life. Nor did he especially want Jaime to see where he lived, but even the short walk from Area 52 to his house was out of the question. He'd never make it. Of all the times he'd been hurt, this was the first time he'd had surgery, and he didn't think he'd ever been so tired in his life.

"I'm glad you like my apartment." There was a funny note in Jaime's voice. What had they been talking about again? Tate tried to focus on the scenery whizzing by the car window.

"Wait. Why are we going to your apartment?"

Jaime snorted out a laugh.

"What's so funny? Then again, maybe I don't want to know. My stomach hurts." The drugs had made it no more than a dull ache, and it didn't hurt like when he'd collapsed at the library. But laughing would be bad.

"Nothing, *mi fuego*. Do you think you can just let me help you out for now, and save the questions until you're on less potent painkillers?"

"Potent painkillers. Potent painkillers." Tate made the *p*'s pop. His mind skittered around, chasing some other words. "What was that you called me? You've called me that before. I think I should know what it means. Is it *stupid* in Spanish?"

Jaime sounded like he was strangling. "You are not stupid."

"Really? Everyone says I am."

"I don't. Mrs. Birenbaum doesn't... never mind. I'll just have to tell you all this again later. But no, it's a good thing. We'll talk about it tomorrow, okay?"

"Okay." Tate looked around. "Hey. What are we doing at your apartment building?"

Another smothered laugh escaped Jaime. "I'll explain tomorrow. I promise. Let's just get you into bed." They pulled into Jaime's parking spot.

"Hmm." Tate considered that. He did love sex with Jaime. "I don't think I can get it up. You're so hot, but I think there's something wrong with my dick. Do you think I broke it when I fell?"

Jaime pressed a fist to his mouth, sputtering with laughter. Tate wished he'd share the joke, but no one ever did. At least Jaime didn't seem to be laughing at him meanly or anything. "No, Tate. Your dick will be fine. It's just the drugs. And we won't be having sex until you're feeling much better."

"Okay."

Jaime came around to help him out of the car, and Tate sagged, exhaustion swamping him.

"Let's get you up to bed so you can sleep this off."

Tate would have replied, but it took all his energy to put one foot in front of the other, endlessly and forever, until they got into Jaime's apartment and Jaime wrangled him onto the bed.

"Thank fuck this building has an elevator." That was the last thing Tate said before he dove into blackness.

TATE BLINKED awake, everything aching, head to toe, but the worst was around his chest and stomach. What the fuck had happened?

He looked around and immediately recognized Jaime's bedroom. His mounting tension flowed away. He was safe at Jaime's. Someone had settled Tate on his back, his head propped up a little, and small cushions supported his knees, making it easier for him to rest comfortably on his back. He was wearing a soft jersey pair of pajamas, one of several sets Jaime used for lounging around the apartment, although he slept in the nude. Tate might like to try sleeping in the nude, but he'd never quite dared, what with the company his mother tended to keep.

Something felt odd around his middle, and he gently probed the area near his ribs. A bandage? He lifted the pajama top and confirmed the presence of a large, pristine white bandage, stark against the blooming bruises on his ribs.

Just like that, the events of the past few days came rushing back, and along with the memories, the realization that he had to piss really bad, but he didn't know if he was too weak to get out of bed. The last thing he wanted was to end up back in the hospital. Everything had been so cold and terrifying, except when Jaime had been there. And Jaime had been there for almost the entire stretch of visiting hours.

Tate turned slightly, hoping to find a glass of water or something within reach—his mouth had never been so dry. It might be a mistake to add more water to the pressure on his bladder, but he wasn't sure he cared.

On the nightstand, easily within reach, sat a bottle of water and a funny brass bell. On it was taped a note that said *Ring me.*

He drank a couple of mouthfuls of water before he gave in to his curiosity and rang the bell.

Almost immediately, Jaime appeared, smiling brightly. "You're awake. How do you feel?"

"Like I'm going to drown in a sea of piss."

Jaime laughed. "Definitely feeling better. Let me help you up."

Putting weight on his feet made him wince, and he realized they were also bandaged up. "What the fuck happened to my feet?" Memories filtered back of the drive home… this morning? Yesterday? There were a lot of muzzy images—the drugs he'd been getting in the hospital had been fierce—but his mind was much less foggy now. "I have other questions too."

"I know, I know. Let's just get you set up, and maybe another pain pill if you need it."

Jaime made as if to follow him into the bathroom.

"I can piss all by myself." His cheeks heated a bit. Jaime was only trying to help, and Tate appreciated that, but he was afraid. Afraid to get used to having someone he could call on for help. Because having that snatched away might kill him, unlike everything else in his life that had tried to drag him down.

Jaime kissed his head. "Don't lock the door. And ring this when you're done." With a brassy tinkle, he set down the bell on the counter, then left, closing the door behind him.

Tate took care of business. Then, smirking a bit, he rang the bell. He had an idea for how to use this bell, but it would have to wait until he was feeling better.

After shuffling down the hall, they finally got Tate installed on the couch, Jaime snuggled in beside him. Tate closed his eyes, letting Jaime's warmth bleed through him, enjoying the unfamiliar sensation of comfort and security.

"Are you falling asleep?" Jaime's voice was soft.

"No. Just resting." Tate opened his eyes. He was tired but not sleepy.

Jaime stroked his shoulder, the touch light and perfect.

They quickly sorted out what Tate remembered and where the gaps were. He had slept all night after getting back from the hospital.

"Okay, so, my feet. I didn't hurt them."

"Uh, yeah, you did. All those busted blisters, and the muddy water you fought in? They were getting infected because...."

Tate squinted. "Because what?" Then it clicked. "Fine. Yes, next time I promise to let you look at them."

Huh. Jaime was a bit of a nag. That simple proof that he wasn't perfect made Tate feel a lot better about the situation.

"Okay, good. Anyway, they fixed up your feet while you were still recovering from the surgery."

"And why am I here? Not that I'm not happy to be here." And he truly was. Feeling like this, needing help getting out of bed to pee? If he was at home, he'd be either dead or dealing with ripped stitches. While lying in a puddle of piss. Jaime's home was happy and bright, unlike his own, which was dingy, dark, and sad.

"Well, your mother and I decided that it would be better if you recovered here. I can spend more time with you."

Tate snorted, then gasped and pressed a hand to his belly. "Fuck. Remind me not to do that for a while."

His momentary spike of pain allowed him to avoid commenting on Jaime's diplomatic statement right away. The only thing he knew for sure was that his mother hadn't been nice about it. She'd been bitching about him living there—whenever he wasn't giving her rent or running her errands. It was unlikely he'd be welcome back unless he paid more rent and begged a lot.

"And my job?"

Jaime looked away.

Shit. "I got fired, didn't I?"

"Well, no. Not exactly. Gary said he'd take your absence as your resignation."

Huh. Could be worse. At least he could say he quit for medical reasons rather than getting fired yet again. But there went any chance of giving his mother more money.

"I'll get a job as soon as I can. Pay you rent. Um…. You were being nice about it, but I'm guessing my mom kicked me out. I wasn't going to be able to pay her rent this month. I know you just feel sorry for me not having anywhere to live and all, but I'll get my own place as soon as I can."

"*Dios*," Jaime muttered. "Tate, I hope you can believe me when I say this. I know this is fucking crazy, living together after dating for such a short time. But I already knew I wanted to ask you to move in. Monday night, when you spent the night for the first time? That was one of the best nights of my life."

"But we didn't have sex." It had been wonderful for Tate too, but he wasn't going to be the best judge of anything in relationships.

"I know, but having you around, sleeping next to you, making breakfast the next morning… I want that. I was going to wait a while before asking, but with this situation we're in? I want to just take that step now. We haven't done anything in the traditional manner before, so why start?"

Tate thought about it. He knew his life and upbringing weren't great, but he'd always wanted someone just for him, someone who wanted him back. He didn't know if God or someone else was responsible for dropping Jaime in his life, but he wanted the same things Jaime wanted. And he was starting to believe Jaime wouldn't get snatched away.

"Tate, listen to me. I don't want you to feel as though you have to do this just because you've got nowhere else to turn. I'll help you get back on your feet no matter what, take care of you until you can get a job and an apartment, but I really want you to think about moving in with me. I'll help out even if you change your mind and feel it's not working out. Whatever happens, you don't have to go back to your mother's place."

Whew. Tate's mother had obviously made quite the impression—she must have been her normal charming self. But if Jaime was lying, he was being consistent, at least. The only thing Tate could possibly give Jaime, Jaime was already getting. Or at least, he was when Tate wasn't all banged to shit. Jaime didn't have any reason to lie to get in Tate's pants, because he dropped them for Jaime just about whenever they were alone together, and most times Jaime wasn't the one doing the asking.

"I want to do this. We can consider this a… dry run? And if it's not working out for you, you have to promise to tell me too. Don't let me stay just because you feel sorry for me."

"I promise. But I can't think of anything that would make me think this won't work out."

"Then I guess we'll have to pick up my stuff from my mom's."

"Uh, yeah, about that."

Interesting. Tate could already tell when Jaime was preparing to say something he didn't think Tate would like. And he already knew Jaime wasn't much of a liar.

"What did you do?"

"I guess you didn't notice the new dresser in the bedroom?" The last word had a hopeful little lilt on it. Like that would help if Tate were upset.

"I already have all your stuff here."

Oh. So he wouldn't actually have to see his mother again if he didn't want to. That probably shouldn't make him happy, but it did. He turned his face into Jaime's shoulder and kissed it. "Thank you."

"Really? I kind of thought you'd be angry."

"About that. What if I actually do get angry with you? I told you, I sometimes just can't help it."

"I'm not too worried. Diego told me about some of your brushes with the law, and you've told me about them. So far every time you got angry and started fighting, you were defending someone else, usually gay kids in trouble. I think I'm safe, but if you're worried, we can see about finding some counseling."

Jaime sounded confident and unafraid, making Tate think about all the other times he hadn't told Jaime about, when his mouth and aggression had gotten him fired but not arrested. He'd never really considered that there had been something similar about all those times, but there was. Somewhere deep inside, a little dark ball of pain, the one filled with fear he was evil and irredeemable, broke open and dispersed.

"I… I can't believe it. But it's true." Even he could hear the wonder in his voice, and Jaime hugged him close.

"You're a good man, Tate. And I'm proud to be your boyfriend."

A new concept for Tate, but with this information, he'd do his best to try to believe it. Maybe he wasn't completely irredeemable.

Jaime cleared his throat. "Since you're not mad about the clothes, there are a couple of other things I did while you were in the hospital."

Curbing these impulsive tendencies might be something Tate would be good for. Jaime obviously didn't have any impulse control.

"I bought you new shoes. I couldn't find any spares at your mother's house, and your old ones were a wreck."

Since his old ones had blistered up his feet, Tate wasn't too upset about that. "And?"

"That obvious, am I?"

"Yes, actually."

Jaime got up from the couch, leaving Tate's right side chilly, but he returned almost immediately. He handed Tate his phone.

"It's your phone. What about it?"

"No, it's your phone. I added it to my plan."

Tate's first temptation was to toss it away from him, but it cost too much money. "What the fuck are you talking about, Jaime?"

It lay on his palm, shiny and new, taunting him. He didn't know if he loved it or hated it, but he couldn't accept it.

"You need a phone. I mean, there aren't really any pay phones anymore. If you get in trouble again, I want you to be able to call me."

"I can't accept this. It's too much." He tried to hand it to Jaime, who closed his hand over Tate's, keeping the phone against Tate's palm.

"Listen to me. This will make me worry less. And you can call the cops when shit happens instead of getting in between bullies and their victims."

"But I told you. I'm not good with phone numbers." Or any other numbers. "I'll never be able to dial people the first time. What if I call China by mistake?"

"If you call China by mistake, well, people make mistakes. But see, if you're calling someone you know, you don't have to dial any numbers."

That couldn't be right. But Jaime showed him how to unlock the phone and navigate to the contact list. He'd already preprogrammed in his own number, Kris's, the library, and his cousin Caleb's.

"We can also set it up so you can access your e-mail here."

"Jaime, I don't know how to thank you for this. This is… overwhelming."

"There is only one way you can thank me. And that's to accept I'm not trying to buy your affection or your time, but I just want to make you happy. Make your life easier, because you deserve it."

Tate tried twisting his body enough to reach Jaime's mouth, but it was too much, and he drew in a deep, shuddering breath, trying to will away the pain.

"What's wrong?"

"I want to kiss you, but I can't reach."

This time Jaime did the moving and brought his lips to Tate's. If romance novels were to be believed, he was definitely falling in love with this man.

Then he pushed Jaime away, panic nearly closing his throat. "Jaime, Jaime, my cock is broken!"

Jaime's eyes flared wide for a moment, and then he started laughing. Laughing so hard he fell off the couch.

"This isn't funny, you asshole. Kissing like that should have made me hard and it didn't!" He'd only just started to believe Jaime, and now his cock refused to work. What the fuck was wrong with him?

"I'm sorry, Tate. But it's probably the drugs, or even just the trauma your body endured. Bodies are smarter than we give them credit for. Don't worry, it'll start working again, I promise."

So many promises Jaime was giving him this day. "You'd better not be lying." He didn't want to end up boyfriendless with no cock to console himself.

Jaime stroked his face. "Just enjoy the kissing. Don't worry about the rest of it. We'll have plenty of time for sex."

Tate had just settled in for some leisurely kissing—he hadn't even known people did such a thing, but he liked it—when the doorbell rang.

Frowning, Jaime pulled back. "I'm not expecting anything. Visitors or deliveries. We could just ignore it and pretend we're not here."

Tate laughed. "I didn't think people did that unless they were hiding from people they owed money to."

The doorbell rang again, and Jaime huffed in irritation. "Let me get rid of whoever that is so we can get back to necking on the couch, maybe watching a movie."

He heard Jaime open the door. "What are you guys doing here?"

Tate wanted to turn around and see who Jaime was talking to, but he didn't dare.

"We're here to meet the man more mythical than a unicorn."

What did that mean?

"C'mon, Jaime, let us in. We brought dinner. Stuff that's easy to eat and digest for the patient, although if he's up for barbecue, there's plenty here."

Shit, shit, shit. Jaime's friends were here? Tate had heard stories, but he never expected to meet them. Not really. After their discussion today, he might have changed his mind about that, but he hadn't had time to consider the fallout of what living together would mean.

"Fine, fine, come in. But go easy on him, okay? He's had a tough couple of days," Jaime said.

Tate took a few deep breaths, trying to control his racing heart. Two strangers came into the living room and introduced themselves.

Caleb, Jaime's cousin, had Jaime's coloring and looked similar, if Jaime's features were thinned out and made more angular. He hardly needed an introduction—it would take someone stupider than Tate not to realize they were related. Raven was dressed in body-hugging black. His artfully spiked black hair with thick blue highlights made him look like an anime character come to life. He was definitely the more intimidating of the two.

Until he sat gingerly next to Tate and grabbed his hand.

"I bet you're glad to be out of the hospital."

"Uh. Yes. I am."

"They're just so miserable."

Tate had forgotten Jaime telling him about Raven's accident. Raven had spent more time enduring medical treatment, including a lot of physiotherapy.

After a bit of mutual commiseration while Caleb and Jaime chatted about nothing, Tate relaxed. A bit.

"Are you all healed up now?" Tate couldn't quite recall how long it had been since Raven's accident, but his memories of being in the hospital were certainly fresh.

Raven grimaced. "As good as it's going to get. I have some residual pain, mostly during storms or if I overdo it, but it's not too bad."

Tate didn't know where to steer the conversation after that. He sort of understood the concept and had had some practice with Jaime, but he didn't exactly want to talk about his employment status or why he was recuperating at Jaime's instead of at his mother's place.

"Caleb, where are the cookies we brought?" Raven asked.

"Kitchen. Let me go make some tea and I'll bring them out."

Jaime went to help Caleb, and in a matter of minutes, the four of them were having tea and cookies. For a moment Tate wondered if he was still under the influence of morphine, because this was the most fucked-up moment he'd never have imagined.

He'd also want some real food soon, but for now he was content.

Jaime started talking about one of the movies they'd watched recently, and suddenly Tate found conversation easier. Movies, TV, books were all things he could talk about, and no one looked at him like his opinions were stupid.

Despite his initial nerves, the evening went well, and by the time they left, he wondered why he'd been so nervous. Raven and Caleb hadn't acted like Jaime was crazy, and they weren't mean to Tate. He should have known Jaime wouldn't be friends with assholes, but proof was nice.

Once he started nodding off, Jaime shooed his friends out and got Tate tucked back into bed. "Oh, I almost forgot. Mrs. Birenbaum stopped by the hospital. She had some things for you, and I forgot to give them to you. Did you want them now?"

"No. Wait until morning." He was tired enough that he could barely get those words out; he'd never be able to appreciate whatever Mrs. Birenbaum had dropped off for him. His gaze fell on the new dresser, about half the size of Jaime's but probably far bigger than Tate needed. Made him smile. Then his eyelids closed.

TATE'S EYES fluttered open. The painkillers made him sleep deeper and longer than he normally did and made him groggy during the day, but it was nice not having to deal with the pain. He was supposed to spend four to six weeks recovering, but he was hoping to lay off the pain meds today. He'd slept enough.

He grabbed the bell and rang it. Calling Jaime for help using a fucking bell seemed weird and demanding, but he still needed help getting out of bed and walking around.

"Good morning." Jaime poked his head into the room. "Hungry?"

Tate sighed. He also had antibiotics to take, and those needed food. Unfortunately, they also made him a bit queasy, so eating had been a challenge. Refusing food made him feel like quite the entitled princess, and he didn't much like that either. "Not yet."

"Okay. We can wait a bit, but not too long. You slept longer than I expected, and it's better to take the antibiotics at regular intervals if you can."

Tate didn't bother answering. His boyfriend wasn't going to let him forget to take his meds. He ran his fingers through his hair, and it didn't fall the way it normally did. "I need a shower."

"Maybe we can try later. But if we do it, we're getting in together. Because there's no way you'll be able to steady yourself if you slip or get dizzy."

Great. That's what he was hoping for. Getting naked with his boyfriend in the shower… so his boyfriend could keep him from cracking his head open. Perfection.

Still, it might be worth the humiliation to be clean.

"Wait. Did you say something yesterday about Mrs. Birenbaum?"

Jaime smiled. "Yep. Want to see what she brought you? She came to visit you in the hospital, but you were sleeping."

Gifts. From Mrs. Birenbaum. She'd always been so nice and gave him special treatment at the library, but he'd never have expected gifts or visiting.

He hated being sick and weak, but he had to admit, it wasn't terrible having people do nice things for him.

AFTER A detour in the bathroom, Jaime helped Tate down the hall. Aside from Jaime's initial tour of the apartment after their second date, Tate had never set foot in the spare bedroom. He'd actually been a little surprised to wake up in Jaime's bed and not the bed in the spare room, but there was a lot of comfort in knowing Jaime was so close during the night while he slept.

Now, Jaime stood close behind him as he opened the door to the spare room. On one wall, a collage of kids' artwork hung, glued in place on a piece of poster board. It was an odd decorating choice, and he didn't remember it being there. He was about to compliment Jaime's nieces and nephews when he realized his name was plastered all over the drawings.

He let out a little bleat of surprise and tottered closer. Colorful pictures in the rough, unfinished hands of small children accompanied simple messages, from *Hi Tate* or *Get well* to the sweet *We miss you*. The kids had signed their artwork as well, and he suddenly realized he recognized the names. He reached out for Jaime, who came right up to steady him.

"These are… these are…."

"From story circle, yes."

Tate hadn't even known Jaime knew about story circle. And it would be a long time before he was going to be able to read to the kids again. Story circle was about the only time he ever felt useful, wanted, or needed. Sniffling, he tried to battle back the tears that suddenly welled in his eyes, blurring his vision.

"But… why…."

"Mrs. Birenbaum said the kids missed you, so she had them make you get-well… not cards, I guess. Drawings? Anyway, she dropped them off at the hospital and said she hoped you'd be feeling up to doing story circle soon."

Hopefully not long. But…. "It's too far to walk."

Jaime snorted. "When you're feeling well enough to do story circle, I'll drive you or make sure one of the boys can give you a lift."

It truly was like Tate was in a fairy tale. He didn't want to wake up and find out this was all a dream filled with things he couldn't have.

"Thank you. This is wonderful." He was going to have to look at each one individually, but not now. He was about ready for a sit-down.

"Oh, one more thing. Mrs. Birenbaum and the other librarians pitched in to get you these." Jaime grabbed a bag from the corner of his desk.

Tate peeked inside and squealed before clasping a hand to his side, covering the bandage. "Remind me not to do that again," he whispered.

When he was breathing normally, he pulled the books out of the bag. The next trilogy in the sci-fi series he'd just finished up. Mrs. Birenbaum had told him it would be a while before she could get him these, but instead she'd bought them for him. His very own books.

"These are mine? Not the library's?"

"Yours. Feel free to use any bookshelf space to store them." Jaime kissed his head. "You want to start reading them now, don't you?"

He did, but he also worried he wouldn't be able to properly stay awake. "Let's have breakfast first, and then I'll see how I feel."

He might just lie in bed and read. That would be so decadent. And would probably surprise the ever-loving fuck out of his English teachers.

A WEEK after Tate's surgery, Jaime was going back to work, on days for now. The past week had been mostly glorious—Jaime had had a couple of nightmares, the worst one on that day he'd had to leave Tate at the hospital. Again, Tate had been the main player out on the sands, dying in Jaime's mind instead of Mario. Jaime's subconscious wasn't exactly subtle, but the subsequent nightmares were weaker, and being able to turn over in bed and watch Tate, hear his breathy snores and smell his skin, did wonders to soothe Jaime.

During the day, Tate living with him and recuperating was still an adjustment—for them both. But Tate's frustration with the healing process meant he'd stopped being so careful and just came out and said what he meant. It was another thing to love about Tate. There was no game playing, just Tate out there for everyone to see. Watching him slowly grow enamored of his new phone had been gratifying too, especially texting—Kris had just about passed out when he got Tate's text. Or so Tate had told him.

Jaime stepped out of the shower and grabbed his towel when Tate rang his bell. Tate had been asleep when Jaime woke up, and he'd let him sleep while he puttered about the kitchen and did some laundry, but he'd lost track of time when he'd hopped in the shower.

"Be there in a second. Hey, what time is it? Is Raven here yet?"

There was no answer.

With one towel wrapped around his waist, he used the other to rub at his hair. "Tate? What time is it? I think I might be running late."

Tate seemed to be awake, but Jaime couldn't be sure without his glasses on, and he hadn't had a chance to put in his contacts before answering Tate's bell. He snagged his glasses from the nightstand and slid them on. Vain though it was, he'd been nervous about letting Tate see him in his glasses—he hadn't even told Tate until after the hospital that he needed them.

Tate had thought they were sexy, though, so maybe Jaime didn't mind them so much. Not that he'd ever become a regular glasses wearer; contacts were so much easier on the job.

"What's wrong?"

Now that he could see properly, he realized Tate was awake, but he was also terrified. His gaze darted from Jaime to the LED alarm clock, his face devoid of all color except those adorable freckles.

He didn't think it was the prospect of him showing up late for work that had Tate in a panic. Carefully, he sat down on the bed and tried to remember exactly what he'd said that might have caused this. Tate's hands were fisted in his lap, but he didn't seem angry, so Jaime wasn't worried about those fists flying. Besides, he'd done enough homework to assure himself that Tate never actually started any of the altercations he'd had.

He'd asked Tate about the time. Time that was clearly visible on the large-numbered LED. There were no signs that Tate needed glasses, and surely poor vision wouldn't account for the panicky fear Jaime could almost smell on Tate. Jaime had seen him read books, and he spent hours upon hours at the library. He wasn't illiterate. There were a number of puzzle pieces just waiting to click into place, but Jaime didn't have the right information.

The time kept ticking away, though, and although he knew this was something he and Tate should talk about, Tate's demeanor screamed that it needed more care and attention than a five-minute discussion before Jaime left for work, leaving Tate to put on a brave face before Raven showed up.

Jaime kissed Tate. "I am running late. But it'll be fine. No need to worry."

Tate visibly relaxed, color wisping back into his cheeks, and his fists unclenched. Tate was getting a reprieve, but only until he was recovered. Then they were going to clear the air.

Wait. Whatever was going on, was Tate afraid of how Jaime would react? Maybe... maybe think he was stupid, a word Jaime had heard altogether too many times in reference to his incredible boyfriend, often enough he was ready to strip the word from his vocabulary.

"You know I love you, right?"

Tate's cheeks pinkened up further, expression adorably confused. "You what?"

"I love you." Those words had been bottled up for what felt like forever, and getting them out there was a relief, for more reasons than reassuring Tate. "Come what may, good or bad." Maybe that laid it on a little thick, but he wanted Tate to believe that more than anything.

Tate's lower lip trembled.

Oh shit. Had he completely deluded himself? Jaime had been so sure they were recklessly barreling toward the same thing, but he had moved fast, especially for a man who'd had very little relationship experience.

"I love you too," Tate whispered.

Jaime almost said Tate didn't have to say it back just because Jaime had said it, but as he stared into Tate's eyes, his doubt vanished. That was love looking back. He hadn't been deluding himself at all—Tate had signed up willingly for this wild and crazy ride they were on.

There was no help for it. He dove in and met Tate's lips. God. He was insane, telling Tate he loved him right before he had to go to work while Tate was still not well enough to have sex, because oh fuck. Hearing those words made him want to strip them both down and spend hours fucking.

Blood thrummed through his veins, thickening his cock and pounding in his temples.... Jaime lifted his head, Tate growling his displeasure.

"Someone's knocking on the door." Jaime was breathless.

"Raven's here." A sneaky look crossed Tate's face. "You could call in sick. Stay here with me."

"Oh, *mi fuego*, if I could." But his supervisor would shit a brick if Jaime took any more time off. Harold had been quite understanding, considering Tate wasn't listed as a dependent and they weren't married, but Jaime didn't want to strain his patience.

Tate's jaw firmed up. "I don't need anyone to babysit me, you know."

"Saying you love me isn't going to change my mind. You don't want me to worry about you, do you?"

Tate rolled his eyes. "No, I suppose not."

"It'll be fun. Raven's a great guy."

Jaime gave him another quick kiss, the knocking becoming too insistent for anything more, and ran to the door, making sure the towel still covered the important bits.

"Hey, Raven. I'm running a little late."

Raven smirked at him. "Gee, I wonder why? But you shouldn't be molesting the patient, you know."

"Shut up. Make yourself comfortable. I'll be dressed in a minute."

"Hold on, hold on."

"What?"

"Give us a spin." Raven made a circular gesture with his fingers.

Jaime obeyed with a grin, even giving a little hip shimmy worthy of the catwalk, if he did say so himself. He was in the best mood, and he knew exactly why.

"Yep. You will look perfect in a kilt."

A what now? Oh fuck. He'd promised Raven he'd be in that damned photo shoot for the calendar. Just because Jaime had put it firmly out of his mind didn't mean Raven had forgotten, though. He'd have to put the pressure on Caleb, see if he could get Raven to drop it, but he had the bad feeling he was stuck.

Still, not even the prospect of parading around half-naked for Raven's inaugural photo shoot was enough to put the damper on today.

In a few minutes, Jaime had dressed, kissed his boyfriend a few more times, then left. In the car on the way to work, he called the library and asked for Mrs. Birenbaum.

"Good morning, this is Mrs. Birenbaum. How can I help you?" Her tone was brisk and impersonal but perfectly polite.

"Morning. This is Jaime, Tate's boyfriend."

"Oh yes, hello. How is he doing? We've missed seeing his smiling face around here." Just like that, her tone warmed up. Jaime bit his lip against a laugh, wondering what Diego would think about a flock of librarians missing Tate's smiles. Diego probably thought Tate didn't even know how to perform that set of muscle maneuvers.

"He's doing well, although he does hate being a patient."

Mrs. Birenbaum huffed. "Well, he's a man, isn't he? Terrible patients, the lot of you."

Jaime chuckled. "That we are. I had a couple things I wanted to talk to you about, though. Could I take you to lunch? Today or sometime this week?"

"Oh, that would be sweet. And just the thing to make Mr. Birenbaum jealous." Her teasing tone assured Jaime that she didn't think Jaime was interested or anything.

"What day would work for you?"

"I'm afraid I have plans today, but tomorrow would be lovely, thank you."

"Tomorrow it is. My job can be a little unpredictable, but I'll try to get there as close to noon as I can."

"That's fine. I'll wait until you show up."

Now he just had to find someone to cover him so he could take a couple of hours off in the middle of the day to go on a lunch date with a woman twice his age.

CHAPTER TWELVE

RAVEN POKED his head into the bedroom. "What did you want to do today?"

"Watch movies?" If Tate was dreaming, he didn't want to wake up. Jaime's—their—bed was comfortable. Jaime's—their—apartment was a pleasant temperature, clean, bright, and smelled good. Jaime loved him, and Tate loved Jaime. Tate would have been happier if Jaime hadn't left him to go to work, but he could live with that. And hopefully when Jaime came back, he'd have forgotten all about how Tate had frozen when he'd asked him what time it was.

"Yeah? I heard you were a bit of a fiend for it now that you had access."

He tried to push himself up to get out of bed and groaned. If nothing else, the pain in his feet and torso still ached enough to reassure him that he wasn't dreaming. That this was his life now.

"Hey, whoa, that's what I'm here for, to help out." Raven dashed around to Tate's side of the bed, and between the two of them, Tate stood without too much additional discomfort. He'd been a little annoyed when Jaime had lined up a selection of babysitters for him; he'd been taking care of himself since he was in elementary school. He hadn't expected how much worse it was recovering from surgery and a beating together, especially since his feet hurt almost as much as the incision.

But he was worried what Jaime's friends would think of him as they got to know him. He still hadn't met Will and Dallas, and he hoped it would go as smoothly as his meeting with Raven and Caleb.

"We could play cards or a game or something. I'm sure Jaime's got something hidden away here somewhere."

"Uh." Fuck no. He was terrible at games. They only made him look stupid. Painfully stupid. "I don't know if I'm up for concentrating like that."

Raven looked apologetic. "Oh, of course not. C'mon, let's get you to the couch. I've got strict instructions to take you for a walk later." He waggled his eyebrows. "Jaime forgot to leave a leash and collar, though."

Tate laughed, then cut himself off with a gasp. "Fuck. Don't make me laugh."

"Oh my God, I'm so sorry."

Waving away the apology, he concentrated on breathing. Jaime had taught him a few types of deep breathing. It made his ribs ache a bit, but it did help control the pain overall. "It's fine. And believe me, it's getting better."

"Oh good."

"Can you grab me that shirt?" He'd slept in pajama bottoms, but Jaime kept the apartment a lot cooler than Tate was used to, and if they were going to sit on the couch, bare-chested would be too cold.

Raven went and grabbed the shirt, but when he turned around, he tilted his head, inspecting Tate from head to foot.

"What?"

"Your coloring is fantastic. And you're adorable."

Adorable? Tate sputtered. "You mean the bruises?" Tate didn't know how Raven equated adorable with looking like a big fat rotten grape. He also wondered if appreciating the rainbow of colors covering his chest was just a little rude. Those niceties escaped him sometimes.

Raven's cheeks went pink, and Tate almost forgot himself enough to laugh. It was so fucking awesome to find someone else who blushed hard. Raven wasn't quite as bad as Tate, but Tate had a new appreciation for the way Jaime compared them both to vampires.

"Of course I don't mean your bruises. But your skin, your freckles, that hair." Raven's tone was frankly admiring, but not weird like he was trying to get into Tate's pants.

Raven helped Tate into the shirt, and they walked slowly to the living room. Tate didn't need support for walking, but knowing Raven was right there beside him in case he stumbled was a comfort.

After Tate was settled, remote in hand, Raven slumped into the recliner.

"Anyway, as I was saying, your coloring is awesome. Beautiful. You'd have made a killing with Idyll Fling."

"What's Idyll Fling?"

"Did… what did Jaime tell you about me?"

"Not much. Said you owned a business called Tartan Candy. He showed me the website. It looks cool. And you look incredible in a kilt."

Raven didn't look anything like the Highlander chieftains featured on the covers of historical romances Tate had seen at the library, but more like a Goth prince, wearing a costume all his own.

"Yeah, well, that's true. But before that, I supported myself for several years and put myself through college doing gay porn. That's actually where I got my name. Raven was my stage name, but I liked it so much more than my real name, I kept it after I was forced to retire. Anyway, Idyll Fling was the studio I worked for. Will and Dallas work for them still—they're the ones who keep the website going. Although they'd be a hit if they filmed themselves fucking."

Tate blinked. So much information in so few sentences, it was almost like he'd been slapped. He'd had a number of guys tell him the exact same thing—he could make a killing in porn—but the guys had been so awful, he'd assumed they were lying. Not that he was considering that as a potential job—he'd developed too many knee-jerk reactions to sexual situations, and he was pretty sure having sex on camera with a stranger would set one or more of them off. But Raven wasn't pervy or gross. He was almost as gorgeous as Jaime.

"Redheads are popular in porn?"

Raven nodded. "Well, it's a certain fetish, to be sure. Not everyone likes 'em, but if you're natural… it definitely has a draw."

Huh. Who knew? Jaime was certainly fascinated by his… naturalness, but Tate had thought it more a contrast thing. Tate was certainly fascinated by Jaime's brown and gold coloring, with his beautiful black hair.

Raven tapped a finger against his lips. "So, one of the ideas I had for growing Tartan Candy was a calendar. You know the ones, a different half-naked man every month."

"Sure. I've seen them." And drooled. Once he'd snagged one out of the trash in January, after the year in question had ended. His mother had found it and set it on fire with her lighter. At the time, Tate thought it was because she didn't approve of him being gay or whatever, but as time went on, he realized his mom didn't care one way or the other. Burning the calendar had probably only been a way to punish him for everything else—not being smart, not making enough money, chasing away his father.

"Anyway, I'm gathering hot guys, and I'm going to put them in kilts. No shirts, just hot men in kilts."

If Tate had disposable income—and a reason to need a calendar—he'd probably buy that. "Sounds like a smart plan."

"Did you want to be one of the models?"

Again, Raven had managed to completely surprise him. "Me? Why me?"

"I just told you. Great coloring. And you're gorgeous. People will want to eat you up. I've already convinced Jaime to be in it—and that took some doing, let me tell you. You're both gorgeous, but in completely different ways."

Jaime was going to do a calendar shoot? Tate shivered. That was so fucking hot. "I'm... are you sure?"

Raven stuck out his tongue, and Tate sputtered. "Of course I'm sure. This is my business. If I didn't think you'd be a good fit, I'd have never asked. In fact, I know just the kilt to put you in too."

There wasn't even a whiff of a lie in Raven's words, and Tate smiled. "I'll do it. Uh. As long as you don't mind waiting until the bruising is gone." Doing something like that with Jaime could be a lot of fun too.

"Duh. Of course. I can pay you too."

"Really?" That would be cool.

"Yeah. I mean, I managed to coerce Jaime into doing it for free, but I think that's only because I caught him when he wasn't paying attention. But seriously. Models get paid, photographers get paid. It's only fair that you do as well, even if you are Jaime's boyfriend."

"Oh. That would be great."

"Okay, so what did you want to watch?"

Tate could hardly believe it. Getting paid to let someone take pictures of him, and he didn't have to show his dick? Awesome. He didn't know what models got paid for something like this, but it didn't sound hard, and any money at all would be a bonus.

AT LUNCH, Jaime was having a lovely conversation with Mrs. Birenbaum. They spoke of Tate's recovery—she truly did care about Tate, and for that alone, Jaime adored her. In many ways, she reminded him of his nana. They also shared a few amusing anecdotes from their vastly different jobs—although any job where one worked with the public would have certain commonalities.

Since he wasn't sure how to broach the subject he truly wanted to ask about, he just... didn't. Lucky for him, though, Mrs. Birenbaum fixed him with a steely look about halfway through the meal.

"Not that this isn't lovely, Jaime dear, but I got the impression you wanted to talk to me about something specific. Tate, I'm guessing. So rip the bandage off and get it out there. If it's something I'm uncomfortable talking about, I'll tell you."

He wiped his lips with his napkin and took a sip of water, but he was stalling, and he wasn't fooling her one bit. "I don't know where to begin. Tate can obviously read, but I think there's something wrong. With numbers. Anything with numbers. Money. Telling time. Phone numbers. Comparing quantities." Jaime could think of all sorts of little examples that fit, although he hadn't really put it together until yesterday morning when Tate had frozen at Jaime's request for the time. Hell, even just Tate's calling 192 by its lesser used alternative of Irlo Bronson Highway should have twigged something.

Mrs. Birenbaum pursed her lips in a disapproving manner, reminding Jaime of one of his high school teachers when the class had been particularly disruptive. "Ah, yes. But that wasn't always the case. That poor boy—I'm not sure if the system just failed him or if he merely slipped through the cracks, but standardized testing didn't do him any favors."

Jaime lifted an eyebrow. He had sort of forgotten she'd known Tate back in his school days, although those days weren't as far back as Jaime's were.

"How so?"

Mrs. Birenbaum paused, as though choosing her words carefully. "Tate definitely has a problem with numbers. I think it's probably an actual learning disability, but of course, I'm not qualified to assess that. But in school, there wasn't the time or money, or perhaps support at home, to get him the help he needed. And I think the math issues were bad enough that they probably assumed he had low intelligence. Low enough that he'd have skewed the average for the school."

No longer hungry, Jaime shoved his plate out of the way. "He's not stupid." Oh, but he was starting to see where all that self-recrimination had come from.

"Oh, dear, I know that." Mrs. Birenbaum patted his hand. She sipped from her iced tea before continuing. "Anyway, schools had some...

discretion. They didn't have to report scores for every student, and Tate, for all that he wasn't left behind on paper, he surely was from an educational point of view. It's possible there were programs that would have helped him, but if they required support, money, or even permission from the parents? I think you know well enough that wouldn't have happened."

He settled for a noncommittal grunt. Jaime didn't want to speak ill of Tate's mother, but she was definitely a piece of work. "So what happened, then? I mean, in the course of my work, I've come across a few illiterate people. They've got all kinds of coping mechanisms to help them function, although it's hardly perfect. But Tate isn't like that. He's not pretending or using social engineering to get people to tell him what he needs to know."

"No, and when he first started haunting the library, he wasn't illiterate, but had a very low reading level. He worked so hard, without any help at all, to get better."

"He's very independent."

Mrs. Birenbaum laughed. "That he is. Perhaps even a little hardheaded about it."

Oh, that was his Tate, through and through.

"He's smart, and he's now an avid reader. But numbers? No, that was a different kettle of fish. Once I realized what was going on, Tate wouldn't have accepted my help, and honestly, I didn't have enough one-on-one time to devote to helping him. He's convinced himself, I think, that anything with numbers is just impossible for him."

"Is there anything I can do? Is there even a name for this disability?" He hated to think of his vibrant boyfriend ending up so discouraged.

"Like I said, I'm not an expert, nor do I have the specialized knowledge to form a true assessment, but I suspect Tate's got something called dyscalculia. Even if that's not what he has, I'm guessing resources available to aid people with that particular learning disability will be of some help to Tate, especially if he got someone to support him, give him a hand when he needs it. Whether he wants it or not."

Ha! At this rate, that was going to become the motto of their relationship. "I've never even heard of that."

"From all accounts, it's rare, but there is some belief that it's caused by excessive consumption of alcohol during pregnancy." With hardly any variation in tone, Mrs. Birenbaum delivered a scathing criticism of Tate's mother.

Jaime shook his head. He'd treated kids with fetal alcohol syndrome, sure, but for some reason, he'd never really thought about what kids like that would go through when they became adults. Not that Tate necessarily had that, but it might explain his anger issues.

And dyscalculia would explain a whole lot else. Like his inability to keep a minimum-wage job, and the habitual lateness. Mrs. Birenbaum might claim not to be an expert, but she was an intelligent, savvy woman who spent her days in a building filled with books. And she'd observed and interacted with Tate on a regular basis for years. If she had incorrectly assessed Tate, she had to be in the right ballpark at least.

"So there are definitely resources out there?"

Mrs. Birenbaum smiled softly. "Yes. I think there's probably a lot of hope. Certainly more than he's had in the past."

Jaime had no idea how he was going to broach this subject with Tate—it would be a thousand times more difficult than it had been with Mrs. Birenbaum—but if Tate wanted help, he was going to get it for him. Obviously there were hurdles like getting his GED and whatnot, but there were a ton of careers out there that didn't use math or lots of numbers. Tate could choose any one of them, if that's what he wanted.

Jaime didn't give a damn if nothing changed at all—he loved Tate just the way he was. But if Tate wanted something more out of life, and Jaime suspected he did, Jaime liked the idea of giving him hope.

"One piece of advice, dear, from an old married woman."

"Uh. Sure." He had no idea what she meant by that but hoped it wasn't anything about his and Tate's sex life.

"You're a health-care professional, so it will be tempting to approach this like Tate's your patient. But he's your boyfriend. Treat him as a partner in this—you're a team."

Uh-oh. She had him pegged. It was sometimes hard to turn off that part of himself. "Sounds like you've had experience."

"Oh yes. Mr. Birenbaum is actually Dr. Birenbaum, retired. Calling him Dr. Birenbaum just gives him a swelled head, though."

Jaime absolutely wasn't going to ask if she called her husband Mr. Birenbaum at home, as though neither of them had first names. None of his business, but he wondered what Tate would do if Jaime tried calling him Mr. Buchanan in bed. Might be fun to try once Tate was all healed up.

She continued as though she hadn't triggered any bizarre thoughts in her audience. "Anyway, he used to be very bad about treating me like I wasn't intelligent, that he had to do my thinking for me. That did *not* last long. But if he hadn't changed his ways? I'm quite certain I wouldn't be Mrs. Birenbaum today."

He'd do his best. The last thing he wanted was to make Tate feel inferior, because Jaime didn't see him that way at all. "Thank you. I can't tell you how much I appreciate your candor."

"That boy has lived through a lot of hurdles, and I only want the best for him. He's a good man."

A good man Jaime loved.

TATE SNUGGLED up against Jaime as they watched a movie. It had been just over two weeks since his surgery, and while he was on the mend, surgery was no simple thing. He'd slept so much—he could only stay awake for a few hours at a time before he needed another nap. Now, he still tired easily but didn't have to sleep quite as much. He wasn't even entirely sure if he was catching up on years and years of being a light sleeper, worrying who might come into his room while he slept, or if healing took such a huge amount of energy, but he did know he felt nothing but safe.

They did get along, so well. The more time they spent together, the more he and Jaime could have fun with each other and talk about—almost—everything, the more he loved Jaime. There were things in his past—ugly things—that didn't affect his relationship with Jaime. How dumb he was with numbers, and how it made it hard for him to keep a job? That could cause problems, and if his newfound love of gay romance novels told him anything, it was that he should tell Jaime the truth, but he couldn't bring himself to do it.

There had been that one scare when Jaime had asked him the time and Tate had panicked. He'd pretty much frozen in fear, waiting for the name-calling, the sneering tone, and maybe even getting kicked out of the apartment, but it was almost like Jaime hadn't noticed. Tate nearly blurted out his inability right then, unable to bear the silence, but Jaime had said he loved Tate for the first time. The moment passed, but a tiny kernel of fear remained. Tate wanted to trust that Jaime would still love him if he found out Tate couldn't tell time, or make change, or figure out a budget so he didn't go hungry, but when his own mother hated him, that trust was hard to come by.

The credits rolled on one of Jaime's favorite murder mysteries—Tate had liked it well enough, but he didn't quite understand Jaime's fascination. Next time he was at the library, he'd see if he could find the book it was based on. Maybe that would help.

Jaime turned to him. "I've been meaning to ask you something."

Everything in Tate froze, including his blood transforming to ice. Discreetly he rubbed at suddenly numb fingers. He just knew Jaime was going to ask about him and his numbers. Maybe he had noticed how stupid Tate was, and was just waiting until Tate didn't fall asleep in the middle of sentences to confront him about it.

"I couldn't help but notice your argyle sweaters."

Tate frowned, but he didn't understand. What did his argyle sweaters have to do with his inability to deal with math and numbers?

"Um. Yeah. What about them?"

Jaime kissed his jaw. "Nothing to get tense about. I was just wondering why you had them. I mean, Raven and Will have some sort of unnatural love affair with plaid, and Dallas has a thing for paisley, so I wondered about you and argyle."

Oh. So not numbers. Tate let out a relieved breath. He shouldn't be so happy to have dodged that bullet, but if he could continue to dodge it for the rest of his life, keep Jaime in the dark, then he would.

"What's Caleb's favorite fabric?"

Jaime laughed wickedly. "That would be a plaid kilt while Raven's wearing it. Easy access, don't you know?" The exaggerated leer Jaime gave him made his cheeks hot, even as he chuckled. Thinking about Jaime's cousin and Raven having sex seemed a little... nosy. Not quite right. Especially since Jaime had told him about catching Caleb and Raven having sex.

"The argyle is kind of like... a lucky charm?"

"Really? I've never heard of anyone with argyle as a lucky charm." Jaime's voice only held an eagerness to hear more, no indication he thought Tate was a moron for having an odd lucky charm. "Then again, I've known a lot of superstitious guys, so I guess anything goes. Tell me about the argyle charm."

Superstition. Yeah, maybe it was that, more than a lucky charm. God knew the luck never seemed to last very long.

"When I was a kid, there was a guy. He wasn't my dad, but he lived in the house and was there for a while. I called him Uncle Phil. He liked me… and not the way some of my mother's boyfriends seem to like me now." Tate rolled his eyes, but Jaime looked slightly horrified. Right. Tate wasn't going to talk about things that no longer mattered. "Anyway, he stuck around for a long time. When he was around, my mom drank less, didn't do drugs, I don't think. He was a good man, respectable, you know?"

Jaime threaded their fingers together, letting some of his warmth seep into Tate's hands.

"But my mother… is my mother, and eventually she slipped back into the drinking. They would fight a lot, and finally, one day, Uncle Phil was gone."

To this day, it still hurt. Uncle Phil hadn't ever yelled at him for being stupid or not doing well in school. He'd even made his mom a nicer woman. But he'd left all the same. Tate drew in a shuddery breath.

"Anyway, after I dropped out of school, I knew I would need some nicer clothes if I was going to convince anyone to hire me without a diploma. In the thrift shop, I found an argyle sweater-vest, and suddenly I remembered Uncle Phil wearing them all the time. Maybe it could make me look as respectable as he was. So I bought it and wore it to my first interview. I got the job, and so whenever I need clothes, I keep my eye open for argyle stuff too."

Jaime picked up his hand and kissed it. "That was mostly very sweet, but I'm still tempted to go back to your mother's and slap some sense into her."

Tate grinned. He loved that Jaime was so protective of him and thought his mother had missed out on knowing a great son. Nobody had ever thought he was great or wonderful or any of the other beautiful things Jaime told him all the time, even when they weren't in bed.

But in many ways, Tate was thankful for his life. Growing up had been filled with hardship, but without it, he might never have realized what a treasure Jaime was.

CHAPTER THIRTEEN

FRIDAY MORNING, almost six weeks after Tate's terrifying collapse and surgery, the vivid bruises on Tate's body had faded, his feet were back to normal, the stitches were out, his incision was healing beautifully, and the day Jaime had been dreading had arrived.

Jaime had done whatever he could to keep Tate from getting bored. Having his friends come by and spend time with Tate had only partially been worry about Tate's health. He'd hoped that they'd get along, enmeshing Tate further into his life and giving Tate something else to think about. It had worked too. Tate got along well with his friends, and it hadn't taken long before they all saw what had mesmerized Jaime.

Jaime had also made a point to get Tate to the library for story circle and out to Area 52 for a few short visits with Kris. But even supplementing those activities with unlimited movie and television watching wasn't enough to occupy Tate when Jaime was at work. Not surprising, but Jaime had hoped to put this day off a little longer.

Tate was making serious noises about finding a job. But Jaime had an idea that—probably—didn't involve another minimum-wage job Tate would suck at. On breaks at work or when Tate was asleep, Jaime scoured the Internet for resources and information. He'd discussed his ideas with Caleb, refining details and marshaling his arguments. His game plan was ready, but all the planning in the world wouldn't help if Tate told him to fuck off.

Jaime had asked for—and somehow gotten—the whole Memorial Day weekend, plus the Friday before, off work. He'd been planning to spend some quality time with his boyfriend, thoroughly reacquaint himself with Tate's naked body, and somewhere in between orgasmic stupors, convince him to come to the family barbecue. Instead, he might not even have a boyfriend by the time Sunday rolled around, but Jaime couldn't wait any longer.

Sitting across the kitchen table from Tate, Jaime pushed his scrambled eggs around the plate. Tate had virtually inhaled his breakfast, but Jaime's appetite had disappeared the moment Tate had said, "I'm going to look for a job after the holiday."

If Jaime had known, he'd have seduced Tate last night, because he suspected there wouldn't be any sex for a while. "You know there's no rush, right?"

Tate ate his last bite of eggs, then stared Jaime in the eye. Jaime hadn't seen much of Tate's stubborn jaw over the past few weeks, but it was waiting in the wings right now, ready to be trotted out at any minute. "The hospital bills will be coming in soon. I can't tell you how thankful I am that you were willing to help out, but I need to start paying you back."

Jaime was thrilled—truly—that Tate had recovered so well, but he really wasn't looking forward to outstubborning his boyfriend.

"Right." He wasn't going to get into this again, because he was hoping to talk Tate into accepting even more money without worrying about paying it back. "Before we, uh, figure out what we're going to do this weekend, I wanted to talk to you about something."

Tate set his fork down and stared at Jaime, expression blank. It hadn't taken long to figure out that Tate used this particular stone-faced expression to hide his emotions or when his thoughts were whirling, even if subterfuge wasn't always possible with his involuntary blushing. But Jaime hated not being able to tell what Tate was thinking.

Pushing his plate away, Jaime gathered the threads of his thoughts. "First things first. I love you, Tate. I don't see anything changing that."

Tate's expression softened. "I love you too."

Good. Because he was going to test Tate's patience, and he wanted Tate to know he was loved before Jaime started probing at something painful.

"If you could do anything with your life, what would you do?"

Tate wrinkled his nose, his confusion evident. "I don't understand."

"Well, is there a job or career you'd like to do? I'm sure you didn't dream of being a busboy your whole life."

Fuck. Tate's cheeks reddened. "I'm a high school dropout. I'm not smart enough to do anything else." His voice lowered. "I'm hardly even smart enough for that."

"Bullshit. Bull fucking shit." Jaime hated this self-doubt of Tate's.

If Tate were a cat, his ears would be flattened against his head, although Jaime couldn't quite decide if he was mad or surprised at Jaime's vehemence.

"Tate, you read more voraciously and with more enthusiasm than most people I know. You're smart and funny, and so fucking determined to do everything on your own that I am not only in awe, but I want to slay all your dragons for you."

The flush got brighter, climbing up Tate's ears.

"If you want to finish high school, you can take your GED. Go to college. I know you can, and I'm willing to help if that's what you want."

Tate's jaw squared off and he stood abruptly, grabbing dishes off the table and dumping them into the sink with a clatter. Then he faced the sink, gripping the edge of the counter so hard his skin whitened.

"I can't pass the tests. That's why I dropped out in the first place. I'm sorry I'm not smart enough for you. I assume that's why you don't want me to meet your family."

Jaime gasped like Tate had stabbed him. He hadn't expected this conversation to go well, but it was unraveling in a seriously unexpected way, and he hadn't even gotten to the part that he'd thought would piss Tate off. "Tate. God. You're smart enough for me. You're perfect for me. And of course I want you to meet my family."

"Right. Uh-huh. When were you going to tell me about the barbecue? Or were you just planning to sneak off? Maybe tell me you got called into work?"

"How did you...." Oh, of course. "Caleb told you."

He got up and stood behind Tate, put his hands on his shoulders, but it was like Tate was all angles and tension. Jaime wanted to wrap Tate up in a big hug, but he didn't think Tate would appreciate that.

"I promise I wasn't trying to hide anything. I wasn't sure you'd be recovered enough to deal with the family. I wasn't planning to go without you."

"Really?" Tate's disbelief was loud and clear. "Why didn't you at least mention it? Give me a chance to think about it and decide if I felt well enough? Or were you seriously going to just wake up Sunday, ask me how I was, and then drag me to your mother's house?"

"Uh. No. I don't know? Honestly, I hadn't even thought too much about it." He'd been too busy planning other things. "Look, I don't want to fight about it."

Tate slid away from him and turned a horrified look on him. "Fight? I don't want to fight."

Jaime blinked, then realized Tate might be taking him a little too literally. "Hey. I'm not talking about physically fighting. That's not how people in love should deal with each other." Or anyone else, really, but he didn't want to sound too sanctimonious when Tate had been involved in so many fights.

"I know. I wasn't going to fight."

Could Jaime screw this up any more? Was that level of fuck-up-itude even possible? "When I said fight, I meant argue. I promise—I had forgotten about the barbecue, mostly because I was trying to figure out how to talk to you about your GED… and other things."

One of Tate's russet eyebrows lifted. "Other things?" He didn't sound impressed, and he looked on the edge of tears, which was killing Jaime.

Jaime stepped close and stroked his hands down Tate's shoulders. "Can we just calm down, please? I hate seeing you upset. If you're feeling up to it, I would love to take you to my parents' house on Sunday."

Tate's nose tilted slightly upward. "I don't want you to take me because I guilted you into it."

"You haven't. I swear." His sincerity must have been clear, because Tate stared at him for a moment before nodding sharply. "I want them to love you as much as I do."

A fine tremor shook Tate, and he took a deep breath. "Okay. What other things?"

"I think if you want to get your GED and go to college, you can. Because I think you're smart, and I think… I think with the right resources, you can work around…." How did he say this? "I mean, I know you have problems with numbers. All numbers. It's a learning disability, but one that you can, if not overcome, work around to get where you want to be."

Jaime didn't let go of Tate's shoulders, but for the longest time, Tate just stared at him.

"A learning disability." The words broke the silence, but without any inflection, Jaime still didn't know what Tate was thinking.

"Yes. I mean, a bunch of those apps I installed on your phone can help you. And I can help too." He'd wondered if Tate would think he'd overstepped, but Tate had definitely used them.

Another dark flush swept across Tate's face. "You… when did you figure this out?"

"There were a few signs, but it was that day I went back to work after your surgery. You couldn't tell me the time. That in itself explains why you had trouble getting to work on time, but with your phone, you could set up reminders instead of trying to figure out what time it is."

Tate wiped a hand across his mouth, shuddered, and then tears streamed down his face. Jaime gathered him close, and this time he melted into Jaime's arms.

When he finally lifted his head, his face was blotchy, but there was a serenity in his expression that made him beautiful.

"Are you okay?"

"I'm not stupid."

"You're not stupid." Or any other awful name Jaime had heard. "You can do this. And you can focus on getting a good job that doesn't include making you work with numbers every day. They're out there, I promise. And many workplaces will make allowances for things like this too."

"Do you think...."

Jaime wiped at the wetness on Tate's cheeks. "What?"

"Would someone who helped kids in a bad situation, like a social worker or maybe at an LGBT organization, need to use numbers?"

Jaime's heart swelled. He wasn't surprised that's where Tate's interests would lie. Given the triggers for his anger, he was clearly passionate about saving people, especially gay guys who couldn't defend themselves. Even that anger was something they could work through. Jaime was pretty sure if Tate was able to exert some control over his life, he'd be in a better position to control his anger, but if not, there was always counseling.

"I am certain there are jobs related to that with few numbers required. We can do some research this weekend."

Tate bit his lip. "But how can I pay for college if I don't find a job? There were times I couldn't even afford to eat every day."

God. Every time Tate said something like that, it gutted him. "If you want the traditional college experience, we can get you loans, but I'm willing to support you in this, in all ways. I wasn't kidding when I told you I was in this for the long haul—we're a team, and we wouldn't be the first couple where half of them worked while the other half went to school."

"This is scaring the fuck out of me, but okay. I... want to try. I want to let you help me."

Jaime hugged Tate again, somehow ending up kissing him. They kissed for he didn't know how long, and then Tate pulled back and looked up at him. "Will you help me out of my clothes?"

Jaime drew in a shaky breath, already so hard he could barely stand. "Did I tell you what I wanted to do this weekend?"

"Fuck me?" Tate said it as a question, but there was a spark in those eyes that said he was going to get demanding, and Jaime couldn't fucking wait.

"Oh God, yes."

Tate reached between them and stroked Jaime's cock, making him moan. Jaime could control himself, but lying celibate next to Tate for a month and a half had him on a hair trigger.

"I need you," Tate whispered.

"I'm here for you, always."

A FEW hours and a couple of orgasms later, they'd showered and emerged from the bedroom. No fucking, because Jaime still worried about jostling Tate's abdomen, but blow jobs and hand jobs were every bit as satisfying.

"Did you want some lunch?" Jaime asked while admiring the hint of beard burn on Tate's pale neck, as well as a darker love bite near the hollow of his throat. Still damp, his bright hair was a darker shade than normal and tousled from being towel dried. Best of all, Tate looked relaxed and happy. So fucking beautiful.

"Yeah, I could eat."

The doorbell rang. "Jesus. It seems like lately, no one ever has to get buzzed in through the gate." Might be broken.

"Are you expecting anyone?"

"No, but maybe the guys forgot I was off today? Who was supposed to be coming over today?"

Tate shrugged. "You made up the babysitting schedule. But maybe Raven? He doesn't normally ring the bell, though."

Jaime strode over to the door and peered out the peephole. "Mama?"

"What?" Tate asked.

Without bothering to answer, Jaime quickly unlocked the door. "Mama? What are you doing here?"

Automatically, he stepped out of the way to let her in, and she took it as the invitation it was. Jaime should have realized avoiding his family the way he had would result in something like this.

"Is something wrong?" Jaime glanced over to the living room. Tate was mostly hidden from view by the back of the couch, but he peered over it, just his eyes, hair, and the bridge of his nose visible.

"Jaime, Jaime." She shook her head. "I have to hear from Maria that you're *living* with a man? When were you going to tell me? Introduce us?"

Damn Caleb to hell. Ever since coming out and clearing the air with his parents, he told his mother everything, including, apparently, details of Jaime's love life. Jaime's mother wasn't angry, but she was annoyed. Jaime couldn't tell if it was that Jaime'd had the nerve to find himself a boyfriend—making the gay obvious—or that Caleb's mom had found out before she did.

He also wasn't sure if she'd care that Tate wasn't even part Latino. All of his siblings had married people who'd at least have some understanding of his culture, and they could all speak Spanish even if they didn't always do so. Tate didn't know any, except for a few words he'd picked up in various restaurants he'd worked in, and most of those weren't fit for polite company.

"Oh, Mama. I was going to tell you. Introduce you. But there was so much going on, with him recovering from surgery and all."

She tsked dismissively. "Your poor old mama has had lots of experience nursing sick people. You should have called me right away."

Jaime bit his cheek to keep from laughing. Tate was so damned skittish, Jaime's overbearing mother would have sent him scuttling away. And Jaime had been desperate to get him to stay.

"Sorry, Mama. Next time, okay?"

Barely mollified, she nodded. "Where is this Tate?"

Jaime glanced over at the couch. Tate had hunched down, but since Jaime's sofa was chocolate leather, the top of Tate's head, covered in that silky red hair, flared like a beacon.

He led his mother into the living room.

"Tate, this is my mama, Rosa. Mama, this is Tate, my boyfriend."

A sure sign of his anxiety, Tate's freckles stood out stark on his face. He was polite but clearly terrified—considering the experience Jaime had had with Tate's mother, Tate had every right to be wary.

His mother settled herself in the overstuffed chair that Jaime never used and chatted benignly about the weather and her grandchildren.

Jaime did his best to rustle up some coffee as fast as he could, opening a new package of cookies and arranging them on a plate. As soon as he returned, though, she began to interrogate Tate. It was a very subtle interrogation, to be sure, but everyone in the room knew exactly what was going on. Jaime tensed, waiting for the explosion or for Tate to up and run out, but Tate held his own and remained as evasive as possible without outright refusing to answer or being impolite. It was more gratifying than Jaime could say that Tate had opened up to him far more than he was doing with Jaime's mother.

When Jaime could bear it no longer, he spoke up. "Tate, are you feeling okay? You look like you could use a nap."

"Oh. Yes, that would be good." He flashed Rosa a wan smile. "I still tire out quickly."

"Of course, *querido*. You must get your rest. I wouldn't want you to be too tired to come to the barbecue on Sunday."

Pink flooded Tate's cheeks. "Right. Yes. I'll be there. Uh. Nice to meet you." He stood up, but not faster than Jaime's mama, who still had the speed of a striking snake when she wanted.

"Lovely to meet you too." Then she hugged Tate and kissed both of his cheeks while he stood there like a cat getting forced affection.

After Tate had escaped to the bedroom—no hiding that he hadn't gone into the spare room—Jaime glared at his mother.

"That really wasn't very nice of you. He's not used to... all of this." Jaime's family could be rather overwhelming, and his mother had been at her overbearing best.

His mother sniffed. "He'll get used to it. If he's intending to stick around."

Jaime didn't like the sound of that. "Can I get you another cup of coffee?"

"No, thank you, *querido*. You make coffee like mud. But I will take some water."

She settled back in her chair and waited. Jaime refilled his coffee—he liked it strong, and as far as he was concerned, he'd brewed a perfect pot. Tate put a lot of cream in his but never complained.

Jaime sat on the couch and faced his mother, waiting. He'd known her too long, and just getting an introduction to Tate wouldn't be enough for her to seek him out in his apartment, although he had no doubt that was a big part of her motivation.

"He is adorable." Her tone said that *adorable* wasn't necessarily a good thing.

"I think so."

"*Mi hijo*, are you certain this is a good idea? He's a lot younger than you. He doesn't have a job, a good family, a good upbringing, and not only have you moved him in when you barely know him, but Caleb says you're going to put him through college? And pay his hospital bills?"

"Mama!" Jaime spoke sharply, but it felt like she'd slapped him. Why had he thought finding someone he loved would be simple? He'd hoped his mother could accept him, but obviously she couldn't. Nor did she trust him to make good decisions. "There is nothing wrong with me supporting my boyfriend—my partner. And how could you even suggest I wouldn't offer him assistance when I have more than I need for myself?"

"Are you sure this isn't just you... taking on a charity case? You have such a good heart, it's easy for people to take advantage. And you've known him hardly any time at all."

"He's not taking advantage." He grimaced and cracked his knuckles. "I have offered him all of these things because I'm hoping to build a life with him, and you're just going to have to accept that. Great Uncle Ricardo left me that money to do what I want. Even after those expenses, I'll have plenty left over. Enough to buy a house and still have investments." After all, the money had just been sitting there, generating interest, since Jaime did not live extravagantly.

"Calm, calm."

Right. How was he supposed to be calm? He kept his tone even and bared his teeth in an approximation of a smile. "I am calm." He wasn't, but he was at least attempting to keep his voice down. He didn't want Tate to hear this.

"Why don't you take your old mama out to lunch. We can talk about it there."

Jaime snarled but grabbed his keys. Presumably she'd only suggested lunch because in a public place he probably wouldn't yell at her. If it weren't for the fact he didn't want Tate to overhear them fighting, he would have told her to go to hell. But nicely, because she was still his mama.

He resolutely didn't think about what would happen if she didn't accept Tate. He didn't want to consider the fact that this might be his last lunch with his mama, because he wasn't giving Tate up. Not because his mother had some weird hang-up about gay men being in a real relationship.

After penning a note for Tate, he slipped into their bedroom. "Tate, are you awake?" he whispered.

Tate had the covers bunched up around his shoulders and didn't stir—he must have been exhausted. Jaime left the note telling him where he was going, and slipped out again.

As tempting as it was, he refrained from slamming the apartment door as they left. However satisfying it would be, he didn't want to disturb Tate.

Seething, he got into the car. He'd been out since fucking high school, and all this time, his mother had pretended to be fine with it, but clearly she wasn't. Not if this was how she reacted in the face of him finding a man he was serious about.

They'd only been in the car for a few minutes before his mother spoke. "You love this young man?"

"Yes. I do. And he loves me."

His mama waved her hand. "Well, of course he loves you. Who wouldn't?"

Her automatic response confused him and blunted his anger a bit. "I don't understand. If you think a guy could love me, why don't you ever tell me I need to get married and settle down like you've said over and over to Alberto, Miguel, and Maribel?"

"Jaime Eduardo Escobar. I was just doing what you wanted."

"What I wanted? You're the one who doesn't believe I could have or want the same things as everyone else. Like a husband and a family."

His mother gasped. "Of course I believe you could have them. I want you to have them. I want all my children to find happiness. It has been so hard to see you alone, and even worse since Caleb found that nice Raven. But I kept silent. Because that's what you wanted."

Oh God. Had his anger triggered a stroke or something? He had no fucking clue what was going on. "Why would you think that's what I wanted?"

"*Cariño*, don't you remember?"

"Mama, I don't know what you're talking about."

The restaurant loomed ahead, surprising Jaime. He hadn't realized they were already there. He pulled into the parking lot and killed the engine. Neither of them made a move to get out of the car.

"Before you went into the Army, you were too young to settle down, and Miguel was already starting to court Diana. There was plenty of time for you to settle down. When you got out of the Army and came home for good, I said you needed to find a good man and settle down. Start a family. Just like I've said to your brothers and your sister, and most of your cousins. But you got so angry. Told me you weren't going to conform to heteronormative values and didn't know why you had to be like everyone else. Said you were never going to... and I think the words were 'become a mindless drone, a slave to old-fashioned, paternalistic traditions.'"

Jaime's mouth fell open. There was no denying he'd been angry—so angry—when he'd come home. The nightmares and sleepless nights had been... nightmarish. Trying to hide it from everyone had made him even surlier. Although he did not remember that conversation at all, he did recall feeling cheated by Mario's death—among other things. Cheated in that he didn't think he'd ever find anyone who suited him like Mario. Almost like he'd bought into the fairy tale that there was only one love allotted per person, and he'd lost his chance at love when he'd lost Mario.

"I'd lost friends, seen so many men die, and I couldn't help them. Mama, when I got home... I wasn't quite right."

His mother sniffed and pulled a tissue out like magic. Jaime looked at her, amazed to see she was actually crying. "What's wrong?"

"*Cariño*, I know you weren't right. You were angry and sad, but you wouldn't let anyone in. You wouldn't talk to anyone. You looked like you were sick, bags under your eyes, and so skinny. I was afraid, for so long, I'd lost the boy who'd joined the Army. You slowly got better, but you never gave any indication that you had changed your mind about starting a family. So I never brought it up."

Jaime's eyes started burning. "You weren't saying anything... because you were trying to do what I wanted."

"Of course. I love you, *mi hijo*. I want nothing more than for you to be happy."

He battled back the tears with effort. A quick swipe of his hand dealt with the excess moisture. "Thank you, Mama, for loving me."

Another sniff, and then she blew her nose before making the tissue disappear again. "Your boyfriend. He's had a hard life, hasn't he?"

"He has. His mother is… awful." And the less said about her, the better. One day he might tell his mama everything, but probably not. She didn't need to know.

"Then I'm glad you found him."

With the crushing disappointment no longer weighing down his shoulders, Jaime couldn't keep from smiling. He got out of the car and went around it to help his mama out. She smiled up at him and patted his cheek. "Does this mean I can start asking about grandbabies?"

Jaime laughed. "You can ask, but Tate's only twenty-two and we haven't even talked about marriage yet, much less kids. So you might not like the answer you get."

Arm in arm, they entered the restaurant.

As soon as Tate heard the door shut, he flipped up the covers and swung out of bed. His stomach roiled, and he wondered if he was going to be sick. Or just cry until he was a dried-up husk.

Jaime's mother hated him. And Jaime loved his mother. If Tate's mother had hated a man he brought home, Tate would know he was on the right track and would probably have suggested eloping to Vegas. But Jaime might listen to his mother. Jaime probably would listen to his mother, and they were going out to lunch, where his mother was going to try to convince him to break up with Tate.

Tate probably shouldn't have listened to their conversation after they thought he'd gone to nap, but he had to know how he measured up in Mrs. Escobar's eyes.

Turns out, he didn't. Not at all. She thought he was a charity case. Worse, she might be right. There had been a number of times Tate had wondered about Jaime's generosity and thought someone else might have easily taken advantage of that.

What was he going to do?

He paced the length of their—Jaime's—bedroom. Just that morning, they'd agreed to spend the weekend making a plan. A long-term plan to get Tate's life where he wanted it. But he'd assumed he'd have Jaime by his side the whole time. After all, they loved each other. Jaime had certainly given him to believe that would be the case, but after hearing Jaime talk to his mother, he was no longer so confident.

All he had to offer Jaime was his love, but what if that wasn't enough?

Briefly, he considered packing up all his stuff and leaving. He couldn't go back to his mother's house, but he could probably convince Raven or Dallas to take pity on him and give him a place to crash. He stood in front of the dresser Jaime had surprised him with after he got out of the hospital. He remembered the get-well cards the kids from the library had made him, and how Jaime had mounted them on a board, which he'd hung in the spare room.

He wiped at his eyes. He couldn't give in to tears. Not yet. Even if the thought of losing Jaime was more painful than anything he'd endured in his life.

Hiccupping slightly, he started pacing again. A plan. He needed another plan. And it had to start with him getting a job.

A job. After snatching his phone, he pulled up Raven's contact information. The job was going to have to pay enough for an apartment and for his phone. Because Jaime was right. It had the potential to help him enormously, and he'd be a fool to give that up if he didn't have to.

Can you get me a job at Idyll Fling? You did say my look might be popular.

There. He flung the phone back on the nightstand. Raven would understand. He'd started with nothing too, and Idyll Fling had been the answer.

Maybe Tate should pack anyway? Just so he'd be ready to go?

Just that thought set his eyes filling up again, and he scrubbed at them with his palms. No. His instincts about people didn't suck. If nothing else, he could have confidence in that. And he believed Jaime wouldn't be a dick and throw him out without giving him a chance to at least pack.

He didn't want to beg Jaime to keep him around, but maybe he could… offer a revision of their plan? Jaime wouldn't stop loving him just because his mother didn't like him, would he?

The door to the apartment slammed open, making Tate jump. He wasn't ready for Jaime to get home yet. He hadn't heard if Raven could get him a job.

He took a deep breath and left the bedroom. "Raven? How did you get in?"

Raven stared at him like he'd lost his mind. "I took the spare key off Caleb's key ring."

"What are you doing here?"

"What am I doing here?" Raven parroted. "You asked if I could get you a job in porn."

Tate took a step back. "Is there some sort of ginger porn shortage? You could have just texted me."

Raven heaved in a deep breath. "Where is Jaime? Surely he's not going to let you do this."

Tate gritted his teeth. "Let me? He's not my father, you know."

"Ugh. That didn't come out exactly right. C'mon, sit down. We're going to have tea and talk."

Tea and talk with an ex–porn star. He couldn't quite believe this was his life now. But then, he also didn't know what had gotten Raven so riled.

Tate sat down at the kitchen table, not wanting to see the reminders of Mrs. Escobar out in the living room. The tea would be a nice change from the coffee he'd had a hard time choking down earlier.

Steaming cups in front of them, Raven stared earnestly at him. "Okay, I wasn't kidding when I said you could make good money, but I wasn't seriously suggesting you start doing it."

"Why not? I need a job."

Raven sounded like someone was strangling him. "Okay, you don't need Jaime's permission, but he will flip his shit if you do this."

Tate didn't want to upset Jaime, but he was half-convinced their relationship was currently fizzling out over pasta with Jaime's mother. If so, Jaime's emotional state would have no bearing on Tate's ability to get a job to feed himself.

So he explained what he'd overheard and why he'd thought porn might be the answer to his job woes.

Raven splayed his fingers and waved them. "A backup plan. That works. You can certainly consider Idyll Fling as a backup plan, but I really don't think you have to worry about anything. Jaime is so in love with you."

A flush heated Tate's cheeks. Hearing it from someone else helped.

"His mom can be a little scary, though. I'm so glad Caleb's mom isn't quite that terrifying. And she's obsessed with her grandchildren. Anyway. I'm not entirely sure porn would be the best job for you, at least, not if you weren't desperate."

"Oh? Why not?"

"I haven't known you long, but you don't really like people telling you what to do, and there's a lot of following the director's orders to get the right shots. That's one. Two, I don't think exhibitionism gets you off. Imagine a thousand horny guys watching you get fucked on film and stroking off to it. Get you horny?"

"Uh, no, not really."

"My point. And how do you feel about having sex with more than one guy at the same time?"

Ew. He loved having sex with Jaime, but he'd spent so long searching men's eyes for ulterior motives, he'd never wanted sex very often.

Raven waved a finger at him. "Yeah. That face there says it all. And if you're not going to have fun with it, you shouldn't get into it. But if you're *desperate*, let me know and I can help you out. One or two films, a little more vanilla, I'm sure I can talk Stefan into that. Only if you're desperate."

"Thanks. I appreciate it."

"Any time. But seriously, you're not going to need it. I've heard all about Jaime's plan. He's done a shit-ton of research and all. He wouldn't go to all that trouble if he was planning to ditch you. He's dated a lot of men, even in the short time I've known him, but he's rarely even wanted a second date, never mind planning things that are going to happen years in the future."

Tate blinked. That particular aspect hadn't occurred to him. Jaime had been full of plans. Long-term plans. It would be an odd thing for him to do if he thought they weren't going to last that long.

TATE TALKED a bit more with Raven, letting his freak-out fade away. He was still afraid, but he wasn't panicky. There was a plan even if Jaime changed his mind, although Tate was going to do a serious job of trying to convince him not to.

Raven knew what it was like to have nothing, and Tate really appreciated his friendship.

Jaime returned home and walked into the kitchen before Tate had a chance to call out a greeting.

"Tate, you're up. Raven, what are you doing here?" He narrowed his eyes. "Tate, are you feeling okay? We don't need to go to the hospital, do we?"

"Nope. He's fine," Raven drawled. "But he was asking me about a career in porn. Wondered if I could get him a job."

Tate's mouth fell open. Why the hell had Raven said such a thing?

Jaime, on the other hand, went about as pale as he'd ever seen him. "Uh. But we had a plan. I mean, I thought we had it all worked out." Jaime clenched his hands into fists before visibly relaxing them. "But if… but if that's what you want to do, I will. Support you." His last words were barely audible, and he appeared to be under great strain.

Tate stood. "I don't want to do that. But I also don't want you to dump me because your mother doesn't like me. I just… wanted to know I had alternatives."

"Alternatives?" Jaime practically shouted the word.

"Well, that's my cue to leave. See you around!" Raven sailed out the door with a cheery wave, leaving them to deal with the aftermath of his probably calculated words.

"I don't understand." Jaime didn't sound angry any longer, only sad. "What happened? I know we still have to plan out the specifics, but I thought… we were both on the same page."

Tate pressed a fist into his stomach, feeling sick. He had a bad feeling he'd misread the situation. "I heard you and your mother talking. She thinks I'm taking advantage of you and that I'm not good enough for you."

Jaime still looked hurt, but his voice was firm, scolding even. "You're wrong. My mama and I… we had a miscommunication, and she was just worried about me. But even if that wasn't the case, I was—and am—willing to tell her she'd have to accept that you are my choice and this is our life. And that you are here to stay."

He took a tiny step forward and flexed his arms as though to reach out for Tate, but then he didn't follow through.

"You are here to stay, aren't you?"

God help him, how could he not? Jaime's desires so directly mirrored his own, there wasn't any other choice.

"Of course I am. I love you. I just… got afraid. I've never loved anyone so much, and it scares me that you could just go away."

"Believe me, I know." Jaime's voice rang with conviction. "So, will you go to the barbecue with me tomorrow? Meet the rest of my crazy family? I promise that my mama doesn't hate you."

Tate smiled and moved into Jaime's personal space. "On one condition."

"Anything."

"Come to bed with me."

Jaime's eyes darkened. "Are you sure?"

"I am feeling much better." Tate grabbed Jaime's hand and brought it to his hard dick. "Much better."

"Oh, yes. Better." Jaime licked his lips. He led Tate into the bedroom and stripped them both.

Tate lay back on the bed, not expecting Jaime to bypass everything else to suck Tate's cock into his mouth.

"Jaime. Oh. So good."

Jaime merely smiled around his mouthful and massaged Tate's entire length with his tongue. All too soon, Tate was pumping his hips up into the volcanic haven of Jaime's mouth.

"I'm close. So close." They were supposed to fuck, but Jaime had brought him to the edge so damned fast, Tate was going to spill in his mouth.

A harsh groan tore from deep in his chest as he pumped down Jaime's throat. He lay, gasping, while Jaime straddled him, fisting his hard cock. Jaime threw his head back and spurted, warm and wet, across Tate's belly.

Jaime slumped to Tate's side and pulled him close. When Tate caught his breath, he pinched Jaime's nipple to get his attention.

"Ow. What was that for?"

"Don't think I don't know what you were doing."

"Having an awesome shared orgasm with my sexy boyfriend?"

"Okay, yes, that too. But you were babying me. And I won't have it. Next time you're going to slide your cock inside me and fuck me like you mean it. Got it?"

Jaime smirked. "Anything you want. Forever and always."

Forever and always. Tate could definitely get behind that.

Chapter Fourteen

Tate had showered first, and lay back on the bed waiting for Jaime to get ready. They'd learned pretty quickly that showering together was fun, but it took them way longer to get ready. Tate didn't want to show up at the Memorial Day barbecue late. No matter what Jaime had told him, he wanted to make a good impression. Besides, he was maybe too nervous about meeting the rest of Jaime's family to be able to lose himself in shower sex. Or any kind of sex.

Jaime came out of the bathroom and pulled on boxer briefs, a pair of beige pants, and a bright red golf shirt. Tate admired the bits of bared brown skin that were all too quickly covered up. Maybe he'd been too hasty to dismiss the relaxation power of a good orgasm.

Then Jaime turned to him. "Wearing one of the argyle vests, I see. You know they'll think you're respectable without that, right?"

Tate lifted one shoulder. "It's also my lucky pattern. And I think I'm going to need all the luck I can get."

Jaime smiled but somehow still managed to look sad.

"Hey. Come here."

Without a word or question, Jaime sat down next to him on the bed. Initiating any sort of affection was taking some getting used to, but Tate could tell Jaime needed something. He pulled Jaime back so that they were lying beside each other. He laid his head on Jaime's shoulder and rested his arm across Jaime's chest.

"What's wrong?"

"Nothing really. Memorial Day isn't exactly easy for me."

"Hmmm. Not surprised, I guess. I have always thought it a bit weird that everyone has barbecues for a holiday that's always seemed a little somber to me."

Jaime hugged him. "See, this is another reason why we're so good together. You get that. My family means well, but I'm the only one who's served, and it's all a bit academic for them. But I… I lost people. And this day is to remember them. It's hard to pretend it's like any other family event."

Tate hadn't missed the tremble. And he knew Jaime had lost people. Not that he'd heard any of the specifics, but the nightmares alone—although infrequent—would have told him that, even if Jaime hadn't.

"Did you want to talk about it?" He'd listen to whatever Jaime wanted to tell him, in whatever detail, if it helped bleed the poison from inside Jaime's mind and heart.

"I met a guy out there. Mario."

It was difficult hearing that, but Tate had had his suspicions.

"We weren't together or anything. For a number of reasons, but mostly because I was going home just as he was starting his service. But we clicked. We were tight. Then our small convoy was hit by an IED. Most of us got out of the trucks, and I started treating the wounded while the able-bodied worked on protecting us, getting help, and trying to gather what supplies were still salvageable. Mario was gunned down by a sniper while he was tying a tourniquet on another soldier. I lost him before I could get to him."

Jaime's voice broke and his chest shook. Tate held him tighter. He almost wanted to be jealous, but that would be stupid and petty, and he couldn't bring himself to make Jaime's grief about his own insecurities. That wasn't fair.

Then Jaime curled into him and cried. Tate rocked him as best he could, rubbing his back, returning all the comforting actions Jaime had shown him since they'd been together. He kissed Jaime's head, his hair soft and smelling like Jaime's coconut-scented shampoo.

"It's okay, it'll be okay," he murmured into Jaime's hair. While he held Jaime, something odd happened. His fears about their relationship washed away. They were a team, and they were stronger together than they were apart.

Sooner than he expected, the emotional explosion was over, and Jaime disentangled them to flop on his back. "You reminded me of him."

"I did?" What did Jaime mean by that? "He was a redhead?"

Jaime let out a wet-sounding laugh. "No. Not in looks at all. But there was something about your... defiance. Stubbornness, maybe, on that first night at Area 52. Mario had been battling against the world too. Until I met you, he was the only man who made me think that maybe I could find someone and settle down. Build a life with. Once he was gone, I assumed it would never happen. Then we answered a call at Area 52, and there you were, reminding me of that defiance. I couldn't stop thinking about you, which is why I had to seek you out again, but I was afraid I'd imagined it all. But I hadn't. You and your spark made me believe in forever again, *mi fuego*."

"I'm sorry you lost Mario, especially like that. But I'm also thankful for him. Without him, you might not have come looking for me, and I'm so glad you did."

"Me too."

"I don't remember if you ever told me—what does *mi fuego* mean, exactly? I mean, I know it's good. I can tell by the way you say it."

"It means 'my fire,' and it's got nothing to do with the color of your hair. It's that incredible spark of life within you. Your determination, your drive."

Fire. Not at all what he'd been expecting to hear, but he liked it. It sounded strong and independent but still warm and comforting. Maybe the best endearment he could have asked for.

Jaime rolled over him and kissed him. Crying didn't make him look like he'd developed some awful skin disease—bastard—but the effects were visible all the same. Even so, Jaime looked happy again, truly happy. "I love you."

"I lov—" Tate's words were swallowed by Jaime's lips. Maybe they could be a bit late to the barbecue after all.

"THIS IS going to be so much fun." Tate was almost bouncing in his seat, making Jaime grin.

He did not agree at all, but Tate's enthusiasm for doing Raven's calendar photo shoot had softened up all of Jaime's objections. He'd even forgiven Caleb for not getting him out of it. If their positions had been reversed, with Tate wanting Caleb for a photo shoot, Jaime would happily have hog-tied his cousin, thrown him in the trunk, and driven him to the photographer's studio.

"I have a little present for you." Jaime had found one of the best ways to get Tate to graciously accept things was to present them as gifts, although he tried not to overdo it. His friends had, however, replaced Tate's ratty old wallet, backpack, and several T-shirts under the guise of "get-well presents."

"Really? Why?"

He grabbed a small gift bag from the backseat and handed it over. He had another gift too, one for their three-month anniversary, which somehow managed to fall on the same day as Raven's damned photo shoot, but that gift was going to have to wait until later. "Just open it."

Tate pulled out the tissue, then a dark green scrap of fabric. He stretched it out. "Boy shorts? These look awfully small." He stroked the fabric. "But they are so soft. Why are you giving me underwear?"

Jaime wiggled his eyebrows suggestively. "They'll be snug, but they should fit you perfectly." And the color would be gorgeous against Tate's pale skin.

Tate rolled his eyes. "And I'll be happy to model them for you. I've never owned anything like this before. But that still doesn't answer the question of why."

"Two reasons, really. First off, this is kind of a new job for you, right?" Jaime waited until Tate nodded. "See the pattern?"

Tate looked closer. "It's argyle!"

The material was solid in color, but a variation in the weave held an argyle pattern. The Internet could be a beautiful thing. "Just a little luck for you for this new job."

"But why didn't you give this to me at home?"

A wave of contentedness swept through Jaime. He loved hearing Tate call the apartment home. In the weeks since Memorial Day, Tate had settled somehow. He was no longer poised with one foot out the door, ready to run, and Jaime hadn't realized how much that had bothered him until he no longer had to worry about it. In the past month, he'd never been happier, and that had made his decision about celebrating their three-month anniversary that much easier.

"You're going to have plenty of time to put it on when we change into our kilts. Which brings me to the second reason for this. Raven will want us to model those kilts in the traditional fashion... naked underneath."

The sudden sweep of red in Tate's cheeks told him exactly what he thought about that.

"You're not serious."

"Oh, I am serious. I know Raven." But he also knew Tate. His boyfriend was not inhibited in bed at all, but the way he'd grown up, with too much prurient interest from unwelcome sources? Jaime knew he'd be a lot more comfortable wearing underwear during the shoot, especially since there would be strangers. "I thought you'd prefer to be safely covered up."

"Thank you. I hadn't thought about it all, but I'm glad you did." Tate stuffed the briefs in his pocket, then leaned over and kissed him. Then he stared past Jaime, out the window. "Is that Officer Hernandez?"

"Oh, yeah. It is. And remember, you can call him Diego now." Tate's cheeks flamed a bit hotter. Introducing Tate to Diego in a social setting had been all kinds of awkward, but eventually they'd get over it. Maybe. "Raven gave me orders to find some guys to bring to the shoot, but I forgot to ask around. Diego was the only one I could strong-arm into coming."

Tate pursed his lips just a bit. He kept his jealousy well under wraps, but knowing it was there gave Jaime a little ego boost. With any other guy, it would have irritated the fuck out of him.

"C'mon. Let's go."

The sooner they got the photo shoot done, the sooner they could start celebrating.

"Diego!" Jaime called out.

Diego turned. "Jaime. Tate." Yeah, still a little weirdness. "I can't believe I let you talk me into this."

"Yeah, well, misery shared is misery halved and all that."

They went into the studio, and Jaime wrapped an arm around Tate. Inside were a number of attractive men, some of them already in kilts and getting their pictures taken. Jaime waved at Dallas and Will. Although Will was the one who liked to wear kilts, Dallas was the one going to be in the calendar. Jaime had requested that he and Tate go last so some of the chaos would recede closer to their scheduled time.

"Well, hello there. Jaime, how did you know I needed a big hunk of man in my life?" Beck, a current Idyll Fling model, stepped right up and stroked Diego's chest suggestively, staring intently. Raven had roped Beck and a few others from Idyll Fling into doing this shoot as well.

Diego cleared his throat. "Hello. I'm Diego." His voice had dropped an octave in the past thirty seconds, and Jaime smirked as Beck introduced himself before neatly directing Diego away to "help" him get changed. Unlike himself, Beck was Diego's type all over. Jaime suspected Diego might be thanking him before this shoot was done.

"C'mon, we need to get changed too."

AN HOUR later, it was their time in front of the photographer. Raven had picked out the perfect kilt for Tate. The dark forest green plaid was shot through with red and yellow pinstripes. It set off his skin and hair to perfection. Jaime's plaid was composed of the same colors, but in vastly different proportions. When he first saw it, he thought he'd be blinded. The dominant color was yellow—bright sunshiny yellow—with thick bands of primary red and thinner, less noticeable forest green. He had no idea how Tate's kilt could look attractive and respectable, whereas his was one shade short of clown fabric.

But then he put it on and realized the yellow and red—similar to shirts he already owned—were a much better match for his brown skin than Tate's kilt would have been. He strutted out of the changeroom, a lot more confident that maybe he wouldn't get laughed out of the building.

"Hey." Tate's gaze swept from head to foot, and the dilation of his pupils told Jaime all he needed to know. Raven knew what the fuck he was doing.

Jaime stepped close. "Hi." Heedless of the makeup and powder and shit that had been applied, Jaime wrapped his arms around Tate. Having their naked chests brush, with Jaime nude under the kilt, was crazy erotic. He understood—finally—why Raven loved his kilts so much. Jaime wanted nothing more than to find a dark room and let Tate explore his easy access.

Tate rubbed his entire body against Jaime, a faint, breathy moan escaping his lips. Jaime kissed him, quick and dirty, then stepped back. He didn't really want his erection immortalized in a calendar, and he didn't have the advantage of underwear that Tate did.

Tate pouted, but not seriously. He wasn't into any sort of exhibitionism, and that was more than fine with Jaime.

Jaime went before Tate, enduring catcalls and whistles from Diego, who had just finished up. Tate watched Jaime with an avid expression, and Jaime had to look away before his cock got too interested in the promise in those fine whisky amber eyes.

By the time Tate, the last one, took his turn, the number of people remaining had reduced to a trickle. Jaime stayed the whole time and watched his boyfriend light up in all his glory.

The photographer nodded at Jaime once he'd finished Tate's shots, and before Tate could walk away from the backdrop, Jaime moved in.

"Looked like you were having a good time." Jaime stroked his shoulder.

"I did. It's harder than I thought it would be, but it was fun too. I can't wait until the calendar comes out. Mrs. Birenbaum said all the librarians she knew were going to buy a copy."

Jaime laughed. That Mrs. Birenbaum was not nearly as prim as she looked.

"I thought maybe we could get a few shots together."

TATE STARED at Jaime. He'd been just a little obsessed by the camera function on his phone, but these would be like formal shots. For the two of them. Maybe as close to wedding pictures as a guy like him would get.

Jaime's eyes were dark and focused on him, making him just a little breathless. "Okay, but nothing… that's going to get me hard, okay? There are too many people here."

However, he'd been skating around arousal ever since he'd seen Jaime in that kilt. He looked strong and gorgeous, and Tate wanted to lick him all over, and he almost didn't care that other people might see him.

Jaime let out a nervous laugh while the photographer snapped pictures all around them. Tate had been expecting some more directions, but maybe that would come once he'd gotten a few initial shots. Establishing, he'd called them when Tate had first stepped in front of the camera.

"I honestly don't know if it'll make you hard or not, but I guess we'll find out."

Tate narrowed his eyes. What was Jaime planning to do?

In the next breath, Jaime dropped to one knee, and Tate forgot how to breathe.

"Tate, I've never been happier than I've been since I met you."

Fingers chilled, limbs rubbery, Tate managed to cover his mouth with both hands. This wasn't happening. He… had to be imagining it.

"I know it's been a crazy ride we've been on. Living together so soon after we met and while you were recuperating from surgery put some übercompression on our relationship. It was either going to make us crack or it was going to give us a diamond. And I think we found a diamond. Please marry me. There's nothing in this world that would make me happier."

Oh God. He wasn't imagining it. Tate couldn't stop the tears, and his hands shook as he reached out.

"Yes. Oh, yes."

Jaime leaped up and kissed him. Tate was dimly aware of the camera clicking and a cheer from the onlookers.

When Jaime broke the kiss, Tate knew he was flushed, but he still smiled at their friends. Caleb looked like he was heading over with hugs and kisses for them both, but the sight of him triggered an unpleasant thought.

"Jaime, your mother is going to hate this. She'll think this is too soon."

Jaime just laughed. "My mama is not going to have a leg to stand on. They don't talk about it much for fear of giving us kids bad ideas, but she met and married my father within six weeks. Besides, we haven't done anything else traditionally. Why start now?"

Jaime pulled out a box and opened it up. Two decorative silver bands lay inside. "I bought us rings. For our engagement. We'll go together to pick out wedding bands."

"Two rings?" Tate wanted to object because that would be too much money, but Jaime looked so pleased. Tate didn't want to mar this beautiful moment. Jaime slipped the matching rings on their fingers, and the photographer snapped a few more pictures. The rings clued him in, but the photographer capturing Jaime's proposal without missing a beat should have made him realize sooner that Jaime hadn't done this on the spur of the moment. Jaime had planned this, right down to making sure they were the last to be photographed.

Somehow Tate had managed to find the sweetest, most perfect man, and that man loved him back. He'd read about karma and wondered if this was the universe making up for the shit show of his younger years. Either way, he was going to love Jaime for the rest of his life.

Raven wheeled out a serving table with an enormous sheet cake on it.

Congratulations Jaime and Tate.

Nope. Not spur of the moment.

A dozen guys in kilts, along with the photographer and his assistant, dug into a rainbow cake with thick sugary icing, and Tate couldn't stop smiling at Jaime, who just smiled lovingly right back.

EPILOGUE

TÍA MARIA came up to Jaime. "The cake is ready, but I can't find Tate. Since it's your engagement party, you both ought to be there."

Jaime had a feeling he knew where Tate had gotten to. He walked down the hall to the large rec room that doubled as a playroom for his nieces and nephews. Tía Maria followed him, and when he stopped in the doorway, his aunt peered around him.

In the middle of a big puppy pile on the floor, Tate was reading to the youngest brood of kids—most of Jaime's nieces and nephews, along with some of his various cousins' kids.

The kids were enthralled, loving Tate's delivery. Jaime hadn't seen him do this for his family, but he'd had the pleasure of watching Tate run story circle at the library a few times. Tate loved kids, and they loved him right back.

"Oh my. I'm going to kill Rosa," Maria whispered.

"Why?"

"Because she's going to get even more grandchildren soon, isn't she?"

Jaime shrugged. "Tate's going to be too busy for a while, but if he wants kids, then we're going to have some." Tate would make a wonderful dad, and Jaime couldn't imagine a better partner to raise a family with.

His aunt hugged him. "Your mama is going to be just insufferable."

Maybe so. She'd definitely been preening, just a bit.

Tate looked up and smiled. Jaime smiled back.

"He is so sweet."

Yes, he was. A sweet tiger with a fiery temper had deigned to spend the rest of his life with Jaime, and Jaime had never been happier.

KC BURN has been writing for as long as she can remember and is a sucker for happy endings (of all kinds). After moving from Toronto to Florida for her husband to take a dream job, she discovered a love of gay romance and fulfilled a dream of her own—getting published. After a few years of editing web content by day, and neglecting her supportive, understanding hubby and needy cat at night to write stories about men loving men, she was uprooted yet again and now resides in California. Writing is always fun and rewarding, but writing about her guys is the most fun she's had in a long time, and she hopes you'll enjoy them as much as she does.

Website: kcburn.com
Twitter: @authorkcburn
Facebook: www.facebook.com/kcburn

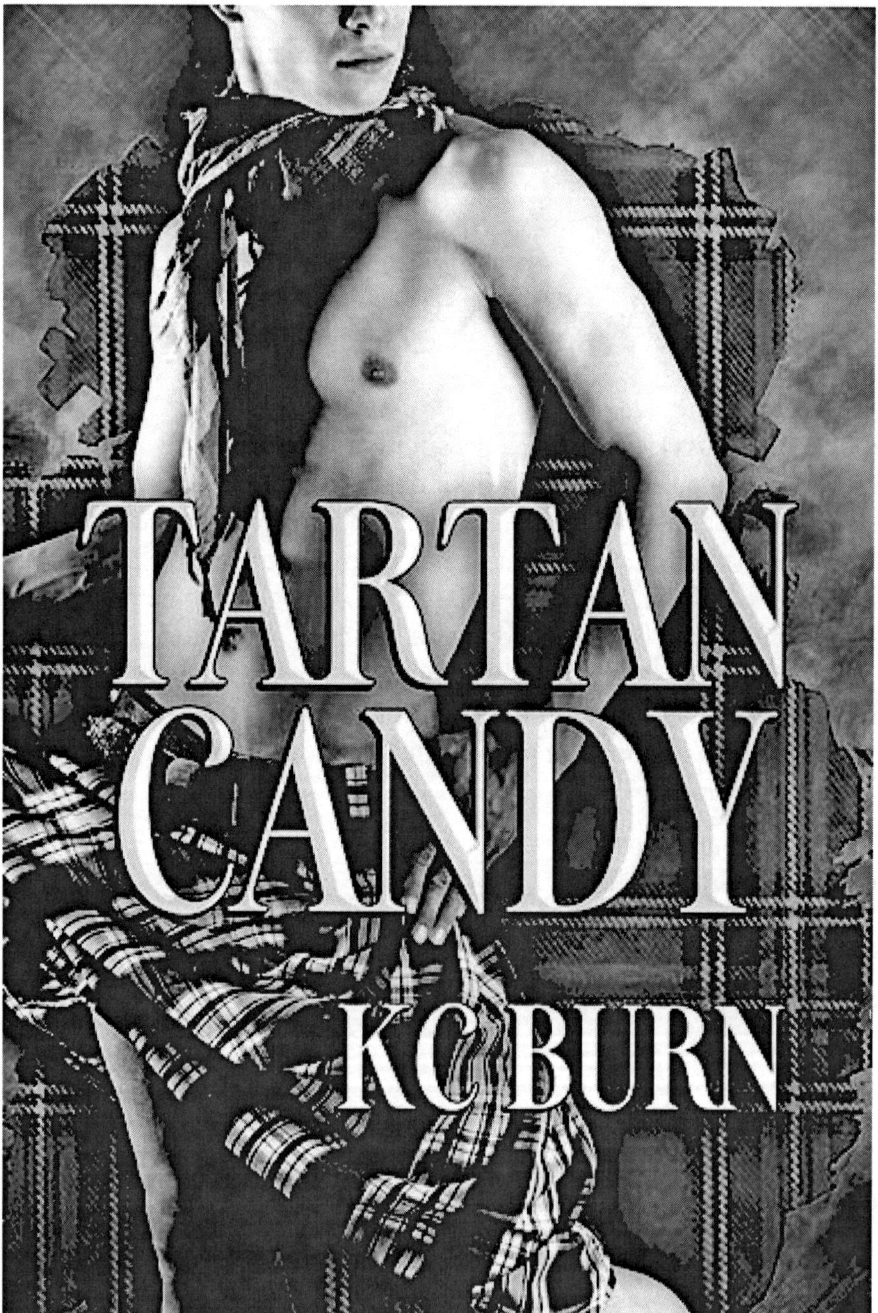
TARTAN
CANDY
KC BURN

A Fabric Hearts Story

Finlay McIntyre (aka Raven) is a successful adult film star with a penchant for kilts, until an accident cuts short his stardom and leaves him with zero sexual desire, lowered self-esteem, and no job. He knew his porn career wouldn't last forever, but he wasn't prepared for retirement at twenty-eight. While trying to figure out the rest of his life, Raven agrees to attend a high school reunion. That's when a malfunctioning AC unit in his hotel room changes everything.

Caleb Sanderson, an entrepreneur with his own HVAC business, has no idea what to expect when he steps into Raven's hotel room to fix his AC unit. They're attracted to each other, but Caleb, closeted, can't afford a gay relationship, not with his mom pressuring him to produce grandchildren. If he wants to keep Raven—who no closet could hold—he'll need to tell his family the truth. But Raven has a few secrets of his own. He refuses to reveal his porn past to Caleb, a past that might be the final obstacle to Caleb and Raven having any kind of relationship.

www.dreamspinnerpress.com

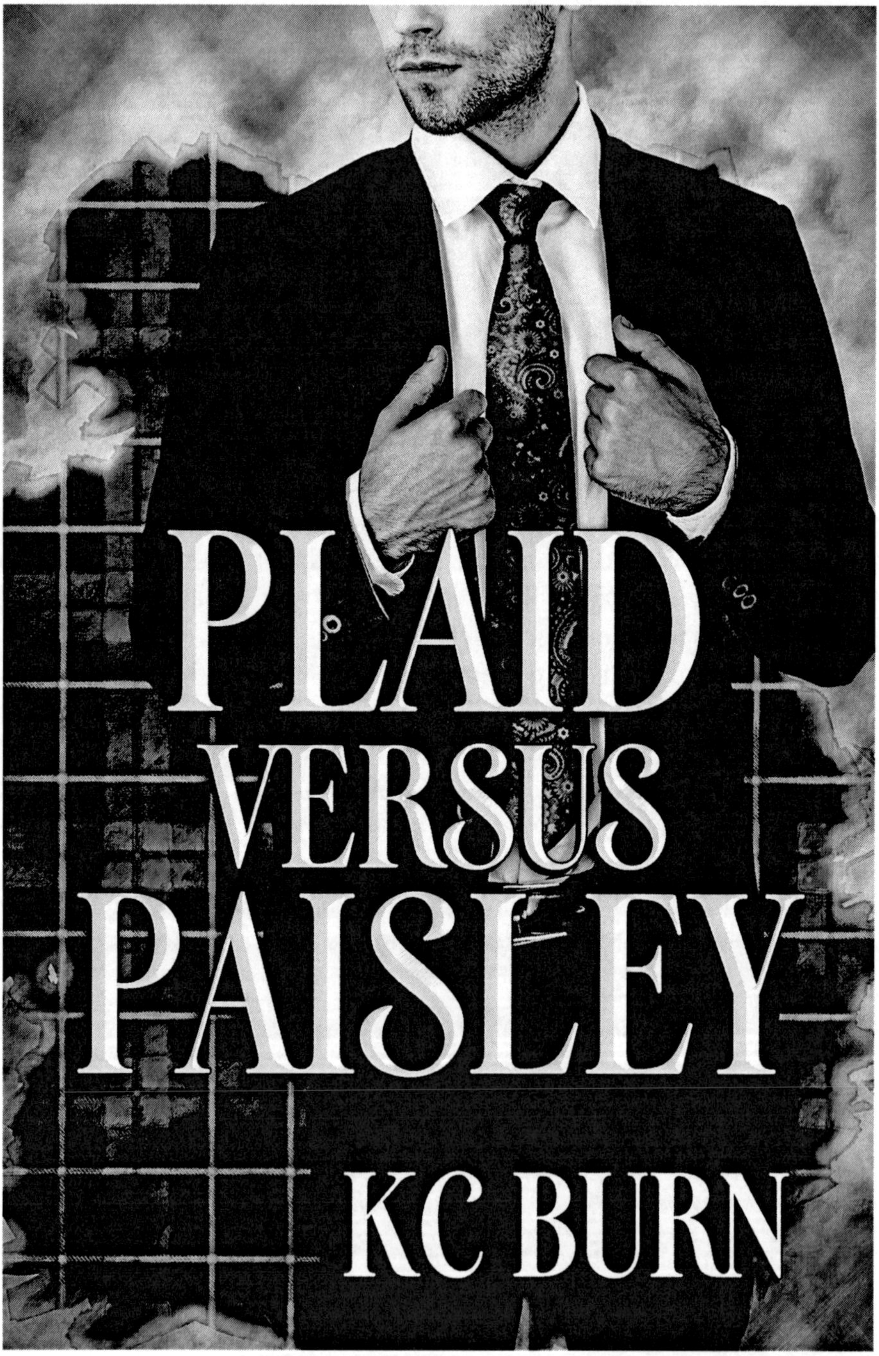
PLAID
VERSUS
PAISLEY
KC BURN

A Fabric Hearts Story

Two years after his life fell apart, Will Dawson moved to Florida to start over. His job in the tech department of Idyll Fling, a gay porn studio, is ideal for him. When his boss forces him to take on a new hire, the last person he expects is Dallas Greene—the man who cost him his job and his boyfriend back in Connecticut. He doesn't know what's on Dallas's agenda, but he won't be blindsided by a wolf masquerading as a runway model. Not again.

Dallas might have thrown himself on his brother's mercy, but his skills are needed at Idyll Fling. Working with Will is a bonus, since Dallas has never forgotten the man. A good working relationship is only the beginning of what Dallas wants with Will.

But Dallas doesn't realize how deep Will's distrust runs, and Will doesn't know that the man he's torn between loving and hating is the boss's brother. When all truths are revealed, how can a relationship built on lies still stand?

www.dreamspinnerpress.com

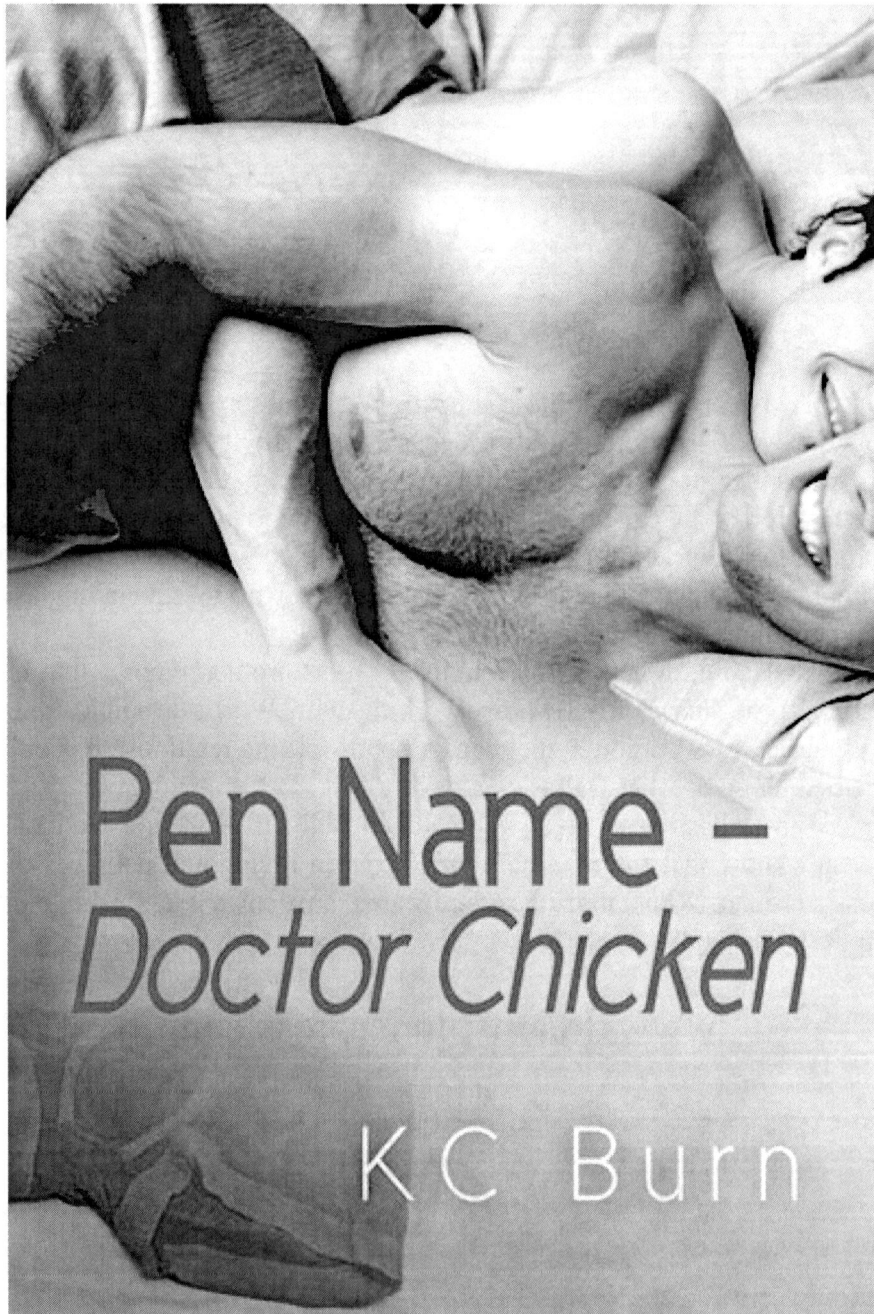

Pen Name –
Doctor Chicken

KC Burn

Sometimes Stratford Dale feels like Doctor Chicken consumes his life. It's his pen name for a series of wildly popular children's books. They were his brainchild; he meant for them to be a way to pay his many bills while he pursued his dream of publishing graphic novels. But the Doctor Chicken contract was a raw deal. Instead, he churns out book after book for a pittance, leaving him broke and no closer to his dreams.

Stratford's dreams of love have fared no better, but he's still trying. After yet another disastrous date, he's intrigued by a man going into a cooking class—so he takes the class too. Vinnie Giani is a successful, self-made man who is charmed by Stratford's bow ties, sharp humor, and clumsiness—which leads to an opportunity to take Stratford in for stitches. Vinnie is, above all, responsible, having taken on the care of his mother and sisters from a young age. Perhaps it's natural when he begins to treat Stratford more as a child who needs a parent than as an equal partner. But when Vinnie tries to "fix" Stratford's career woes—including the Doctor Chicken problem—and ends up making the situation worse, their fledgling relationship may not withstand the strain created by blame and lies.

www.dreamspinnerpress.com

RAINBOW BLUES

KC Burn

Having come out late in life, forty-three-year-old Luke Jordan is at a loss about how to conduct himself as a gay man. As a construction manager, he's not interested in being out at work, but he'd like to find a boyfriend or at least some gay friends. Two years after his wife got all their friends in the divorce, he's no closer to the life he wants.

Zach, Luke's adult son, takes charge and signs him up for the Rainbow Blues, a social group for gay blue-collar workers. At an event, he not only finds friends but meets Jimmy Alexander, part-time stage actor and full-time high school biology teacher. Jimmy loves the stage but wishes potential boyfriends weren't so jealous of the time he devotes to it. When he meets Luke and finds him accepting of his many facets, he thinks it's a dream come true.

Their relationship quickly moves into serious territory, but their connection is tested to its breaking point by the offer of a juicy movie role that takes Jimmy to the opposite coast and into the path of a very sexy costar.

www.dreamspinnerpress.com

CPSIA information can be obtained
at www.ICGtesting.com
Printed in the USA
LVOW07s1300170517
534806LV00033B/1599/P